Rules of Survival
A Post-Apocalyptic EMP Survival Thriller

JACK HUNT

DIRECT RESPONSE PUBLISHING

Copyright (c) 2019 by Jack Hunt
Published by Direct Response Publishing

Copyright © 2019 by Jack Hunt

All rights reserved. Direct Response Publishing. No part of this book may be reproduced, scanned, or distributed in any printed or electronic form without permission. Please do not participate in or encourage piracy of copyrighted materials in violation of the author's rights. Purchase only authorized editions.

This eBook is licensed for your personal enjoyment only. This eBook may not be resold. If you would like to share this book with another person, please purchase an additional copy for each person you share it with. If you're reading this book and did not purchase it, or it was not purchased for your use only, then you should return to an online retailer and purchase your own copy. Thank you for respecting the author's work.

Rules of Survival: A Post-Apocalyptic EMP Survival Thriller (Survival Rules Series Book 1) is a work of fiction. All names, characters, places and incidents either are the product of the author's imagination or used fictitiously. Any resemblance to actual persons, living or dead, events or locales is entirely coincidental.

ISBN: 9781797756967

Also By Jack Hunt

The Renegades
The Renegades 2: Aftermath
The Renegades 3: Fortress
The Renegades 4: Colony
The Renegades 5: United
Mavericks: Hunters Moon
Killing Time
State of Panic
State of Shock
State of Decay
Defiant
Phobia
Anxiety
Strain
Blackout
Darkest Hour
Final Impact
And Many More…

Dedication

For my family.

Chapter 1

Ten minutes late. He should have known it would end badly from the moment the cabbie swerved into Las Vegas rush hour. Tyler Ford leaned forward in the cab and glanced out the windshield. Vehicles were bumper to bumper, silhouetted by the sun setting between the buildings of the concrete jungle. He sighed as the cab crawled forward a few inches and then the driver slammed the brakes on again. Tyler jerked forward. Exasperated, he fished into his pocket and dropped forty dollars over the driver's shoulder before getting out.

"What the…?"

"Keep the change. I gotta go."

He hopped out just as a green Kawasaki dirt bike with

two people on darted through the narrow space between vehicles and nearly plowed into him. The bikers shouted something before slaloming around him and the next vehicle like a professional racer. Tyler glanced at his phone to see if she had replied to his text. Nothing. That wasn't a good sign. Damn it. He didn't want to screw this up. She looked good, really good and pickings had been slim lately. He was still two blocks from the restaurant but at the pace the traffic was moving he would be lucky to get there within an hour.

He took off running, adjusting a green backpack as he went. The damn thing was the last and only attachment he had to his family. Over the years the bag had changed but the contents really hadn't. A few items had been rotated but not much. Still, he found ways to use it and avoid explaining why he took it everywhere he went.

Moving traffic honked as he darted between vehicles, trying to get to the sidewalk. "Hey!" someone shouted, shaking an angry fist at him as he slid across the front of their hood just as they were moving forward. He didn't stop to argue, he simply threw up a hand to acknowledge and apologize.

Downtown Las Vegas was buzzing with activity. It was always like that. Not much had changed in the years he'd lived there. Old flea-infested motels were always being replaced by larger upscale hotels, billboards updated every month as new acts and services came to the city. Casino lights shone brightly, luring in another sucker with the hopes of riches only to spit them out with empty pockets.

"Hey darlin' you need someone to keep you warm tonight?" A prostitute walking her stretch of road tried her worn-out line only to have him ignore her. He used to stop and chat to them with the grand ol' hope of convincing them that it wasn't the life for them but it never worked. The second they knew he wasn't interested, they moved on. Vegas was all about commerce. Getting people in the door, relieving them of money and keeping the circus going twenty-four seven. It wasn't like he wasn't used to a tourist town, he was born and raised in Whitefish, Montana, but a population of 7,000 was a far cry from 641,000, at least that's what his father said before he departed at the age of eighteen for college.

But that was nine years ago.

The truth was he couldn't wait to get away. It wasn't that the town was awful, it was his father's strict rules. Had it not been for his Uncle Lou who now resided in Las Vegas but at one time lived in Whitefish, he might have still been there.

Sweating and out of breath, Tyler arrived at Andiamo Steakhouse on Fremont Street. It was a swanky upscale restaurant, certainly not the type of place he frequented. That was what worried him. He wasn't exactly rolling in money and the thought of having to act different from who he was only brought up painful memories of the past. It hadn't been selected by him but by her. In fact, she seemed quite adamant about where they would meet even though he'd been the one to suggest dinner. It struck him as odd. Previously, when he'd taken out other women on dates, they'd allowed him to select the place, and in all cases, he went for something middle of the road. Of course, he'd done his homework on the restaurant and that was when he balked. One glance at an uploaded menu online and he realized either she had a taste for the finer things in life or didn't care because she wasn't going to be footing the bill. As it would be their first date, and he didn't want to screw it up before he had a chance to meet her, he decided to give her the benefit of the doubt.

Tyler reached into his bag and pulled out some deodorant and gave himself a spray. He was wearing the only dress jacket, shirt and pants he owned. It was terribly wrinkled. In fact, the last time he'd worn the clothes, it was to his grandmother's funeral. He was more accustomed to wearing jeans and a T-shirt than anything fancy. He glanced at his reflection and quickly ran a hand through his dark floppy hair, breathed into his palm and sniffed. Okay, good. Stay calm. It had been a while since he'd gone on a date — at least eight months but that was because of his job. Management had put him on the night shift, and it had taken a while before he'd managed to convince his boss to give him days. Still, regardless of night or day shifts, his uncle had given him heck, trying to persuade Tyler to work for him, but he was done with all of that. It served a purpose when he first arrived but the whole point of getting away from Montana was to carve out a life of his own, free from the past.

Tyler stepped inside and walked through the brick archway and breathed in the smell of fine food. The sound of cutlery and glasses clinking could be heard as he caught a glimpse of the dining area which was partially exposed through a narrow doorway.

A well-dressed woman in a dark navy suit and white blouse, stood behind a leather counter looking down. Behind her was an elegant gold sign with the restaurant's name affixed to the hardwood wall.

The woman's gaze lifted, immediately making him feel self-conscious, as if in some way she was trying to suggest that maybe he'd walked into the wrong establishment.

She lifted her nose ever so slightly, all snooty like. "May I help you?"

"Yeah, I have a reservation," he said as he tried to peer around her shoulder and see if he could spot his date. All he had was a few photos from her Tinder profile. The woman in front of him shifted into his field of vision.

"Can I get a name?"

"Of course. Um. Ford. Tyler Ford. My date should already be here. I'm running late. Do you think I could just go through and see if I can find her?"

"I shouldn't be a second here," she said gazing down and running her finger over a page. As she was doing that, Tyler spotted her. His eyes widened. Holy cow, she looked good. Too good for him. Erika Lyons was sipping on a glass of wine, wearing a tight-fitting black dress. She had dark wavy hair that came down to her shoulders, and intense green eyes. Her profile pics didn't do her justice.

"Ah, yes, here we go." The woman glanced at her watch and made a huffing sound as if she wasn't impressed by his tardiness. She scooped up a menu. "Follow me." Her high heels clattered across the hardwood floor as she escorted Tyler into the busy room.

Either side of the room were private booths with brown leather backing, down the center were a dozen white cloth-covered tables each surrounded by four green leather chairs, and at the far end was an illuminated bar. Waiters in white dinner jackets, bow ties and black pants threaded around tables filling up glasses and smiling. He'd specifically requested a private booth, and he was relieved to see they'd accommodated. But not as relieved as he was to see Erika. She glanced up from her phone as they got close and Tyler smiled warmly before immediately rolling into his rehearsed apology.

"I am so sorry. The traffic was a nightmare," he said. As he slipped in across from her, his foot caught on the table and her drink toppled over. "Oh shit!" he said without even thinking. He snatched up a handful of napkins in front of him and immediately started patting down the table. "Again, sorry. I…"

"It's okay. Just um…" she said as the woman who had guided Tyler to the table shook her head and called out to a waiter to give him a hand. By now he was feeling like a complete fool. The look on Erika's face said it all. The chance of getting a call back, let alone experiencing a pleasant evening, was out the window. A waiter rushed over and within a matter of minutes he'd changed out the tablecloth and had everything dry. What he couldn't do was mop up the wine that had spilled on her dress. Erika dabbed at it and waved a hand when Tyler offered to help. "Just give me a minute," she said getting up from the table and swaying her way to the women's bathroom at the back of the room. As Tyler sat there feeling like a chump, he glanced at the menu and balked again at the prices.

The same waiter who'd assisted in the clean-up returned with a notepad in hand. He said, "Can I start you with a drink, sir?"

Tyler chuckled thinking of the irony. "Yeah, I'll take a beer."

"What kind? We have…" he began rattling off a whole host until Tyler told him to make the choice for him. As he walked away, Tyler noticed Erika's phone across from him. It began buzzing. He pulled out his own and tried to relax and act as though he wasn't fazed but the truth was, he felt like a world-class buffoon. Erika's phone buzzed again and he looked towards the bathroom. She still wasn't back. He envisioned her standing near a hand dryer vent cursing under her breath. Her phone buzzed again. He wasn't one for poking around in anyone's business, and certainly not someone he'd just met or planned on dating, but call it a gut feeling or the fact that he'd shown up late, he couldn't resist leaning forward. The cover was open leaving the messages she got in full view. Maybe that's why he didn't feel too bad turning it ever so slightly as one message after the other came in. That's when he noticed his name in a reply. A wave of guilt hit him and he leaned back in his seat as the waiter returned with his beer.

"Thanks," he said as he tried to push the thought of reading the message from his mind. *Who was it? A friend, brother, mother? Ex?* It wasn't like he needed to know. They were probably just wishing her all the best with the date. Or... his mind started churning over. Every few seconds he glanced up to check that she wasn't on her way back. And then, after waiting a few more minutes he couldn't resist. He took a swig of his drink and leaned forward turning her phone around, and reading the last message that was in full view. There was a comment from someone called Trish.

"Ha, order the most expensive thing on the menu. Will serve him right. Anyway, there is Michael on Saturday, and Darren on Sunday. I'm choosing the next restaurant."

Tyler frowned as he looked up again, then flicked the screen. There was no password so it opened and the text message system was in full view. He flicked it a few times to go back and see what Erika had said.

"Let's hope he wasn't using a fake photo on his profile," Erika said.

"Ah, like that slob who showed up on Tuesday? Oh well at least the meal was good."

"Yeah."

"What are you going to do about Chad?"

"I'm still meeting with him tonight. If this guy doesn't show in the next ten minutes I'm leaving."

"Even if he does, I would block him."

"Already have," Erika replied.

"Ha! At least this one will make a good blog post."

"I'm thinking it would get a lot of hits on it."

What kind of game was she playing? Tyler glanced up. Still no sign of her. Her purse was still on the seat so she hadn't gone out the back. He continued reading and it didn't take him long to realize that she was a serial dater. A woman who used online dating sites to fish for men and then have them bankroll her dinner, only to later go on and blog about the encounter in unflattering terms. More emojis were posted, along with a link to her last blog post from the day before. Tyler scanned it quickly and made a mental note of the blog. The post was about telling a guy she would go back to his place after dinner only to bail on him after finishing dessert. The blog came across cold, heartless and kind of shallow.

He closed the message program and turned the phone

around, pressed the button on the side to make the screen go dark then leaned back waiting for her to return. A number of thoughts went through his mind. He could get up and leave. He could out her and tell her the gig was up. Or they could order a number of expensive items and he could do exactly what she'd done to the fat slob (her words) the night before, and bounce before the bill showed up. He frowned, and drummed his fingers on the table. Before he could make a decision, he looked up and she was there.

"Ah that's better."

"All dry?" he asked, trying not to give away that he really didn't care. Within a matter of minutes his view of her was tainted. Her beauty was now seen through a dirty lens. Even the least attractive woman in the restaurant looked more appealing than her.

"Yeah," she said with a wave of the hand. "Anyway, let's order."

"Let's do that," he said running his hand over his chin and wondering how someone could be so cold and calculating. Was she hard up for cash? Hell, he wasn't living the high life, but stooping so low as to date men only for a meal at restaurants she'd picked, now that was below the belt.

"Tell me, you ever dined here before?"

She swallowed some wine. "No," she said looking around. "But I've been meaning to."

"Yeah, I bet you have," he said. "What about Vic and Anthony's Steakhouse?" He'd seen it mentioned in her blog the night before. Curious to know what her response would be, he tossed it out there.

She glanced up and without hesitation said, "No. Can't say I have."

Tyler took a sip of his beer and his lip curled at the corner. He'd recalled the names of a few other establishments so he threw those out for good measure, and one after the other she denied it. Wow, this girl was damn good at lying.

The window of opportunity to walk away soon came and went as the waiter took their orders and brought them from the kitchen. Still unsure of what he was going to do, he'd begun to think that perhaps turning the tables on her would be best.

"So, you work as a tour guide?" she asked.

"Yeah, most days I take folks out to the Grand Canyon but I sometimes do runs to Area 51. It's whatever they want."

She nodded and smiled. "I always wondered what that was like."

Knowing that she was lying about the restaurants he wondered what else she had lied about. Was her name even Erika? And why had she been so elusive about telling him what she did for a living?

"Ah there's not much to it. Doesn't pay too good but it beats being stuck behind a desk. I get out there in God's country and there's nothing better than seeing smiles on family's faces. The nice part is I only deal with folks who are having a good time. What about you?"

The waiter returned and began mixing up a Caesar salad in a wooden bowl in front of them. He'd just expected them to bring it on a plate but no, they had to send a guy to create the dressing and give some long-winded speech. Once it was dished up and she tucked into it he waited for her to reply. She didn't. She stuffed her face and began chomping on the romaine lettuce like a cow eating its cud. Not wishing for her to duck out of it, he asked again.

"So, what do you do for a living, Erika?"

She swallowed hard, dabbed the corner of her mouth and took another large gulp of her wine while eyeing him over the rim. He maintained eye contact to let her know that he wasn't going to drop it until he got an answer. It wasn't like he was asking her if she slept with a guy on the first date, or how much she earned.

Erika placed her drink down and stabbed another piece of lettuce then looked at him. "I work in…"

C'mon, think up your best lie, he thought.

"Advertising."

"You do. What kind of advertising?"

She jammed the lettuce into her mouth almost

immediately upon hearing the question. An attempt to not answer? More delays? He was beginning to think that everything she was telling him was a lie. Who cared what was truth if she wasn't planning on seeing him again?

She never did give an answer. Maybe it was her smooth ability to change topic or the annoying waiter that kept coming over and asking how their meal was, but she ducked out of it and they spent the rest of the evening in small talk with him doing most of the talking as she seemed distracted.

As the evening came to a close, the waiter slipped the bill across the middle of the table. She looked at it and pulled out some makeup from her purse and began to touch up her lips. No doubt getting ready for her next date with Chad.

Tyler didn't turn the bill over. He didn't need to know the total. In his mind it would be expensive. She'd gone through four appetizers, three drinks, a large steak, small potatoes, veggies, and polished all that off with cheesecake. Even after all that he expected her to ask him to foot the bill for a cab home.

He contemplated going to the bathroom and ducking out. It would have been really easy. A quick chat with the waiter on the way to let him know she would be paying, and the rest would be history. He'd head home with a story to tell, and she'd finally know what it felt like to be the punch line.

But that wasn't how it ended. Instead he decided to drop the truth on her, and go one better, making it clear that she hadn't got to him.

"So, what are your plans tomorrow?" she asked while glancing around the room. It was obvious she didn't give a crap. So, he thought he would catch her off guard. No one had probably done it before. He took the bill and motioned to the waiter to come over. He handed off his credit card, and said, "Take 15 percent for yourself, and would you mind paying the bill of the table behind us and the one ahead of us as well as ours? No need to tell them who paid. Let it be a surprise."

"Of course, sir. Thank you. That's very generous."

He didn't look forward to getting his statement. It was going to hurt, that was for sure. Without missing a beat, he turned back to her with a smile on his face. "Tomorrow? I'll probably look for someone else on Tinder to take out. Someone who's not in the habit of serial dating and taking advantage of men. Maybe we'll date some more, and who knows… but you…" he turned his phone around. "I would have blocked you but you had already done that. But of course you're used to doing that. I'm sure you'll do it with Chad tonight, Michael on Saturday and Darren on Sunday, won't you, Erika? Or is that even your name?" Tyler cocked his head to one side and waited for the response.

Her cheeks went a deep shade of red and she slipped her phone and makeup back into her bag, rose from the table and went to walk away. She took about ten steps before she turned around and came back. "My name is Erika and I wasn't lying. Chad is my brother. And as for Michael and Darren, those are two people my friend has arranged dates with, not me. But I guess you didn't dig far enough inside my phone to realize that."

With that said she turned and walked to the entrance where she collected her jacket and exited into the evening. Tyler sat there finishing off his drink, mulling over what she said. He wasn't sure whether to believe her or not. It didn't matter now anyway. He didn't want to hook up with a girl who hung around with friends that treated guys like that. Sure, guys might have done it to them but he wasn't like that.

The waiter returned with his card. He signed off and thanked him. Tyler got up and smoothed out his wrinkled jacket and headed towards the exit. As he walked through the lobby, he noticed Erika had returned and was standing by the main counter talking to the restaurant employee. She glanced at him and turned away. He shrugged and walked out into the night trying to hail a cab. It was a terrible night but just the beginning of something far worse.

Chapter 2

Minutes earlier

The nerve of the guy. Erika exited the restaurant and took a moment to text her friend and update her on the situation. Trish shot back a response almost immediately.

"Don't worry, darlin', you've just saved yourself a whole world of heartache. Even if he was good looking, a tour guide and capable of taking you up in a helicopter. There are plenty of ways to see this great city from above, and lots of men ready to take you out. You want me to pick you up for drinks?"

"I can't. I promised I'd go out with Chad. He's only in town for the evening."

"All right, hon. Keep your chin up."

"Trying."

As soon as she disconnected, she slipped the phone into her bag and looked back inside the restaurant. She had a good mind to go in and chew him out some more. Going through her phone? Who the hell did that? She looked off to her left and figured she'd have to call a cab to pick her up. No sooner had the thought passed through her mind than she heard an engine, then felt a tug and before she knew it her handbag was gone — torn straight off her shoulder.

"Hey!" she yelled at the thieves who were on a green dirt bike. One was driving, and the person on the back had her bag. They looked back and stuck up a finger before disappearing into the busy crowd. She tried to get the attention of people around her but they just looked on bewildered, thinking she had mental problems. Erika gave chase for a couple of minutes but it was useless. She returned to the restaurant even more pissed than when she exited. She couldn't believe that anyone would have the nerve to do that. Erika peered inside the steakhouse hoping to not see Tyler again. She didn't have much choice but to go in and see if they would let her use a phone to call Trish. She trudged in scowling and angry.

As soon as the woman at the counter saw her, her eyebrows shot up expecting the worst.

"Everything okay?"

"No. I just had my bag stolen and it has my phone in. Could I use your phone?"

"Of course."

Right then as the greeter handed her the phone, Tyler came out and cut her a glance. Erika turned her back not wanting to engage with him. Quickly she dialed in the number and prayed that it would connect so she didn't have to enter into an embarrassing conversation. No doubt he would see this as another lie, or an attempt to get what she wanted. Trish picked up.

"Trish. Thank God. Look, I'm in a bit of a bind here. Some asshole just swiped my bag and now I'm without my phone, money or means of getting back to the hotel. Do you think you can swing by and give me a lift?"

"Oh shit."

"Oh shit, what?"

"Had it been five minutes ago, I would have said yes

but I ended up grabbing a ride with Rachel and Kelly. I'm headed south to Kelly's place."

"Oh great." Erika sighed. "This night is just getting worse by the minute."

"I'm sorry, hon. Let me see if I can get her to swing back around." Erika heard Trish put the phone against her body as the voices and music in the car became muffled. She turned to see if Tyler was lurking but thankfully he was gone. A few seconds later, Trish got back on. "Ugh. No can do. Kelly told Brianna that she would be swinging by to pick her up in a few minutes and with the way traffic has been today…"

"I get it. Don't worry, I'll…"

"You could always call—"

"I'm not calling him."

"He would pick you up."

"Yeah and probably have her with him. I'm not doing it." She sighed and then Trish said she would call her later. After hanging up she thanked the greeter and ran a hand through her long hair. The thought of calling up her ex was nearly as bad as the idea of phoning her mother. Both would be embarrassing and she wouldn't hear the end of it. No, she would rather trek through the city on foot.

"Anything else we can help you with, ma'am?" the lady asked behind her.

Erika turned and smiled. "Can I borrow your car?" she said jokingly. The woman let out a chuckle and was about to answer when the phone rang. The greeter snatched up the phone to quickly bury herself in her duty.

"Andiamo Steakhouse."

Erika knew that was her cue. She trudged out into the humid evening, pissed off and frustrated. She weighed her options again. The journey to the hotel had been a twenty-minute car ride, on foot it would take her at least an hour and a half and that was if she double-timed it and knew her way. Having only lived in Las Vegas for the past year, she'd become accustomed to the main veins of the city but had always driven or been driven. She adjusted her tight black dress and was about to set off south for Las

Vegas Boulevard when a familiar voice called out to her.

"Erika."

She grimaced and turned to find Tyler leaning against the wall, one foot up on the brick, the other straight against the asphalt. He flicked a cigarette on the ground and blew gray smoke out the corner of his mouth before strolling over. A smoker? He'd said nothing on his profile about smoking. Had she known she wouldn't have given him the time of day. Her ex was a smoker. It was like kissing an ashtray.

"Go away," she said as she walked off into the crowd.

A few seconds later he fell in step. "I couldn't help but overhear that—"

"Just as you couldn't help look at my phone?" she said cutting him off and not looking at him. She didn't slow for even a second. The hope was he would get the point and vanish like all the other guys she'd dated.

"I guess I deserve that." They slipped through a loud crowd of college students and Erika felt a pang in her stomach for the old days. The days when life was easier.

The days when she didn't have to try and prove anything to anyone.

Tyler continued. "Look, I know we didn't start off on the right foot. But I can assure you I didn't intend for this night to go the way it has. In fact, I was really hoping—"

"That you would take me back to your place? Go for a nightcap? So you could have a wild story for your bros about how you got laid? Is that right? Please!" she said shaking her head and walking on. Tyler stopped and for a brief second, she thought she was free of him but no, just like an annoying fly he came up alongside her again.

"You know, it's not exactly like you helped yourself. Why did you block me?"

"What?"

"You blocked me on Tinder before our date was even over. Before I had even had a chance."

"Actually, I blocked you because I thought you were going to be a no-show and message me a bunch of excuses. I did it before you showed up."

"Fair enough. But what about…"

She'd had enough. Erika stopped in her tracks, turned and jabbed a finger against his chest. "Look, I don't need to explain myself to you. The fact is I was still there when you showed up late."

"I told you why I was late."

"And I'm meant to believe you?"

"Yeah, just like you want me to believe you don't serial date men."

"I don't want you to believe anything. I want you to disappear. Leave me alone," she said as she walked away. Now anyone with a lick of sense would have taken the hint and written off the night as a bad date. Not him. No, he was persistent.

"How are you going to get home?"

"Walk."

"To where?"

"None of your business."

"Erika, look, you don't have any money or a phone. Let me call a cab for you. We can share the ride."

"Uh, no," she said glancing back. "But thanks." A

flicker of a smile appeared on his face as if he thought it was some kind of game.

"I'll drop you off wherever you want. I promise I won't say another word."

"Nope."

The heat and humidity of the summer was almost too much. She could feel beads of sweat rolling down to the small of her back and she'd only been walking a few minutes. The thought of hiking for over an hour in high heels was already giving her mental blisters. There was no way she was going to take off her shoes. The grime of Las Vegas was gross. Besides the few places she had visited, overall, she found the city had a tacky feel to it, making her feel used and always in need of a shower.

"Man, you are stubborn."

She stopped and turned around and glared at him. He was standing a few feet from her with one hand on his hip, and the other wiping sweat from his brow.

"All right," she said walking back.

"All right, what?"

"Hail a cab. But this isn't an invitation for a nightcap."

He grinned. "I didn't say it was."

"And this doesn't mean that anything has changed between us."

"I didn't expect it would," he said turning and raising a hand to try and get the attention of a cabbie. They walked down Carson Avenue for a good five minutes before he managed to flag one down. After it swerved over to the sidewalk, Tyler opened the back door and gestured for her to get in. She slipped by him without making eye contact and he hopped in after her. Inside it smelled like an Indian restaurant. The cabbie was holding a half-eaten donair sandwich with one hand and he had the other on the wheel.

"Where you heading?" The driver asked.

Erika leaned forward. "Lyons Grand Vacations at the Flamingo."

The driver gave a thumbs-up, tossed his sandwich on the passenger seat and hit the button to start the meter. He cranked up the volume for a local radio station and rolled out into the clogged-up streets.

Tyler nodded thoughtfully. "Hold on a minute. You said you are in advertising. What are you doing staying at the Lyons? You meeting Chad there?"

"No, I live there."

He chuckled and glanced at her as if trying to gauge if she was telling the truth. That's when the penny dropped. "Erica Lyons. Lyons Grand Vacations. You own the chain?"

"No, my mother does but if she had her way, I would be spending every waking hour there."

"But you told me you were in advertising."

"I am. Hotel advertising."

Tyler nodded. "Advertising your mother's chain of hotels and restaurants. Right. Got it. Why didn't you just say that?"

Lyons was a large chain that was in forty different countries. Her parents had started out with one hotel back in their early twenties and over the course of their life branched out into franchising. Since the 1990s business had exploded and they were now a household name synonymous with elegance and clientele with deep pockets. Of course, they had another chain of hotels that catered to families and those who didn't have a taste for the finer things in life, but those didn't produce anywhere near the income the Lyons chain did. In Vegas alone, there were eight hotels.

"Would you have paid for the meal if I had?"

His eyes widened and his jaw went slack. "So that's why."

"No, that's not why."

Tyler laughed. "Of course it is. You feel self-entitled. Mommy has been paying for everything since you were born and you don't expect anything less from guys you date, except…" he trailed off raising a finger to his lips. Before he could finish his thought, Erika interrupted him.

"You are such an asshole. I don't even know why I agreed to go out with you."

Tyler shifted in his seat to face her but she wouldn't look at him. "Okay then, while we are on the topic, why did you?"

"Uh, how much further?" she asked the driver trying to avoid answering.

"Erika, don't dodge the question. Why?"

"Because I thought you were different."

"Really? In what way?"

"I…" she trailed off and looked out the window.

"C'mon. Why did you agree to go out with me? You must have known from what I told you about my work that I wasn't exactly Lyons material."

She scoffed. "Please. Give me a break."

"Oh, so you're in the habit of dating guys who probably make less money in one year than you make in one month. Hell, one week!"

"Money. It's always about money. That's why I didn't say anything. I wanted to see if someone would like me for me not for my family ties."

"And you think Daddy would be real pleased if you bring someone like me home?"

She turned and looked at him and Tyler must have

assumed she was analyzing his clothing as he was quick to continue. "Yeah, that's right. This suit. It's the only one I own. And did you know I wore this to my grandmother's funeral? Yep. Same one." He smiled and sniffed his armpit as if finding satisfaction in telling her that he hadn't put in any effort for the date.

Erika narrowed her eyes. "Actually, I was looking at that dusty old bag of yours but thanks for the additional information, it confirms my belief about you."

His eyebrow went up. He looked at the bag but said nothing.

She shook her head and looked towards the front, hoping the driver would reach the destination soon. The sooner she could get out of the vehicle and away from him the better. She really didn't want to have a conversation but something had been bothering her ever since the night went south. "So why pay for the other meals back at the restaurant? Was that meant to impress me?"

"No, it was to show you that money doesn't mean shit

to me either. I figured if I was going to be the next post on your blog I might as well make it worth reading."

"That's not my blog. It's Trish's."

"Really? And so the text that mentioned a post getting a lot of hits — that wasn't you gloating about what you were hoping to achieve tonight?"

"Such an asshole. It was meant for Trish. It wasn't directed towards you."

"Oh well that makes everything better."

She fixated on his eyes. Close up and under the lighting, that was when she noticed they were a deep blue. Back in the dim lighting of the steakhouse she thought they were a different color. She looked away realizing that she had stared a little too long.

"I didn't tell you about the hotels because I wanted you to get to know me. Me," she said again emphasizing the word. "And as for my father. I don't give a damn what he thinks. He's barely been around most of my life, and that includes my mother." She paused. "I was raised by a nanny."

Tyler rolled his eyes. "First world problems, what a tragedy," he replied before glancing out the window. "At least you had someone around."

She narrowed her eyes, pursed her lips, folded her arms and looked ahead. She would have asked what he meant by that but she was already trying to crawl out of the conversation. "Can't this heap of crap go any faster?" she asked the driver. Instead of answering he simply gestured to the road ahead which was chock full of vehicles. She was contemplating getting out and walking the remainder of the way. Sure, it would kill her feet but she was more than willing to suffer a blister than deal with him.

Out the corner of her eye she could see him tapping in a number on his phone before lifting it and waiting for Facetime to kick in. An older man appeared. He had to have been in his late sixties. Bald, a thick gray beard and large shoulder muscles. Behind him were numerous clothes hangers.

"Hey Uncle Lou," Tyler said. "Sorry I had my ringer off. I got your texts. What's the matter?"

"Are you near a radio?"

"Yeah. Why?"

"Tune into 92.3."

"Look, I'm on a date."

"You were," Erika chimed in to correct him.

Tyler shot her a sideways glance before looking back at the screen.

"Tyler, just do it. Now."

"Okay, okay." He leaned forward "Hey, mister, you think you can tune into 92.3 and turn up the volume?"

"No. I'm listening to my jams."

Tyler shook his head and got back on with his uncle. "He won't tune into it. Just tell me what's going on."

"There is something big happening, Tyler. I was chatting with a buddy of mine out in L.A. and he was telling me there have been power outages across the west side of the United States and reports of telecommunication outages. It doesn't look good."

"Uncle Lou, what have I told you about this?"

"Tyler, I'm not messing around here."

"Did he put you up to this?"

"No. Listen."

"I'm done listening. I will be home later."

With that said Tyler hung up and shook his head as he looked out the window. He tapped his phone against the bottom of his chin and looked lost in thought. Erika noticed something she hadn't seen before. Tattooed between his thumb and finger was a small dove, and beside that a number three.

"Um. Do you live with your uncle?"

"Unfortunately, yes. I'm planning to get my own place soon but…" He shook his head and she kind of figured that money must have been tight. What other reason would someone who was in their late twenties have for staying with a family member unless times were hard. She might have probed him more had they been on better terms but after the way the evening had gone, she opted to let it go. Instead she asked him about what he'd said.

"You seemed pretty dismissive of what he had to say."

"If you knew him like I did, you would too."

"But he sounded concerned."

"They always do."

"They?"

He groaned and shook his head again. Obviously, a touchy subject, and one that didn't seem as if it could be cleared up in a few words.

"Would you mind if I used your phone? I should call my brother. Uh. He was flying into Vegas this evening and I was going to meet him at the hotel."

"Knock your socks off," Tyler said handing her the phone without looking at her. He certainly had been disturbed by the call. Gone was the smile. Erika tapped in Chad's number and waited. It rang a few times but went straight to voicemail. She didn't bother to leave a message as she didn't want him calling Tyler's phone. Instead she tried to reach the hotel and speak to Luanne, the hotel concierge.

"Oh hey, it's me. Has Chad arrived yet?"

"I haven't seen him, Erika."

"No phone messages?"

"Let me check."

She placed her on hold for a minute and returned to say there had been one, something about his flight had been cancelled. All flights were grounded until further notice.

"And power outages?" Erika asked.

"Yes."

The moment she said that Tyler's head turned. Without saying a word to her he leaned forward and grabbed hold of the cabbie causing him to swerve in the road. "Tune into 92.3. Please."

"Okay. Geesh. You know I don't have to put up with this. This is my…"

"Yeah, yeah, yeah, just tune in."

Static fuzzed as he turned the dial and the station kicked in. He turned it up. Two people were in the middle of a serious conversation about what was happening on the West Coast. "They are still trying to determine what has happened. Bob, can you…"

Before they could hear any more the signal went fuzzy

and in the next second the car stalled and all of them jerked forward in their seats.

"What's going on?" Erika asked.

The driver tried turning over the engine but it wouldn't start.

He wasn't the only one. A large number of vehicles on the road had stopped working. The newer ones at least. The working ones, which were older, couldn't drive on as the others were now blocking the way.

"Tyler."

Tyler ignored Erika as he stepped out, his eyes widening as he watched light after light blink out. Vegas was the city of lights. A concrete jungle that was lit up twenty-four seven but here he was leaning against the car witnessing something he'd only ever heard about as a youngster. "No. It can't be true. No."

"Tyler. What is happening?" Erika asked as she got out. She along with many passengers began to fill up the road, all perplexed by what was happening and all they were seeing. The entire city was shrouded in darkness.

Chapter 3

It was to be a simple transfer of seventy-nine prison inmates from North Dakota's State Penitentiary to a Washington state facility to ease space and staffing issues. Overpopulation of county jails, treatment facilities, pre-release centers and state prisons had become a chronic problem across America. North Dakota was no different. Earlier that evening, Gabriel Johnson had been in his cell getting some extra needed shut-eye when a correctional officer banged on his single cell and told him to pack his belongings. He was being transferred. There was no warning. No explanation. Any attempt at asking questions was met with shouts to keep quiet. Keeping them in the dark. Keeping them guessing. That's just the way they liked it. It was all about control and they had been trying to control him for the past six years since he'd been incarcerated for armed robberies and killing a cop. In those six years things hadn't got any better for him.

Three failed attempts to escape had ended with him bludgeoning to death a correctional officer, being given more time and thrown in solitary confinement. It had taken the better part of a year before they changed their minds and put him back into general population where his twin brother Marcus was serving time for the kidnapping and murder of three women. Since then he'd been doing his best to keep his nose to the grindstone and avoid trouble if only to figure out how he could escape again.

Heavily shackled and dressed in the usual orange prison garb they shuffled onto the plane and were directed to their seats. For the first hour of the journey, on the bus from the pen to the airport, Gabriel had no idea if Marcus was being transferred. He recognized some of the men — Jericho Wells, Bill Pope, and Torres Hernandez just to name a few. These were guys he'd shot the breeze with in the courtyard. The others? He looked around and spotted those he'd got into a fight with in the cafeteria. They sneered at him as if making it clear that if shit went south, they'd be there to settle the score. It was only when he boarded the plane did he see Marcus seated near the back.

"Hey Marcus."

He grinned, looking relieved. "Gabriel."

Marcus was identical in appearance. When they were kids, they would play tricks on their teachers and people in the town, pretending to be one another. They'd even used it to their advantage in the prison, styling and cutting their hair to create confusion just for the heck of it. The only way anyone could tell the difference was Marcus had a birthmark on the back of his shoulder. Beyond that, they were similar in practically every way.

"Inmates. Silence!" Ted Stevens, a correctional officer, said. Stevens was a brooding individual, six-foot, buzzed white hair, previously in the military. Although he once may have looked intimidating, whatever muscle had been there had turned to fat now that he was a few years out from retirement. His tolerance for insubordination bordered upon psychotic. Rumors had swirled about him arranging for beatdowns of anyone that looked at him wrong. Of course, they were nothing more than rumors to most but not to Gabriel. He'd felt first-hand the harsh consequences of crossing him. After Gabriel killed that correctional officer in a failed escape, Stevens soon got his payback. It occurred sometime after two in the morning on a weekend. The door to his cell abruptly opened, and he was torn from his bed, dragged to the floor and beaten within an inch of his life. The brutality was so severe that he couldn't speak because of the swelling. No charges had been brought, and it was unknown what excuse he came up with but it must have stuck. The prison administration had no idea what took place on shifts. Stevens made sure of that.

Gabriel took a seat two rows back from Torres. He had a teardrop just under one eye, and more tattoos covering his shaved head and throat. Once part of a gang, his reputation preceded him. A ruthless killer who wouldn't think twice about snapping someone's shit up. He was inside for drug trafficking, running a prostitution ring and multiple murders.

Gabriel turned and tried to make eye contact with Marcus.

It burned him to know that his brother was inside but it was to be expected. Their upbringing hadn't been exactly ideal. Their mother was a whore, their father absent and so it wasn't long before they were thrown into the system and shopped around like pieces of meat to different foster homes. Abuse both sexual and physical came with the territory and it wasn't long before they ran away and got caught up in the wrong crowd. Petty theft soon morphed into armed robberies, and although Gabriel tried to keep Marcus away from it, it was a losing game. What drove him to kill those three women vacationing would forever be a mystery as Marcus wouldn't discuss it and no amount of threatening him seemed to help. After a while Gabriel just let it slide.

"Hey Johnson," Jericho Wells said leaning in his seat across the aisle from him. A pale albino, he'd got the attention of the prison when he first arrived. "You heard anything?" Jericho was a complete lunatic. Though short in stature, he made up for it with his unpredictable and unstable nature. Gabriel had seen him rip a guy's penis off with his bare teeth. The victim was twice his size, a meathead who when he wasn't pumping iron in the yard, he was in the habit of doing the rounds and picking someone new as a fuck buddy. He made a bad choice when he selected Jericho. *Keith Anderson.* How could he forget that guy's name? How could anyone? After cornering Jericho in the showers with two of his pals, he thought he had the upper hand, that was until Jericho decapitated his nether regions. His pals got the hell out of there and by the time prison guards showed up, Anderson had bled out. No one touched Jericho after that. Hell, no one barely talked to him. Gabriel had. That kind of aggression just needed to be channeled and he intended to use it when the time was right.

"Nothing. No idea where we're going," Marcus replied.

"Washington state," Bill Pope said without looking at

them. He was seated three rows down from them.

Jericho frowned. "Yeah. What facility?"

"Does it matter?" Pope replied. Bill Pope was the grandfather of the group, though unlike Stevens, he didn't look his age. He was serving life inside for stealing vehicles, and the murder of a family and four police officers. No one would have guessed how violent he could be. On the surface he was a mild-mannered individual. He had a trimmed salt-and-pepper beard, round spectacles and an athletic appearance. He often caused people to wonder if he was on the same diet as the others. He radiated health and that was an unusual thing for anyone locked up. The food was shit. The conditions even worse. And yet he thrived. Pope continued, "It's the same shit just packaged differently."

"You've got that right," Marcus said from behind him. "Though it would be good to know what we're heading into."

"It's larger than what we just left," Pope said turning his head. He squinted at Gabriel and a thin smile flickered across his face. "Overpopulation in the pen. Look around you. The only ones that are being moved are high offenders, or those serving life sentences which means it will be years before any of you return to Dakota for parole. I imagine they are sending another group to another state."

"They can do that?"

"Sure they can. They do it all the time. In the forty-three years I've been inside, I've been transferred three times. They keep the low-risk prisoners in county jails and then move us to another state before they transfer in more."

"Essentially refilling it. How the hell does that help them? It's no different," Marcus said.

"It makes room for more in county, numbnuts," Jesse Walker, a guy that had been at odds with him, said.

"Hey asshole. Watch it," Gabriel said.

Walker laughed. "What are you going to do, beat me to death, Johnson?"

Gabriel knew any attempt on Walker would be an

attempt on Stevens. While he wasn't buddy-buddy with him, they had some kind of arrangement going. Gabriel was pretty certain that Walker was feeding him information, keeping him in the loop of prison conversations, specifically ones involving escape plans.

"It's not just that," Pope said. "It's a matter of cost. It costs them more to house us in Dakota than in Washington state."

The doors closed, sealed by another correctional officer named Martin Lee. He was a young guy, early twenties, Chinese American and overall friendly, maybe a little too friendly. Friendliness was seen as weakness. Inmates were always looking for ways to exploit the system and new correctional officers were prime targets.

It wasn't long before they felt the rumble of the plane and it took off down the runway. Gabriel was pressed back into the seat. He clutched the armrests and closed his eyes as they soared up into the night sky. It wasn't meant to be a long flight, roughly two hours and thirty minutes. He glanced out the window of the plane as it gained altitude. It had been a long time since he'd seen the state from above. In the forty-two years he'd been alive he'd only been on a plane once and that was to visit his mother a year before she passed from an overdose. The landscape soon disappeared as the plane tilted and changed course. As the plane climbed higher, time seemed to slow. He watched as others looked out the windows, most probably yearning to be free again.

He never knew how much he could miss his freedom until it was taken away.

"Soak it in, Johnson. It's the last time you will see the outside." Stevens chuckled looking over at Lee who wasn't smiling. Lee wasn't tainted or jaded by the system yet. He was an idealist like many that came through the doors. They worked there thinking they could make a difference. That somehow a word said, a kind action might change them but there was no changing lifers. The only escape from the claustrophobic environment was an hour in the yard, a family visit or the kiss of death.

For the first hour of the journey the inmates were

silent. A few chatted quietly to the man beside them but most kept to themselves and slept. Gabriel turned to face his brother who was two rows back in the seats across the aisle from him.

"You remember when mom took us camping in Theodore Roosevelt National Park?" Gabriel asked.

Marcus nodded. "Cottonwood Campground. Yeah. I remember not wanting to go."

"Then you loved it."

Gabriel gave a longing look out the window. "What I would give to go back to that weekend."

"One day, brother."

Gabriel inhaled deeply than sighed. "Just a few days under the open sky, a tent, good food, and…"

"And… shut the hell up!" Jesse said turning in his seat. "I'm trying to get some shut-eye here. I don't want to hear about your shitty weekend."

"What did I say?" Gabriel asked, leaning over testing to see if he could reach him. His shackles jangled. What he would give to be able to wrap the chain around Jesse's neck and strangle him. He'd already attacked his brother once inside, cut him across the abdomen and promised him the next time would be worse. But Gabriel. He didn't come near him. He knew better than that.

His conversation was interrupted by Stevens. "Johnson!" he said from his seat upfront. Stevens shook his head and Gabriel scowled and leaned back in his cramped seat.

"Don't we get peanuts or a drink on this shitty flight?" Torres asked.

"Yeah," a few others joined in.

Stevens just looked at them. Even if they could have a drink or a bite to eat, he wouldn't have let them know, or allowed it. He enjoyed watching them suffer. Any chance he got to take away an inmate's privileges was a good day in his books.

Gabriel turned to his brother. "You know—"

The plane lurched violently, and dropped before leveling out.

"Whoa. What the hell?" Jericho yelled.

"It's just a little turbulence," Stevens said. "Calm down."

Again it occurred. The plane heaved and they were forcibly pushed forward in their seats. Gabriel felt his seatbelt cut into him. It was tight around his waist, holding him securely in place. A few seconds later the plane was calm again. He craned his neck around to check on his brother. He knew he was afraid of heights. Even as a young kid he wouldn't climb many of the trees Gabriel would, he had to literally coax him and even then he never went high. Marcus had his eyes squeezed tightly shut and was white knuckling it.

Another jolt in his seat, and the overhead lights flickered.

The plane felt like a rocky van ride. It kept bumping up and down.

"How long we got left?" an inmate asked.

"Long enough," someone replied.

A few more minutes of turbulence and it eased off again. From his seat, Gabriel noticed Lee leaning over and talking to Stevens. He nodded with a scowl on his face and Lee unbuckled himself and motioned to another correctional officer. They disappeared behind the divider and emerged with a cart. He began rolling forward and handing out packets of chips, and asking if anyone wanted a drink.

There was a cheer that washed over the inmates but not Stevens. He gave Gabriel a cold stare as the smile left his face. For a short while he thought the rest of the flight would be peaceful. That soon ended when the lights flickered again and this time went out. Someone yelled, asking what was going on.

That was followed by the plane banking hard and Lee and the other correctional officer losing their balance and falling into the laps of inmates. In the darkness shouts could be heard but Gabriel was unsure of what was going on. He was too busy clutching his seat and hoping it leveled out like it had before.

It didn't. In that moment it dropped fast, several feet at first then that was followed by at least thirty feet in one swoop. Gabriel slammed into the seat in front of him and then was thrown back.

More yelling and cursing before it finally leveled out.

He glanced out the window trying to get a bearing on where they were. It was hard to tell at night what the landscape looked like. It was cloudy and dark. Were those trees or mountains?

"My God, I want to get off this plane," Marcus said.

"Don't be a pussy," Jesse said.

The overhead lights didn't come on so one of the correctional officers turned on his flashlight. Something wasn't right though. They could no longer hear the rumble of the engines. It was quiet. Too quiet. They were gliding. Only the rush of wind could be heard as it passed over the plane.

"Lee. Palmer. Get back in your seats," Stevens said.

They hurried back, taking the carts with them as the plane continued its descent.

"We're not near an airport, are we?" Gabriel asked grabbing Lee's arm as he passed him. He shook his head and pulled his arm away before moving quickly back to his seat and strapping in.

"There's no engines. We're going to crash," Jesse said. "We're going to crash."

"Who's the pussy now?" Gabriel said.

"Fuck you, Johnson."

Everyone was gripping their seat. Unlike a traditional flight, no one had gone through what to do if the plane had to make an emergency landing. He looked back at his brother, fear masked his face.

"Put your head between your legs."

"What?"

Gabriel showed him as his words just went in one ear and out the other.

Others who weren't doing it followed suit. Many were already preparing for the worst. The rumble of the plane got stronger, making it feel like it would tear wide open. As he sat there gripping his legs tight, Gabriel thought of all the people he'd ever cared about and every decision he'd made. What if he didn't survive this? Had he wasted his life? He looked up and saw Stevens trying his phone. A look of surprise and anger on his face as he showed it to Lee. It wasn't working.

From his crash position he glanced out the window and watched the puffy clouds wash over the plane. They were losing altitude fast as the plane took another sharp dive. Oxygen masks dropped down and all of them struggled to get them on their faces. His pulse sped up, and sweat formed on his brow as he clutched tightly and looked back at his brother one final time. Would this be the last time he saw him?

"Everyone keep your heads down," Lee yelled out.

Stevens gripped his seat, a look of fear masking his face as his body was shaken. Hierarchy no longer mattered. The playing field had been leveled. They were no longer prisoners and correctional officers but humans stuffed into a metal tube, praying and holding on for dear life. Each of them had been given the same sentence, the same chance of life or death, and each of their fates were sealed.

Adrenaline pumped through his body, and

overwhelming fear took hold as the plane shook and shuddered and he felt the violent grip of the air take hold in the final minutes before they would merge with the earth.

Then it dawned on him. Where were the exits?

He looked up briefly and made a mental note. Eight rows from the left exit at the front of the plane. He turned and yelled to Marcus. "When this bird lands, if you're still alive head towards the exit on your left."

Marcus didn't reply, his head was down and he was too scared to look up.

The plane began vibrating so hard that Gabriel was sure that it would tear apart in midair. Then came the sound of something hard slapping the bottom of the plane, thump, thump, thump. Metal creaked and bent, and it sounded like a piece was severed. Out the corner of his eyes he caught sight of trees and mountains, and then he prepared for the impact, he prepared for death.

Chapter 4

Around the same time, not but a few blocks from Las Vegas Boulevard, Nate Griffin was finalizing a deal with a guy only known as X. A red light flickered inside giving the whole interior of the apartment an exotic feeling. He'd been coming to X for the past two years. The gig was simple. He stole bags, phones, anything of value that he could snatch out of people's hands or off their shoulders. In return X would give him top dollar for every credit card and electronic device he had — phones, tablets, computers — everything had a monetary value, and back in Nigeria it could be sold for even more. Previous to meeting X he'd been taking it to another buyer but the payoff was peanuts.

X never showed his face. He wore a skull bandanna covering the bottom half of his jaw, and sunglasses and a beret. He always met him in different locations throughout Vegas and Nate only knew where to go about five minutes before meeting him. If he was five minutes late, X would be gone.

Nate arrived with his buddy Zach. Both of them were always dressed in tight leather motorcycle gear. Zach had long blond surfer hair that he usually tied back in a man bun when he wasn't wearing a helmet. He banged on the door and after a few seconds it opened and he was led in by an armed guy. X surrounded himself with armed heavies, guys who wouldn't think twice about blowing a hole in someone. Initially when he made the contact, he was worried that X would rip him off, kill him and throw him in a shallow grave but he'd been reassured that would have cost him money and he wasn't frivolous with his cash. No, as long as he delivered, and there was no heat following him, X would pay good money.

"So, what you got today?"

"A nice little stash," Nate said pulling off his backpack and emptying out the contents. In the course of an hour he could steal upwards of twenty phones. Many times he could take three or four on the same street before disappearing down the back streets. Cops didn't bother him. On the odd occasion they had been in the neighborhood or had given chase, Nate was able to lose them because they were always driving cars, and some of the narrow streets in Vegas were only accessible to bikes. They often changed out the bikes, many of which were provided by X himself. He had a collection of upwards of fifteen dirt bikes. License plates were stolen, clothing was changed, locations were never the same on any given day. The police didn't stand a chance. That was why he'd managed to elude them for the past three years. He and Zach would take turns riding a dirt bike. Whoever wasn't riding was the grab man.

"iPhone 10, an iPad, two Samsung phones, three Mac Airs and a whole range of other makes and models." Nate laid them out on display while X ran the numbers in his head. He pulled out a huge wad of notes from his leather jacket and thumbed off hundred-dollar bills. It was a good day. Seeing all that green made the risk worth it. It was more than enough to cover him and Zach if they wanted to take the rest of the week off but that wasn't like him. Nate had a goal to leave it all behind. Long before he'd got caught up in the criminal underbelly of Vegas, he'd been trying to pay his way through college where he was taking a game programming course. Everything was going well until his mother became sick and he had to quit to look after her. He had no siblings. An absent father. And no prospects on the horizon. It was like life wouldn't give him a break. After the death of his mother in Colorado he'd dodged creditors coming after him for money and packed up what little he had and headed for the city of lights. He had no idea what he would do or even where he would stay. But that all changed when he took a job at a local gas station, and met Zach. At first, Zach had been a little hesitant to tell him but when he got to know him more, he asked him if he wanted to make more money. The rest was history.

Nate counted the money and nodded before clasping hands with X and smiling. "Good doing business with you again." He gave half to Zach and they turned to leave.

"You guys interested in doing another job for me? Pays three times what you're earning now."

"What do you have in mind?" Zach asked.

"Bikes. I have a client that is interested in a large purchase but that means getting my hands on them and well, that's where you two come in. I have a few others guys who are up for it, so you wouldn't be going in alone."

Nate threw up a hand. "Nah, man. We'll stick to what we're doing, but thanks." He slapped Zach on the arm and turned towards the door. A few seconds and Nate looked back. Zach hadn't moved.

Nate frowned as Zach threw up three fingers "Three times, Nate."

"Are you serious?"

"Of course I'm serious," X said. "You won't be doing this alone. I'll provide the muscle, you just have to take the bikes. You call up the restaurants and fast food establishments and ask them to deliver. We already know they send out guys on bikes. They arrive. My guys will take care of the rest while you drive the bike to the drop-off point. Boom. You get paid!"

Nate stared at X and then his eyes darted to Zach. He couldn't believe Zach wanted to get involved in that shit. He'd heard about it happening. Delivery guys getting robbed at knifepoint, some of them ending up with acid in the face, all so bikes could be stolen and resold. Maybe he might have got involved had he never worked as a delivery driver. That had been his first gig when he came to Vegas. He knew the blood, sweat and tears those delivery guys had to go through to earn minimum wage for their families. He couldn't do it. Stealing phones was one thing, hurting people was another. Besides, if they were caught doing that, the time behind bars would be a hell of a lot longer.

Zach walked over to him and placed a hand on his shoulder trying his best to convince him that it made sense. "We make good money, Nate, but this shit is small time compared to what X will pay."

"Doesn't matter. It's too risky."

"You didn't hear the offer," X said.

Nate looked past Zach. "I already know. People talk."

"Do they?" X asked motioning to two of his guys. They strolled towards Nate and shoved him back into the center of the room.

Nate took off his bag and scowled at them. "What the fuck is this?"

X rose and walked over. "Who talks?"

Nate shrugged. "You know, people."

"Like you?"

Nate threw his hands up. "Whoa, dude, I did not say that. How long have we worked together, X? You know I have got your back."

"And yet here you are wanting to walk away from good money."

"It's not the money. It's the risk."

"I told you. My guys will handle it. You're just paid to be a driver. No different than what you are doing now, except you earn more."

"Yeah, because if we get caught, we'll go down with your guys. I'm sorry that's not happening."

For the first time ever, X dropped his mask, removed his glasses and hat and revealed who he was. Nate couldn't help but stare. He was a black guy with a scar down his cheek. Now he could see why he wore the bandanna, it was as much a cover for his disfiguration as it was to prevent those around him knowing who he was. Nate didn't recognize him but he knew immediately what X was doing. It was a form of blackmail.

"Now you've seen my face. You know what that means?"

Nate nodded.

"You're going to do the job, Nate. Okay? You're doing it. Now you can either get paid and keep your mouth shut or…" he trailed off. He didn't need to finish, Nate knew what would happen to him. Long before he met X, Zach had warned him not to fuck with X. Not to argue. Not to get into negotiating with him. What he said was gold. Untouchable. Even as far back as three years ago, he understood the risk but back then he didn't have a pot to piss in so he did what Zach said.

"Fine. I'll do it," Nate said.

Zach smiled.

"Good man," X replied before waving him off. His guys stepped out of the way of the exit and he and Zach left the apartment.

They hadn't got but a few yards down the hallway when Nate dropped his backpack and ripped into Zach, pinning him up against the wall. Through gritted teeth he spoke. "You ever do that again, and you and I are done. You hear me?"

"Get the hell off me. If it wasn't for me you would still be filling up gas tanks."

Zach pulled Nate's hands off his leather jacket and straightened out his top.

"What the fuck is up with you? You used to be cool."

"Yeah, well maybe I've changed."

"A leopard doesn't change its spots," Zach said turning to walk away. They walked over to the elevator. Nate kept his distance, watching the lights illuminate on the elevator as it came up.

"You know, Nate..." Before Zach could finish what he was saying, the lights flickered and then suddenly went out in the building.

"What the hell?" Nate said looking down the hallway. They saw the silhouettes of people coming out of apartments wondering what was going on.

Zach tapped the elevator button a few more times. "C'mon, man. Shitty, low-end apartments. Doesn't this elevator have a backup system in place?"

"Not a place like this," Nate replied.

From inside the elevator they could hear a woman crying out for help. Nate put his ear against the steel and listened. "Someone is stuck down there."

"Tough shit. The janitor will have to get them out when they get the power back on!" Zach said out loud as he strolled off down the corridor heading for the stairwell.

"Zach. Wait up." Nate adjusted his backpack and hurried over to him. "There's people in the elevator."

"And?" he said pushing into the stairwell as if it didn't matter to him.

"I heard a kid in there."

Zach stopped at the top of the stairs and walked back to him. "This is not the time to grow a conscience. Let's go, I'm hungry."

"Is that all you think about?"

"That, money and pussy, yeah," Zach said with a smile forming on his face. He headed down a few steps before he realized that Nate had gone back into the corridor heading for the elevator.

"Nate. C'mon, man. You are really getting on my last nerve."

"I want to see if I can help."

"Now you want to help? Maybe you should think about a different profession," Zach said coming up behind him as he raced towards the elevator. On some level Zach was right. He didn't owe those people anything. The fire department or the janitor of the building would probably get them out but that didn't mean he had to ignore the plight of others. Call it his one good deed for the day, or a guilty conscience from having stolen one too many iPhones from unsuspecting tourists, but he couldn't in good faith head out without at least seeing if he could help. People from the apartments were in the hallway talking, others trying to get their phones to work, while several more were at the far end looking out of a window. Nate leaned up against the elevator door.

"Can anyone hear us?" a male voice cried out followed by a young girl wailing. Their voices echoed inside the shaft. Nate banged a few times just to let them know that someone had heard them. He called out to tell them that help was on the way and not to panic. With that said he turned and looked around for anything that might be used to open the doors. Zach was leaning against the wall smoking a cigarette.

"You want to give me a hand?" Nate asked.

"You need a key to open it," he said pointing to a hole near the top of the elevator doors. "Only the fire department or janitor has that. That's what I was trying to tell you but oh no, don't listen to me." He took another puff of his cigarette as Nate hurried down the hallway to the knot of people staring out of the window. He was going to head down the stairwell and see if he could locate management but he didn't get that far. He paused at the stairwell, one hand on the door, and glanced at the window everyone was looking out. A few of them gasped. He jogged over to see what had their attention. That was when he got his first sight of the ensuing chaos. Far below the city was blanketed in darkness. A few lights were on, emergency backup generators kicking in, but for the most part the city was shrouded. Cars, trucks, motorbikes and large eighteen-wheelers had come to a standstill, though there were others that were operational. Strange. How had the entire city's power gone out? Was it a terror attack? He thought back to some of the incidents that had occurred over the years. Many of them coincided with natural disasters but there had been no earthquake, and the weather was as good as could be.

The people around him were talking about their phones not working. Nate pulled out his. The screen lit up because he still had battery life but there was no signal, and no internet. Turning on the flashlight portion of it he cast the glow down the corridor towards Zach.

"Zach. You need to see this," he said before he realized that Zach was gone. "Zach!" He hurried back towards the elevator and on to the next stairwell at the other end of the hallway. Inside, he could hear and see a number of residents making their way down. He called out to Zach but got no response. *Asshole.* He'd ditched him.

Just about to head down, he heard a scream coming from the knot of people at the far end of the hallway. They all began rushing towards him, fear gripping their faces. "Go. Go! It's a plane," a red-headed woman closest to him yelled in terror just as he glimpsed the nose of the airplane. It all happened so quickly. He lunged forward towards the staircase as did several of the people nearby. What transpired next came in a series of loud bangs mixed with glass breaking, and the entire building shaking. He was sure he was going to die as his body tumbled head over feet down the staircase along with other people. No other thoughts went through his mind. Not the money he'd earned. Nor any of the hopes and unfilled dreams, everything vanished in a blur of pain, and screams.

An explosion ripped through the building, and then nothing but darkness and smoke.

Chapter 5

The Boeing 737 shook violently as it clipped the tops of Douglas fir trees over Glacier National Park. Gabriel knew the odds of experiencing a plane crash were low compared to driving but surviving a plane crash at night when the plane had no power? With his head between his legs, he began to pray. He wasn't a religious man but with all his transgressions he wanted to stack the odds in his favor. Air whooshed, and treetops snapped over and over again as they slapped the plane causing them to rock in their seats.

Around him he could hear some men asking forgiveness of their sins, others crying and one person singing an old hymn. It was strange to see hardened criminals buckling under the expectation of death. Death had a way of breaking through even the hardest of hearts and leveling the playing field.

The belly of the plane was no longer slapping against

flexible treetops. There was a huge bang, followed by another as the trunks of trees tore into the guts of the plane splitting it wide open like a can opener.

Gabriel tilted his head and looked out and saw what appeared to be water before one of the wings of the plane must have sheared off, sending the rest into a death roll. Whoever was flying the plane had to have been exceptionally skilled as no sooner had that happened than the nose hit the surface of the water, sliding through its murky depths at a tremendous speed. There was nothing more than a blur as his skin was slapped with water and the sheer force of metal hitting the water tore the cockpit away, sending a wave of frigid water into the cabin. Several rows of seats were ripped from the floor and forced back into the cabin. Gabriel saw four men disappear over his head, along with pieces of the pilot. He saw a North Dakota Penitentiary badge, along with the body of a correctional officer. He never saw the person's face but he hoped it was Stevens. Men cried out as each of them thought they were seconds away from death's door.

It was like watching everything play out in slow motion. There was a loud sound of metal snapping, and bending under the weight of water as the plane broke apart on impact.

What followed next was a large whoosh as water that had flooded in was sucked back as the plane began to slow its descent. Gabriel smashed his head into the seat in front of him and then rocked back and forth as he moved in and out of consciousness. With air trapped inside, it wasn't long before it began to partially bob in the water but it wouldn't end there. The heavy plane let out a groan and began to dip. Within seconds it would be fully submerged, along with all of them.

Gabriel wasn't sure at what point he blacked out, only that when his eyes snapped open, he took in a large lungful of air and gasped as his body began to shiver. It felt like a Mack truck had hit his head. Blood was trickling down the side of his face and droplets hit the surface of the water. Surface of the water? That was when he noticed that it was up to his waist.

The plane was banked to the left and quickly sinking.

In near darkness he gazed around and could see other men submerged. Whether they had survived the initial impact or not was neither here nor there, they were now dead.

"Marcus. MARCUS!" he yelled trying to get his attention without turning his head. His body was in so much pain and he was unable to move. He was sure he was paralyzed. But it wasn't that. It was just the cold. Shock was setting in and with it hyperthermia. If he didn't get out of there soon he would sink to the bottom of some unknown body of water, and that would be the end of his lineage.

"Hey. Let us out!" a voice yelled from behind him.

"Darius?" Gabriel yelled, recognizing his voice. Darius acknowledged him in his panicked state. A few others, hearing them, called out. More were alive. Hope rose in his chest at the thought that one of them might have got loose from his chains. Metal had twisted and wires were exposed, leading him to believe that maybe, just maybe some of the inmates' chains might have snapped. Sections of the floor had been torn apart and bent upright. Several of the food carts were floating on top of the water, one kept banging against a dead inmate's head.

More yelling ensued. This time it was Torres calling out for one of the correctional officers. "Lee. Let us out." All of them were secured with waist, wrist and ankle chains. It was meant to prevent them from starting problems on the plane, and it had, but now it would be a one-way ticket to an early grave if someone didn't let them out.

Gabriel craned his head around the seat in front of him. He could just make out Martin Lee who'd been sitting next to Stevens up front. Stevens was no longer there but Lee was, strapped into his seat with his head slumped forward.

"Lee. Wake the hell up!" Gabriel joined in, trying to get him to stir. He shook the chains around his wrist violently in an attempt to move but it was useless. The plane groaned and sank a little more bringing the water up to his sternum. "Shit!"

Fear turned into panic as the men cried out for help.

He twisted trying to see his brother but it was so dark he couldn't tell if he was alive or dead. It was then that Gabriel saw movement up ahead. Sloshing through the water, Stevens came into view. He had a gnarly gash on his forehead. Blood covered one half of his face, and there was a piece of metal sticking out of his thigh. He stumbled as he tried to make his way to Lee.

"Hey. Stevens. Let us out!" all the surviving inmates cried. It was hard to tell how many were alive. Darkness hid faces, and some of those who looked like they were moving were actually dead and just bobbing on the surface of the water. Stevens turned his face towards them, sneered and then focused on Lee. He clasped him by the shoulders and slapped his face a few times until Lee came to and started coughing. Unbuckling his belt, he helped him up.

"Lee!" Gabriel yelled finally getting his attention. He looked disoriented and bewildered. Stevens wrapped his arm around Lee's waist and tried to guide him towards the large opening where the cockpit had once been. "Stevens, you bastard, let us out!" Gabriel shouted. Stevens turned and flipped him the bird. That only infuriated Gabriel more. He tugged at his restraints like a penned animal. Stevens was going to leave them there to die. He didn't give a shit. Retirement would be a whole lot sweeter knowing that they were dead. He'd probably come up with some tale and Lee would have to corroborate his story, and being a newbie, he would.

Then the unexpected happened. Randall White, a raving lunatic who had gouged out the eyes of another inmate, suddenly emerged from the shadows, wading fast towards Stevens from behind. Stevens didn't know what was happening until Randall looped his handcuffs over his head and fell back into the water behind him. Torres started yelling, "Strangle him!"

Stevens fought for his life, trying to pull the chain away from his neck, but without being able to get a good footing on the ground, he was at a loss. All he could do was extend a hand to Lee who was still reeling from being unconscious. Gabriel heard Stevens cry for help. That was when Lee staggered forward, pulled his pistol and aimed it at Randall. "Release him. Now!"

"Not until you give us the keys."

That crazy fuck was doing it on behalf of all of them. That was the thing about inmates. You never quite knew who was going to stab you or have your back. They were a dying breed, literally.

All the while Stevens was yelling for him to shoot.

The metal of the plane groaned and creaked and it sank a little more, another reminder of their fate if Lee didn't act fast.

"We just want to get out."

Lee nodded, reached into a pocket and pulled out a set of keys.

"Let him go."

"The keys. Set them on that metal counter over there."

Lee hesitated for a second then waded through the water and placed the keys on the counter. Unknown to

Randall, Stevens was still packing a firearm. Because of how tight the chain was around his neck, and attempting to prevent Randall from strangling him, Stevens was unable to reach his service weapon. That all changed the second Randall eased off the pressure. A momentary lapse in judgement was all it took.

A fist punched out of the water holding a gun.

Before Randall had waded within a foot of the keys, Stevens unloaded a round into the back of his head. His skull vanished in a mist of red before he slumped into the water. Lee rushed forward yelling. "What did you do?"

"What you couldn't!" Stevens replied rubbing his neck. "Now move before this bird goes under."

Stevens began making his way out but Lee stood there looking at the body. Gabriel had seen that look in other correctional officers' eyes. Those who hadn't been hardened by years on the job found the reality of death hard to see.

"Lee. Let's go!" Stevens bellowed, stopping for a second. Lee shook his head, waded over to the keys, grabbed them up and began going to those who had survived to release them.

"Did you hear what I said?"

"I'm not leaving them here to die."

"They are already dead. Most of them are lifers."

Lee turned, a look of disgust on his face. "It's not right."

As he proceeded to unlock the binds of Torres, Stevens came towards him. Expecting that, Lee pulled his firearm but kept it out of view. Only Gabriel and the others could see what he was doing as he turned and told Stevens to back off.

"Drop the keys."

"No."

There was a second of tension before Stevens lunged at Lee and they fought for control. The keys dropped from his hand but were caught by Torres, who quickly used them to finish unlocking his waist and ankles. "Torres!" Gabriel said. Torres waded back and released Gabriel while Lee and Stevens continued to fight. Gabriel hurried back for his brother and found him slumped over. The only thing that had saved him from drowning was the tray in front of him had fallen forward and his head was resting on the top. "Marcus. Wake up." He unlocked his binds and then gave the keys to Torres to help Bill and Jericho out of theirs. Marcus was out cold so Gabriel wrapped his arm around him and dragged him out into the aisle.

A gun went off, a loud crack echoed in the fuselage and Gabriel turned to see Stevens slumped against Lee's body. He rolled him off and they watched as Stevens disappeared below the murky waters, a look of shock and horror on his face. A few bubbles came from his mouth and then he was gone. Lee stood there unable to believe what he'd done. Shock masked his face. He turned and looked at them. "I didn't mean to…"

"Doesn't matter now, kid, you're one of us," Pope said brushing past him, trying to get out. Another groan, and the plane let out its final death cry and the water began rushing in faster as it started sinking.

"Go. Move it."

The group waded through the water towards the opening, seeing only a faint glimmer of the moon's reflection on the surface before the front end disappeared below the water trapping them inside. "Help us out!" A few more inmates who were still locked in cried out but it was too late to save them. Torres had done the best he could, releasing a large number of inmates.

Marcus was still out cold so Gabriel held on to him tightly, took a deep breath and dove beneath the surface that was already up to his chin. Below the water it was just pitch dark. He swam forward towards the last glimmer of emergency light. He could see the silhouette of the others' legs as he swam hard out of the opening and headed for the surface.

He gasped as he emerged with his brother still in hand.

A cold breeze blew against his skin, carrying with it the scent of pine.

"I got you, brother. I got you," he said. More faces appeared to his left and right. Torres, Harry, Lee, Jericho,

Bill and several others. Around them, floating on the surface of the water, were bodies of inmates and floatation devices from the plane. A flock of birds broke from a nearby cluster of trees, wheeling overhead before heading towards the hills. For a second he was disoriented as he turned and looked around him. Where the hell were they? There were mountains surrounding them and a landscape of pines and fir trees. In the distance he could make out where the plane had gouged the trees and earth. A huge gash in the earth split the landscape. Turning 360 degrees in the water he could tell the plane had gone down in what appeared to be a large lake. Gabriel rolled onto his back, hooked his arm around his brother and swam backwards to the shore. They had survived the unthinkable, and were now free but it was only the beginning of trouble.

Chapter 6

Whitefish, Montana

Ten minutes earlier, Corey Ford was settling in for a night with his pregnant fiancée when the call came in from Flathead County Search and Rescue. After eight years in the Marines, he'd returned to his hometown to put down roots and had taken a position at his father's army and navy surplus store. Searching for a way to give back to his community, and use the skills he'd gained from his father and the military, he'd opted to volunteer for FCSAR. Calls dealt with everything from water and technical rock rescues to county disaster response, evacuation and emergency medical assistance.

Terry Murdoch, a close friend and co-worker, had called to see if he was available to respond to a mayday issued from a plane somewhere over Glacier National Park. A small team was assembling as they spoke to head out.

"Ah man," Corey replied, casting a glance at Ella. He'd been meaning to have some quality time with her. They were planning to get married in a year and had already moved in together, to the disgust of his father. She looked at him and turned off the TV and shrugged. She'd become accustomed to his need to drop everything and head out. Other women might have taken offense and guilted him out, but she was different. A medic for the local hospital, she understood more than anyone the responsibility he had. She mouthed the word go, and he told Terry to hold for a second. He placed the phone against his chest and said he would make it up to her.

"Don't make promises you can't keep."

"It's not a promise."

She smiled and walked off.

Corey got back on the phone.

"You got the coordinates?"

"Yeah, looks like the plane was close to Lake McDonald."

"That's some rocky terrain out there."

"Yeah, can you bring your 4 x 4?"

Before he could reply the call dropped, and the lights went out.

"Terry. Terry?" Corey said. He tried to phone him back but the line was dead. He leaned forward in his seat and yelled out, "Ella. You messing with the fuse box?"

"No," she said reentering the room. Corey got up and headed over to the window and looked out to check on his neighbors' homes. He lived on a stretch of road in the north end of town, not far from Whitefish Mountain Resort. It was about a fifteen-minute car drive from the downtown, and his father's store.

"Great, looks like we have a power outage. I hope this doesn't last. Fire up the generator. I've got to head out."

Corey hurried upstairs to get ready, slipping into warm outdoor clothes and collecting in a bag everything he would need. As he filled it, he looked at the worn-out green army backpack that his father had given him so many years ago. Tyler also got one. Its contents he knew by heart. Their usage had become second nature. At one time he carried everywhere he went. Not anymore. He scooped up his regular bag and went down.

"You got the keys to the truck?"

"Your father took it," she said.

"What?" He ran a hand through his curly brown hair, and then over his bearded jaw line. "Ah, man, when?"

"This morning when you were out."

"And he didn't think to ask?"

She shrugged. "You know him."

"Yeah, all too well." He glanced at his left hand and looked at the number three between his thumb and finger. He remembered the day he got the tattoo. It was on his tenth birthday. What it meant was only known to them but served as reminder, that was its purpose. He recalled the school phoning his parents to ask why both of their sons had tattoos on their hands. His father's response was clear. It was none of their business and perfectly legal in Montana with the parents' consent. For whatever reason the school didn't buy it. Child services were called and showed up at their home wanting to check on their welfare. The whole thing was made to be something much more than it was. Anyway, that was the last day they were a part of a public school. He yanked them out and homeschooled from then on. Never once did his father ask whether they wanted to leave. Nor did he consider the friendships they would lose because of it. The whole event was embarrassing, and their mother never said anything. She stood by his decision until the day she died.

Yeah, his relationship with his father had been a turbulent one, as had Tyler's. Both had dealt with him in different ways. Both carried more than physical scars. In recent years after returning from the military he'd tried to patch up things and forgive, but his father didn't make it easy. From an early age, his father had raised him and his younger brother to be prepared for a doomsday event. If there ever was a man committed to survival it was Andy Ford. He lived and breathed the prepper lifestyle. Whereas others merely did the bare minimum, his father had spent most of his life building and outfitting his home and outbuildings for the worst. Although he believed it would be an economic collapse, he had left no stone unturned in ensuring that his home was ready for any disaster. For the longest time the shelter was located at the end of a cul-de-sac, beneath their home. Over many years his parents had accumulated enough supplies to feed a hundred people. They had filled it with everything that was needed to survive: a bomb shelter, coal furnaces, kerosene refrigerators, a survival library stacked with books, bunk beds, barrels of dried food, multiple kitchens, showers, washers and dryers, generators, air filtration system, alternative sanitation and additional supplies. The only mistake he made was letting neighbors use the showers after the street lost power for three days. That was their mothers fault. She had a big heart for the community and had convinced him. What should have been a secret quickly became known to more than friends and family. It was the last time he let her good nature get the better of him.

Still, none of it mattered now as she no longer was

there.

Their mother suffered a stroke that left her partially paralyzed, and the doctors said she had less than a year to live. His father had taken out a large loan on the house to ensure those final months were the best. He'd taken her away on multiple trips and financed most if not all of her dreams. The problem was she lived another four years, and the cost of ongoing care and trips soon racked up. With a lack of work as a carpenter, upon her death he could no longer pay the bills so the bank foreclosed on the house. It was a terribly trying time. Not only were they dealing with the grief of losing their mother but they now had no idea where they were going to sleep. At that time, Lou, their uncle lived in Whitefish and he'd offered them a room but their father wouldn't accept it.

Fortunately, a family from a local church took them in and let them use the RV in their yard. Had it not been for their kindness he was sure child services would have moved in and taken them away. Their father was already walking on shaky ground with them and that was when their mother was alive. Those final days in their childhood home were spent carting out 300-pound barrels of dried food from the basement before the bank blocked their father from the property.

Had it not been for all the food that had been stored over the years, life might have been harder than it was, and it was hard. The years after their mother's death, their father lashed out at the drop of a hat. Without their mother to provide balance, and intervene, Corey would often take the fall on the bad nights in order to protect Tyler.

"Okay, I'll swing by his store on the way out of town. Any problems and—"

"I can handle it. Okay," Ella said, walking up to him and giving him a kiss. "Go on. Get going before they leave without you."

Corey gave her another hug and then collected his jacket and the keys to his old blue and white Yamaha XT225. His father had bought it back in the late eighties and gave it to him as a gift when he turned sixteen. It was still in mint condition, though it had racked up a fair number of miles. He wheeled it out of the garage, and kick started it to life. A few revs and he zipped away down Iron Horse Road. It was only then he was able to fully appreciate the gravity of the situation. All the homes were in darkness barring a few that must have been running generators. The outage didn't concern him too much as back in 2017 extreme winds had knocked down power lines and caused power outages to over 12,000 residents in northwest Montana. Whitefish, Columbia Falls and the West Valley had all been hit hard. Back then the community rallied together and within a matter of four hours they were back up and running. Of course his father had overreacted but that was to be expected. Pine trees blurred in his peripheral vision as the bike curved around the road into Lakeshore Drive. Corey felt the bike rattle between his legs as he powered forward out of a bend. He shifted through gears, upshifting to third, then fourth. Fifth gear. The wind whistled in his ears, and vehicles parked at the side of the road receded into his rear view. It had been a while since he'd driven the bike. It had been sitting in the garage gathering dust. Even though it was an old relic from times gone by, it still held up. He pushed it to its top speed. To his right was Mountain Harbor and Monks Bay, the southwestern area of Whitefish Lake. Many a summer he'd fished down there with Tyler, spending lazy Sunday afternoons drinking beer and talking about getting out of town. So much had changed since they were kids. He hadn't heard from his brother in over three years. Attempts to get him on the phone had failed, and the few visits he made to see him at their Uncle Lou's in Vegas didn't end well. Tyler blamed him for leaving to join the military, and in some ways maybe he was right, back then he'd grown tired of taking the brunt of their father's anger and demands. The military was an escape, a walk in the park compared to the years of his father's daily routine. He didn't linger thinking about it. The very thought of it made him anxious.

The closer he got to town the more concerned he

became. He'd pulled out his cell phone from his pocket in the hopes that he could get a signal but there was nothing. Lights all over town had gone dark, cars and trucks had stalled, traffic lights were off, and there was a heavy police presence out on the streets. Though there were no sirens, or strobe lights flashing. For a small tourist town in the height of summer it wasn't strange to see many people out on the streets, going to restaurants and bars, but something was different about this picture. Still, Corey tried not to read into it as he curved onto U.S. 93 South which ran through the heart of the town. His father's army and navy surplus store was one of a kind. While the town offered numerous sports, fishing and hunting stores, there was only one that catered to military surplus. Several years after losing their mother, his father had snapped out of his grief with the help of his brother Lou, and had taken on the Whitefish store while Lou moved to Vegas to branch out, get better deals and extend his family business. It was a win-win situation in some ways. It gave their father purpose and a sense of renewed pride, and it also meant he couldn't spend his days drinking heavily. Beyond the standard camping and outdoor gear that could be purchased, he carried footwear, knives, sports gear, optics, self-defense and surplus items.

Corey veered into the parking lot and glanced at the army green half-track out front. It was used to catch the eye of drivers and draw them in. Around the left side of the building there was a camouflaged K-711 general utility truck that was his father's pride and joy. Now and then he would use it in a town parade as a way of advertising his business, otherwise it remained on the property.

He pulled up outside and killed the engine before heading into the lit-up building. As he entered, he could hear the generator churning away and see his father hunched over taking out items from a large box. Andy Ford was in his late sixties, but those who knew him said he didn't look a day over fifty. He was bald but sporting a frequently dyed goatee. A strict diet, no alcohol and an active lifestyle had served him well. Those who didn't know him and walked into the store for the first time figured he was a veteran as he was always seen wearing military clothing and given the opportunity, he would let anyone who would listen know how proud he was of his Marine son.

"Hey Dad, you got the keys to my truck?"

"Yep," he said without looking at him.

"Well can I get them? I've got a call of a plane in trouble somewhere over Glacier National Park. I'm heading out with Terry and crew."

"No can do. We're going to need it."

Corey shook his head in disbelief as he threaded his way through the main store, which was filled with shelves packed with camping gear, and below that were clothing racks. Above were kayaks attached to the ceiling, and on the far wall were snowshoes, skis, snowboards and a glass case full of military and naval pins. "Look, whatever you've got going on, I'm sure you can use the K-711. And where is your Titanium truck?" Corey asked.

Andy emerged from a rack of clothing and continued, "Haven't you seen it out there?"

"Yeah. A power outage. And?"

"And this is it."

Corey chuckled to himself. "Like 2017 was it? Or 2014, or how about 2012? Like when are you going to stop acting so damn paranoid?"

He shook his aged finger at him. "Boy, I taught you better than this. Watch your mouth."

"Yeah, I think I'm a little old for that, Dad. Look just give me the damn keys and I'll be out of your hair."

"I just told you. The 4 x 4 stays here."

"Like hell it does. It's mine," Corey snapped.

"It belongs to the business," he replied. "I pay for the lease. You drive it. Or have you forgotten?"

"How could I? You just love to keep bringing it up."

Corey watched him loading up several duffel bags with various items. He could tell from some of the items what he was doing. He sighed and leaned against a rack of jackets. "Go on then. What's it this time? An economic collapse, a solar flare, an EMP?"

"Don't be sarcastic. And help me gather up items. We're heading up to the cabin."

"I'm not heading anywhere, Dad. I have responsibilities. People are relying on me."

"People are going to die. Do you want to be among them?"

"Geesh. I told you enough with this crap. I'm heading out. You don't want to give me my truck. Fine. I'll take your utility vehicle. But I'm not heading to the cabin." He stopped and grabbed up a duffel bag to fill with some essentials like a medic kit, flashlights, tarps, insulated blankets. In the past his father had been cool about it as he got compensated by the town. He said he was only doing it for the extra money but Corey knew better. "You don't mind if I take a few things? Better to be on the safe side." He scooped up a Mauser M18 rifle and collected ammo.

"You going hunting?"

"Might have to," Corey replied before dumping it all

into a cart and collecting several jackets, multiple cans of Sterno and a box of MREs. His father watched him with a scowl on his face.

As Corey rolled the cart towards the door, Andy called out. "You ever known your Uncle Lou to jump the gun?" Corey stopped walking and looked at his father in the reflection of the window. While he had doubted his father many times, Lou was different. Although a prepper, he wasn't given to paranoia, or running to the bunker at every news alert or change in weather. Corey turned his head and his father continued, "I was talking with him before the lights went out. There are outages all over the West Coast. Phone lines are down. Power is out. Vehicles are stalled. This isn't an isolated issue, Corey. Listen, I know I've been wrong before but this is different. Now you can either get on board or be left behind but I for one am making damn sure that we have what we need."

"You mean what you need."

His father shook his head. "Look, we need to be ready when this town wakes up to the cold reality."

"Which is?"

He rolled his eyes. "An EMP, Corey."

Corey snorted. "Yeah, I'm sure it is. Just like 2017 was a solar flare, and 2016…"

Andy stabbed his finger at him and bellowed, "Don't you patronize me, boy! I get enough of that from your brother."

"Huh! Been in contact with him, have we? Or are you referring to the last time you spoke? When was that? Oh, that's right, on his eighteenth birthday."

"We never saw eye to eye."

"Maybe you would if you had taken the time to listen. Tell me, Dad, have you even made an effort since Tyler left?"

"No more than you."

"Hey, at least I've tried," Corey said.

"Whatever. He made his choice."

"As did you," Corey said before turning and walking towards the door.

"So that's a no?"

"I'm going to help, maybe you should do the same instead of looking out for number one."

"Everything I did was for you boys."

Corey turned, one hand on the door, the other still on the cart. "Yeah? I appreciate that, Dad. I really do but what have you got to show for it?" His father offered back a blank stare as Corey exited into the humid June evening. Despite his father thinking he wasn't seeing the forest for the trees, Corey was well aware that cars didn't stall in an isolated power outage. But that didn't mean he was ready to neglect his duties. One thing the military had taught him was to show up, and go above and beyond when others would run the other way. This wasn't a time to shrink back. EMP or not, lives were at stake and he'd be damned if he would turn away now.

Chapter 7

The Glacier National Park ranger stood on the upper banks of Lake McDonald with a rifle in hand as he watched the soaking wet inmates and correctional officer wade onto the rocky shore. Gabriel had seen his silhouette as he climbed down. A full moon shone brightly giving him a clear view of the weapon in the ranger's hand. With the other he aimed a bright flashlight beam towards them. Gabriel imagined backup was already on the way, and yet he'd already cautioned correctional officer Martin Lee that if he did anything, he would join the ranger in death.

"Stay right there!" the ranger bellowed as he raised the rifle. He was short in stature, balding through the middle of his hair, and slightly chubby. The ranger pitched sideways making his way down from the embankment to the shore. Loose soil and stone broke away and rolled. Although it was summer, the evening had robbed the water of what little heat had been on the surface. It was now frigid cold and all of them were shaking. Gabriel's teeth chattered. He laid Marcus back and slapped his cheek a few times to get him to stir before turning him on his side. Within seconds he was spewing up water.

"There. Welcome back, brother," he said before looking up at the ranger.

Lee stepped out from among them with both hands raised. "Whoa. It's okay. They are low-risk offenders. Petty crime. We were transferring them from North Dakota to Washington when our plane went down," he said thumbing over his shoulder as if it wasn't already obvious. The ranger didn't take his eyes off the inmates, and kept a safe distance slightly uphill from them. He raked the barrel of the rifle back and forth making it clear any sudden moves would be fatal.

"Backup is already on the way," he said.

"Where are we?" Lee asked.

"Montana. The northwest side of Lake McDonald. You're in the national park. How many others are alive?"

"It's just us," Lee said wrapping his arms around his

body and shivering. "No one else survived that I know of."

"Well you all just… take a seat on the shore. We'll soon have you out of here."

"Mister, we are freezing," Lee said. "We need some blankets. Somewhere warm to stay."

"Can't be of much help there. The ranger station is a few miles up the road but until backup arrives, I don't feel comfortable heading that way. We'll just stay here for now."

Niles, one of the inmates, stepped forward. "And freeze to death?"

"Don't move!"

"What, you going to shoot us?"

"If I have to."

"Then shoot us but I'm not staying here. It's too cold."

Lee turned and tried to get him to calm down but he was adamant. He took a few more steps forward and the ranger aimed the rifle at him. "Stay where you are!"

"Niles, get back," Gabriel said.

"No, fuck this."

"I said stay back."

Lee rushed forward to intervene. He got between them. "Just calm down," he said, his eyes darting between them. "We can figure this out."

"We'll figure it out when I'm warm."

Quickly, the distance between Niles and the ranger got less. Lee kept backing up trying to stay between them. If the ranger wanted to shoot Niles, he would have had to blow a hole through the back of Lee, and it was clear he was already as nervous as hell. "Get your guy to sit back down," the ranger shouted backing up more and almost losing his footing on the steep incline.

"I'm trying. Niles. Listen to me."

Then it happened. As Niles shoved Lee, he fell back into the ranger. That was all it took. Lee twisted around and grabbed the rifle. It went off twice but thankfully no one was injured. Both of them were on the ground wrestling for the gun when Niles rushed forward and slammed a boot into the ranger's face, twice. He would have done it a third time and probably continued until he'd killed the ranger if it hadn't been for Gabriel.

"Enough." Gabriel grabbed him and tore him off. The ranger was out cold, his face covered in dirt and blood. Gabriel scooped up the rifle and checked if it was loaded, and then relieved the ranger of his sidearm, ammo and radio. He tossed the handgun to Marcus, the only person he trusted in the group. "Now listen up. You want to get out of here, we have to work together. None of this every man for himself bullshit."

"Fuck that. I'm not staying with this group," Jesse said elbowing his way forward. "They're going to be looking for all of us. We need to go our separate ways."

"We stick together," Gabriel said.

"You all can but I'm going my own way." He nodded and turned. He had only made it a few feet when a gun went off and he collapsed. Gabriel turned to see Marcus holding the handgun out. Marcus strolled over to Jesse who wasn't dead but trying to crawl away. Gabriel might have stopped him had he seen any use for Jesse but the guy was a loser. He'd been nothing but trouble in the pen, a thorn in Marcus' side. He never told him what had taken place but it didn't take much to figure out what was going on between the two of them.

Marcus kicked him over so he was looking at him. He placed his boot on his neck and without saying another word fired another round straight into his face. With that done, he turned to the rest of the group. "Anyone else want to go their own way?"

Murmurs spread. "Nah, fuck that. I'm good," Hauser, another inmate who had looked like he was about to follow Jesse, replied. Lee looked on in shock, saying nothing. He knew better.

Gabriel reached down and relieved the ranger of his summer jacket and slipped into it. It wasn't a good fit but was better than being cold. "We'll see if there is a vehicle up by the road. Maybe find some additional clothes."

"What about him?" Torres asked pointing to the ranger.

Gabriel cast his gaze down, turned the rifle on him and

squeezed a round into the unconscious ranger's temple. "Who?" A smile danced on everyone's lips as he jerked his head and told them to move out. As they climbed the embankment, he knew Niles was confused. Why had he stopped him from killing the ranger only to end his life with the man's rifle? It was a power move. Give a man an inch and he'd take a mile. Gabriel had no qualms about killing to keep his freedom but he would decide who lived and died, and in a group of this kind, first kills always established pecking order.

They scrambled up the embankment to a dusty narrow road hedged in on either side by thick trees. At the top they could just make out the silhouette of the landscape surrounding the lake. There was no vehicle to be seen so they trudged in the direction the ranger had pointed, northeast.

As they pressed on, Gabriel fished into his pockets and pulled out a pack of cigarettes and a lighter. "Oh, it just gets better," he said. He took one out and tossed the pack to Torres to share among the others. After sparking it to life he took a hard hit and let the nicotine flow through his system. It was like instant relief. A wave of a calm and a sense of well-being came over him. He blew out smoke and gazed up into the night sky. It was crazy to think they had survived a crash and were now free men. All those years wasted. It would all be different now.

"Why did you have to kill him?" Lee said catching up with him. "He was no threat. Guy probably had a family."

"Yeah? So did I. I didn't see anyone crying when they tossed me inside. They might as well have put a bullet in my head."

"But you're responsible for your actions. He was just doing his job."

"So was I," Gabriel said looking at a confused Lee. "Do you think I wanted to hit those banks? If there could have been another way I would have taken it but that's not how this world works. The government steals from us all the time but people sit back and do nothing because it's okay for them to do it, but when we have mouths to feed, rent to pay, we're supposed to grin and endure the hardship. Well fuck that. I did something about it. Robbing banks was my job. And I was damn good at it."

"Until you got caught."

"No, until an asshole cop decided he was going to be a hero."

"Is that why you killed him?"

"He got in the way. I gave him a chance."

Lee shook his head. "Gave a chance."

"You think you're so much better than us because you wear that uniform, because you're on the other side of the bars? Then answer this, Lee. Why did you kill Stevens then?"

Lee's chin dropped. He opened his mouth but then shut it.

"That's right. Because he got in the way of what you wanted." Gabriel took another drag on his cigarette. "Sometimes we have to do what we have to do to survive but don't ever think you are different."

With that said Lee fell back into the group.

It didn't take them long to see a few cabins between the trees. Torres cast Gabriel a glance as if requesting permission to explore. Gabriel gave a nod and Torres and three others hopped over a fence ahead of them and went in as scouts. They heard the sound of glass shattering and then Jericho returned and beckoned them in. "They're empty."

Some of the others rushed in eager to find food and something warm to wear.

"Are we staying here?" Marcus asked.

"No. We need to keep moving but no harm in looking. Keep an eye on them."

Marcus gave a nod and hopped over the fence, hurrying with the others through the darkened woods towards three cabins. "Lee," Gabriel said before he followed.

"Yeah?"

"When we make it to a town, you're free to go."

Lee shook his head. "Yeah right. I'll believe that when I see it."

"I mean it. What you did back there for us on that plane. I respect that. Human decency goes a long way in my books."

Lee snorted. "Human decency. How can you say that after what you just did?"

"It's what I had to do, just like what you did with Stevens."

"I did what I had to, you did what you chose to. Don't confuse the difference."

Chapter 8

The explosion shook the ground, shattering windows in surrounding buildings and vehicles. It was the first of many they witnessed over the course of ten minutes. Tyler was escorting Erika back to her hotel when the 737 nose-dived into a huge apartment block. A billowing cloud of black smoke and tongues of fire rose into the night sky, illuminating the street they were on. Screams cut through the silence as people sprinted away from the crash site. It was like witnessing 9/11 all over again. Tyler recalled the sight on the news as the twin towers collapsed and a tide of gray smoke and debris pushed through the streets of New York, smothering everything and anyone in its path.

Tyler peered around the vehicle from his crouched position. His body was partially covering Erika, shielding her from some of the flying projectiles of debris. In the distance he saw another plane swoop down erupting in a fireball. They were less than twenty minutes away from McCarran International Airport. It was as if every plane that had taken off was bombarding the city. His immediate thought was a terrorist attack but how could they take control of that many planes?

"You ready? We need to move," Tyler said in a strong tone as he tried to guide her along the chaotic street. Off to their left they saw people on fire running from the building, screaming before they collapsed. A reel of video footage played back in his mind from when he was a kid. In an attempt to toughen his sons, Tyler's father had shown them footage of wars, genocide, and plane crashes. He'd lived with nightmares for months after that. Of course, their father said it was a matter of conditioning the brain to respond to the chaos so that when they eventually faced such situations, they wouldn't fall into shock and buckle. Right now, all he wanted to do was get her back to that hotel, make sure she was safe, and then head to Uncle Lou's.

"We should help," Erika said looking off towards the

apartment block.

"We need to keep moving."

"You want to leave. Leave. I'm helping these people," she said, breaking away from him and jogging towards the rubble and smoke. A large section of the building was gone from where the airplane had ripped through it. Blackened sections of the airplane were scattered, some parts had traveled several blocks down the street.

"Erika."

Unaware of the dangers, she didn't listen to him and pressed into the dark smoke.

Another explosion erupted, and the force of it hurled them back against a vehicle. What caused it was anyone's guess but it could have been any number of things from gas pipes to a fuel tank. Tyler was briefly knocked unconscious. When he came to, he was visibly shaken and now blanketed in soot. He shook his head and turned to see Erika gripping her arm and groaning. He scrambled over and saw her jacket was torn, leaving the upper portion of her arm exposed. There was a five-inch gash that was bleeding badly. She had her hand wrapped around it and her fingers were now gloved in blood.

Without even giving it another thought he slung his backpack to one side and reached into it and pulled out a small med kit. From it he pulled out an antiseptic towelette and cleaned her wound, then applied gauze and began wrapping a bandage around her arm.

Erika looked at him in astonishment. "You always carry that with you?"

"Would you think it's strange if I said yes?" He paused for a second before continuing. She continued to watch as he tended to the wound with all the proficiency of someone with first-aid training. To him it was nothing, no different than tying his shoes each day. His father had ingrained certain habits in them when they were younger. At the time he didn't understand why, now it made more sense.

"You know what you're doing?"

"I know enough," he said before switching the tone of the conversation back to what had annoyed him. "What the hell were you thinking?"

"I'm not standing by and doing nothing."

"You're not emergency services."

"No but until they get here someone has to help."

"You're liable to get yourself killed. It's volatile. This whole place could erupt again in a minute. The building is unstable. Now, are your legs working?"

"Of course they are," she said as he helped her up.

"Then let's go."

Erika looked back towards the building. Tyler could see her reluctance to leave despite the danger. Bodies were lying throughout the street. A mother crouched over a child cradling her and sobbing. "My baby, my baby!" Further down four people were carrying a guy whose leg was gone. A woman was performing CPR on an older woman without much success. Were they friends or strangers helping? Did it matter? His father's voice came back to him as clear as the day he heard it. "When all hell breaks loose. Get out. Get back to the cabin. Don't be a hero. Don't be moved by what you see. It will only get you killed. Safety first, and that means you."

"Erika," he said.

She looked at him. "Why did you help me a minute ago?"

"Because it was the right thing to do."

She nodded. "Exactly," she said as she walked back towards the building. Tyler sighed and shifted from one foot to the next. He glanced down the road. Right about now Uncle Lou would be moving into phase one of his plan of survival. Common sense told him to leave her. He didn't owe her anything and after the shit night they'd had, it wasn't like they'd made a connection, and yet… he looked at her as she stooped down to check on someone and saw something that reminded him of his mother. Unlike his father, she had a warm and caring heart. It had been her idea to open up their house to the street when the power went out. She had been the one to convince their father that it was the right thing to do. Maybe that's why he didn't walk away but followed Erika into the midst of the chaos. All around people were shouting for help but there were no medics to be seen. Even if they were on the streets, they would have had a hard time getting through the bumper-to-bumper traffic. Stalled vehicles, no telecommunications and multiple downed planes would have placed a tremendous strain on emergency services. He imagined they were out there just as they were on 9/11. Courageous men and women running into danger to help. They weren't alone. Erika wasn't the only person risking her life. There were others. It was a given. Even though there was no telling what or who had caused this, the people of the city were rallying together, lending a hand if only to comfort the injured and dying.

* * *

Trapped beneath a chunk of concrete with exposed rebar, Nate came to, coughing and spluttering. He inhaled hard trying to catch his breath like a man coming out of the ocean for air. The first thing he saw was the face of the young woman who had pushed him into the stairwell. Her face was covered in blood, and it was clear she was dead. Her body was buried beneath rubble. A shot of pain went through him. He let saliva dribble out his mouth to determine which way was up. It was a little trick he'd learned back when he was snowboarding in Colorado as a kid. Avalanches were common and if you lived through one, disorientation could be a killer. He looked down and saw his jeans and red hoodie were covered in plaster and drywall. He wiggled his Nikes to make sure his legs weren't paralyzed before he tried to shift position and find a way out. His first instinct was to call out for help and he might have done that had he not seen Zach's jacket. How many floors had he dropped? A flood of memories came back to him. Zach leaving him behind, the nose of the plane, the woman pushing him towards the stairs, and then the building collapsing like a stack of cards.

"Zach?"

He shuffled forward, climbing over the dead woman and squeezing through a gap where a shard of light filtered through on the jacket he'd been wearing. He got as close as he could before he realized that it was pointless. Zach had been crushed below heavy blocks of concrete and all he was seeing was his arm in the jacket. The rest was gone. Horrified, he scrambled back and began screaming. "Help. Help! Get me out of here!" He headed for the spot where the light of the moon was filtering through the darkness. The smoke and fire began to make him cough even more. He pulled his top over his mouth and nose and tried to climb his way to the surface. Every step felt more precarious than the last. Placing his foot on a ledge of concrete, he pushed up only to have it give way. Nate fell back, and had he not moved fast he would have been buried below rubble.

Fear gripped him at the thought of being trapped inside the fortress of concrete, or worse succumbing to smoke inhalation. In that moment he regretted ever stepping foot inside that apartment, he regretted leaving Colorado, and he especially regretted the path he'd chosen up until this point. Nate began praying as he clawed away sections of concrete and plaster, slipping his body around jagged rebar. "God, if I get out of here, I promise I will change my ways. I won't steal anymore. I'll do good to people. I'll..." He stopped and looked at the area he was trying to get through, it was blocked by a huge piece of metal. "No. C'mon!" He was so close to the surface. A warm breeze blew in through the tiny gap, teasing him. "Help! Help. Anyone out there?"

He could hear people crying, and reassuring words from people trying to help. A sense of doom and hope mixed together. How many others were trying to get out? How long would it take before they would find him? He'd seen some of the shots on the news of earthquakes out in California — people trapped, emergency services finding them days later and then stories of survivors having lived on bugs and rainwater. Oh God, the thought of spending even another minute below the surface was bringing on claustrophobia that he didn't think he even had. He continued to cry out for help as he backtracked and looked for another way out. He'd passed several people who were alive but unable to move as they were pinned under fallen walls. All he could do was tell them that help was on the way and if he made it out, he'd let the rescuers know where they were. The truth was, he had no clue, and all he could think about was himself.

As he navigated his way through the rubble, he was beginning to think he would never get out. Every band of moonlight turned out to be too small for him. Hope rose then fell. Fear gave way to panic at the thought that the concrete above him could be unstable. What if it gave way? What if it crushed him but didn't kill him? He slumped down feeling defeated, then it dawned on him. He reached into his jacket feeling the weight of the piece against his chest. He'd never had to use it. It was there simply as a means of threatening anyone who fought back. The Glock was loaded. His mind switched to thinking the worst. He felt like he was seated at the edge of an abyss, and any minute he could plummet into it. He took the gun and lifted it to his mouth, thoughts of suicide racing through his mind. If he wasn't found he could always shoot himself. It would be far better than starving to death.

As he sat there in the darkness his eyes began to see thing that weren't there.

He tapped the barrel of his gun against his temple.

How long would it take before thirst gave way to dehydration and he started to hallucinate? *Water.* Then he remembered he'd been carrying that girl's bag with him. Inside of it was water. He scrambled through the grime and debris trying not to make eye contact with any of the survivors that called out to him. There was nothing he could do. How could he help them? It took him a while to find the dead woman and where he'd woke. With only a few faint bands of light he had to feel around for his bag. How long he spent searching for it was unknown as time seemed to cease down there. Eventually, though, his fingers clawed at the leather bag. It was partially buried below plaster. He dug it out and fished inside for the bottle. The second his hand clasped onto it, he felt a wave of peace come over him. Unscrewing the lid, he chugged it down, then about halfway through the bottle he realized he had to slow down. If he was going to be trapped for a day or more, he would need to ration it. He was about to screw the cap on when he heard a groan to the right of him. "Water. Water," someone said. He squinted into the darkness and saw a young boy. A section of rebar had impaled him and even if emergency services reached him in the next ten minutes, he would likely not survive.

At first Nate ignored him but then guilt took over.

He glanced at the young boy. Questions flooded his mind. If he gave him the water there would be less for him and right now, he had a better chance of survival.

Again, he turned his face away, hoping the boy would stop.

In his mind he kept saying shut up, shut up. But the injured boy never did.

Call it an act of mercy or simply a desire to have him stop speaking but Nate slid up beside him and unscrewed the lid, brought the bottle up to the kid's mouth and poured in some of the water. He swallowed hard, stared at him and thanked him.

"Yeah. No problem. It's going to be okay, kid." He felt a twinge in his gut. Guilt was eating away at him. He knew it wasn't going to end well. The boy would be dead before the hour was over. "Who are you?" he asked.

The boy replied, "Samuel Richards."

"How old are you?"

"Eleven."

Nate clenched his jaw. Why? Why did bad shit have to happen to kids?

"Well Samuel, my name's Nate."

He felt Samuel touch his hand and he realized he wanted to hold it and feel some sense of comfort in his final moments. Although uncomfortable, Nate wrapped his hand over his and squeezed tightly. "It's all right, kid. I'm here." He wanted to ask him about his parents, his life in the city but instead he sat there clutching his hand until Samuel breathed his last. When he knew he was gone, Nate felt a sense of despair.

The smell of smoke was getting stronger. If he didn't

die from starvation or thirst, he was liable to die of smoke inhalation. Choking to death. The thought scared him.

"Please. Help! Anyone out there? Dear God. Help me!" he bellowed as loud as he could, over and over again for what felt like five minutes but was probably only thirty seconds. Exhausted and frustrated he stopped and began to accept his fate.

He wasn't getting out of here.

Who was he fooling?

He took out his gun again and brought it up to his temple. *Squeeze it. It will only take a second. It will be all over. No one will miss you.* He could see his mother again. That was the only person that ever meant anything to him. He had no siblings, no girlfriend, no real friends.

Nate closed his eyes and prepared to squeeze.

As the fleshy part of his finger touched the trigger his body tensed up.

Hand shaking, he was just about to release the round when he heard her.

"Anyone down there?"

For a second he thought he was imagining it but then her voice echoed in the dusty chamber. "Hello. Can you hear me?"

"I'm here. I'm here!" Nate bellowed. "Where are you?"

"Follow the sound of my voice," the woman said.

He scrambled through the dirt and darkness like a man lost in the desert, thirsting for water. "Keep speaking to me."

"Over here. We're here."

It didn't take him long to make his way there. When he did, he looked up through a crack in the concrete and saw her fingers. Nate reached up and touched them, a renewed sense of hope followed. "Give us a moment. We'll get you out."

"Okay. Just don't go away."

"We're not leaving you," said a male voice behind her. He could hear the sound of rubble being moved. Small and large boulders being pushed, and pulled and lifted. They had their work cut out for them. Nate looked back into the darkness and thought of Samuel. Had God heard his prayer? Was this Samuel's way of repaying his kindness?

"What's your name?" the female asked still touching his fingers. He'd never felt such a sense of peace and overwhelming gratitude for human life. To be alone in death was awful, but in life, that was a tragedy.

"Nate. Yours?"

"Erika, and this is Tyler."

Chapter 9

Not long after they pulled Nate from the rubble, an emergency crew of six arrived on scene without vehicles. A collection of police officers and rescue volunteers dressed in orange vests began the arduous task of combing through the aftermath searching for survivors. The welcome sight of uniformed officers handing out bottles of water, must have given Erika enough reason to feel the situation was being handled as she began talking about heading back to the hotel. Tyler didn't have the heart to tell her the truth. When he was a kid, his father had run him and his brother through various scenarios — EMP, virus, economic collapse, natural disasters and many others. While other kids grew up watching MTV, listening to rock and rap music, they viewed prepper videos and recited the three rules of survival. While other kids wrote assigned essays on the great American novel, they digested FEMA, government and town emergency plans, searching for weaknesses, discussing alternatives and preparing for every outcome. He would test them on the four phases of emergency management, the six critical areas of emergency response, what to do in a disaster, what to carry on them at all times, where to go, who to contact, when to use a bunker, how to fire weapons, the keys to living off the land, and so much that Tyler could practically quote verbatim large sections of text from government emergency response plans, and identify and name wild plants that could be used for food and those that were a danger. Andy Ford believed that knowing a few things was not enough. It was never enough for him. It needed to become second nature, instinct, so when the shit hit the fan they weren't just physically, but mentally and emotionally ready.

A show of strength by the government was always the way. It wouldn't last.

But there was no way to convince anyone of that. The gullible, the untrained, the unprepared and the reckless believed the nation or world around them would come to their aid. Presidents, prime ministers and the powers that be would ensure their survival. Sure, they would suffer for a day or two, a week even, or at worst a month but total collapse? It was unheard of, rarely talked about and certainly not the kind of conversation heard in homes of America. No, the government would send out the National Guard, police would patrol the streets, curfews would be put in effect, martial law would be declared, guns confiscated, looting banned, generators freely handed out and food and water would continue to flow abundantly to those in need. But Tyler knew different. That was nothing but a pipe dream. Oh, there would be an initial push, an initial show of strength. It was humanity's way. Its first reaction was to respond, revive and rebuild. It was what anyone would do. It was why Erika reacted. And, often that was all it took to turn the tide on a small-scale disaster — people rallying together, emergency response crews working around the clock, Red Cross out in full force, and emergency funds set up to raise money. So, no, the government wouldn't sit by idly and just allow chaos to rule, and society wouldn't immediately start attacking each other, but given enough time, given enough pressure, and given the right circumstances, people would eventually revert to their natural instinct to survive. How and when that would happen would vary depending on where the disaster occurred, his father would say. The lawless had no gatekeeper, they were opportunists. That's why looting in riots usually began within the first twenty-four hours if opportunity presented itself. The L.A. riots stemming from the beating of Rodney King were a prime example of that. And that wasn't even a natural disaster, just a tragedy. The fact was even those who would have never dreamed of stealing might run into a building and snatch a case of water if they saw enough people doing it, and they knew they could get away with it.

Tyler glanced at his watch. Seconds, minutes, hours meant more to him than others. They weren't just the signposts for the passing of time. They were a countdown, red flags and sirens. He'd been keeping an eye on the time ever since the lights went out. Every minute that passed without heading for safety reduced the likelihood of surviving.

"What happened to helping those who can't help themselves?" Tyler asked curiously. He was keen to see what caused the change of heart.

"Bailey," Erika replied, carefully stepping down and hopping over large chunks of wall.

Tyler frowned. "Who?"

"It doesn't matter. I need to get back to the hotel."

"I'll walk you."

"I'm fine."

"Look, I said I would get you there and I meant it."

"That was before this. Let's just call it a night. I appreciate your kindness, Tyler, but I think I can find my way from here," Erika said.

Nate coughed and squinted at them. "You two an item?"

Both of them replied in unison. "No."

Nate was seated on a collapsed concrete wall. "Hey,

you think I can tag along with you?" Nate asked Erika. "I need to contact a friend and it seems cell phones aren't working. Maybe a landline will."

"I doubt it," she replied.

"No, he's right. There is a good chance they will," Tyler said. "Cells, that's another thing entirely. Not all cell towers have generators but the ones that do are weak at best. They might last anywhere from four to six hours but they can't handle a mass of people calling all at once and in an event like this…" He didn't need to fill in the blank.

"Bullshit," Erika said. "Generators last longer than that."

"Permanent ones. Yeah. You might get an extra day or two but you think they have the kind of money to install those in every cell tower? Think again. Besides, it happened in Hurricane Katrina. Look it up when the net comes back up, which will likely be never," he said getting down off the rubble and wiping his hands clean on his pants. She eyed him with a look of concern. Tyler scooped up his backpack and put it on then rolled his shoulder, feeling a twinge in his muscle. "Anyway, you will find that landlines as long as they aren't wireless tend to work in a power outage. It's because the power sent to the phones comes from the power companies and they will often have battery backup and other forms of generators to keep operations ticking over for at least a week during a power outage."

"Then how come the power didn't come back on for four days when we had a power outage a couple of years back?" Erika asked.

He smiled. "I said they would have power, I didn't say you would. Besides, I don't know what the situation was. Maybe it was a downed power line. Power without a way to get it to you — ah, I'm guessing it could be a problem," he replied and she must have read into it as sarcasm because as he headed away from the site she followed eager to ask more questions, no doubt about why he was going her way.

Nate wasn't far behind. "So, is that a yes?"

Neither one replied, there was too much happening around them. Along with the brave few who chose to help, many residents and tourists took to the streets, some trying to leave the city, others to return home or to hotels, probably assuming that was the safe thing to do. It wasn't like all of New York left the city when the twin towers came down but you could be damn sure no one stayed in the neighborhood unless they had a good reason. With Vegas drawing in upwards of forty million people a year to its attractions, there were many options for tourists, and by the looks of the downed planes, travel by air was cancelled. That meant overly crowded streets even if the vast majority were sightseeing outside the city limits, or holed up inside hotels.

Another explosion erupted farther away but it was powerful enough to rock the ground. Shock and bewilderment masked faces as they passed people in a hurry to get to safety. But was anywhere safe?

"Hey, you know what caused this?" Nate asked.

"EMP, I think. It has all the hallmarks of one but in

this day and age there is no telling what or who could be behind something like this," Tyler replied.

"You think it's terrorists? I mean with that plane, and all," Nate said thumbing over his shoulder.

"Look, I don't mean to be rude but don't you have a place to go to?" Tyler asked.

"He could say the same about you," Erika said casting him a glance.

He refused to bite for a second or two but then felt the need to respond. "I told you I would get you home."

"Yeah, and that involved not walking but I'm back to doing that, so…"

Nate asked, "How do you two know each other?"

Tyler glanced at him. "We went out on a date."

"A bad one," Erika was quick to clarify.

"Ah, and there was me thinking you were engaged."

Erika blew out her cheeks. "To him?"

"To her?" Tyler mirrored what she said just so she could feel how rude it sounded.

Nate rubbed the back of his neck. "Yeah, you two have

got issues to work through."

"What about you?" Tyler asked. "Was that your apartment?"

Nate hesitated before he responded and then replied, "Yeah. Actually, that's where I lived. I don't have a place to stay now, and that's why I was hoping to use the phone at your hotel. See if I can get hold of my…" he coughed, "mother."

"Oh, your mother lives nearby?" Erika asked.

"Yeah, um, not far from here," he said.

Erika glanced at him and squinted. "Why do you look familiar?"

"Well I'm from around here. Maybe you've seen me," he said clearing his throat.

She looked him up and down but before she could say any more, he changed the topic. "So what hotel are you staying at?"

"You mean which hotel does she own?" Tyler added.

"I don't own the hotel. I run it."

"What?" Nate asked.

Tyler decided to fill in the blanks. "Lyons. Her parents own the franchise."

Nate put a fist up to his mouth and smiled. "Wow. You must be loaded."

"That's what everyone assumes."

"C'mon, are you telling me daddy didn't set up some nice trust fund that you got when you hit eighteen?" Nate asked. She didn't respond to that but quickened her pace as if to make it clear that she was against them going with her.

Tyler nudged him. "Ah don't mind her, she has trouble with anyone calling her out on the truth."

"You know I can hear you," she replied, looking over her shoulder. He smirked and reached into his pocket and pulled out his phone to check one last time, just to be sure it wasn't some fluke event. He didn't want to believe it was an EMP. He'd spent the last nine years trying to distance himself from that world of doom and gloom. It wasn't that he had turned off his mind to it all, if he did, he wouldn't have carried around the backpack with him.

Tyler caught up with her. "Listen, this friend of yours. Bryan or…"

"Bailey," Erika said correcting Tyler.

"Right. Bailey. What is she, your sister?"

"Not exactly."

"A cousin then, or a co-worker?"

He heard her sigh as they got closer to the building. Erika sped up. "Thank God. I don't know what I would have done if…"

"Your inheritance was in ashes," Tyler said sarcastically.

"No, asshole, if my dog was hurt," she said looking back at him with a glare.

Tyler stopped walking. "Hold on a minute. Bailey is a dog? We're going back for your dog?"

Chapter 10

The third cabin wasn't empty. A couple in their late sixties were enjoying a quiet evening meal by candlelight when the home invasion occurred. Despite his age, and being outnumbered, Gabriel had to admit the old-timer had balls. He'd made a move for his shotgun only to get slapped down by Torres. With his head now bleeding, his wife crouched over him, crying. "Shut up, or you'll be next," Torres bellowed.

"Steady, Torres," Gabriel said before gesturing to the others to help themselves. They spent the next twenty minutes drying off, eating the remainder of the couple's supper and rooting through the cabin for items that could be of use. There weren't enough clothes for all of them as they learned the place wasn't the couple's permanent residence, just a summer retreat. Gabriel sat at the table mopping up the last remnants of soup from a bowl with a chunk of bread. He studied the old-timer across the room. "You got a vehicle?"

He didn't reply so Torres pulled his hand back as if to gesture he'd better answer.

"Not one that's working," he said, his eyes washing over their group.

"You lying to me, old man?"

"The keys are on the hook. Check it yourself. Do you think we would be here if it did?" Gabriel glanced at his brother who was standing beside the log fire stoking it with the metal poker. "Bill, you want try it?"

"Do I look like your whipping boy?" he said smoking a cigarette in a recliner chair. Gabriel smiled. Bill listened to no one except the correctional officers and even they gave him a wide berth at times.

"I'll see," Lee said.

"No. You stay where you are," Jericho said. "We're keeping a short leash on you."

"I'll do it myself." Gabriel got up and scooped up the keys and headed out to a carport around the side of the cabin. Inside was a large silver 4 x 4 Ford truck. He hopped inside and tried firing it up. It didn't respond. *Weird.* He tried again without success. The damn thing looked brand-new. He popped the hood and took a look to see if there was an issue with the engine. Nothing. It was as clean as a whistle. Slamming the hood down he headed back in and tossed the keys on the counter.

"What year is that?"

"2018."

"Why isn't it working?"

"Couldn't tell you. When the lights went out, we gathered our things together planning on heading back to Whitefish but it wouldn't start. It's not the only thing that isn't working. Cell phones aren't either. Internet is down as well."

Bill picked up the guy's cell to check. "He's telling the truth," he said before tossing the phone to Gabriel to see for himself. Gabriel stood there trying to piece together what was happening. He figured the plane going down was pilot error or engine trouble, but no cells, vehicles or internet?

"Any ideas?" Gabriel asked the others.

He thought one of them might know. No one did.

Gabriel scowled. "Whitefish. That's the closest town? How far away is it?"

"About an hour southwest of here. There are small villages along Highway 2 but that's where we're from."

"Villages?"

The old guy squinted. "Where are you all from?"

Torres leaned over him and replied with a smirk on his face. "Hell."

The smile left the man. His wife was tending to his wound with a cloth. There was a nasty gash on his head where Torres had struck him across the forehead.

"These villages…" Gabriel continued prompting him to answer.

The old man shook his head before rattling them off. "Apgar at the tip of the lake, West Glacier, Martin City, Columbia Falls and then Whitefish is just northwest of that."

Gabriel nodded. "All right, old man, I guess we'll

follow your lead."

"What?" Torres said. "We're not taking them with us."

"You know the area, Torres?" He waited for a response but got none. "You want to spend a few days hiking through the outback? No? Neither do I."

"But his vehicle isn't working, Gabriel," Marcus said adding in his two cents. "And look at them. If they could have walked out of here, they would have done it by now. Besides, I'm guessing he's saying it's an hour by car."

The old guy nodded.

"It could take upwards of half a day to reach it by foot," Marcus said. "And the cops will be out looking for us."

"Not if vehicles aren't working," he said. Suddenly a sense of peace came over him. Maybe the situation could work in their favor. With no communications operating, and no vehicles — had that ranger even managed to call for backup? Did anyone else know they were there besides prison officials? Other than those who tracked planes, who even knew where that plane had gone down? And if their plane went down, how many others did at the same time? The plane was now at the bottom of the lake. Hidden. Out of view. Would anyone be looking for them? A smile broadened on his face.

* * *

Corey met Terry Murdoch at the rendezvous point in the heart of Whitefish. Prior to the line going dead they'd arranged to meet at the crossroads, where Spokane Avenue met Second Street just in front of the Firebrand Hotel. With so many vehicles not in operation he didn't imagine anyone would show up but he was wrong. As he swerved the army utility vehicle to the side of the road, he saw that Terry was there with two of the twenty-five that would often head out. Depending on the situation, there could be more but under the circumstances he was surprised it hadn't been cancelled being as the rescue team was mostly made up of volunteers. Noah and Vern both lived in the downtown so walking to the rendezvous point hadn't been a problem but the others were further afield. The utility truck kicked out a plume of gray smoke as he turned off the engine and hopped out.

Terry approached, arm extended. Corey shook it. "Glad you could come. We're still trying to decide whether or not it's worth driving out there. You're the only one with a working vehicle. I managed to contact Matt, Kevin, Jules, Gina and Darren, and a few others before the power went out. We've been here for over twenty minutes and no one has showed except you, Noah and Vern. Vern thinks we should stay here to help the town."

"And you?" Corey asked.

"There are enough capable people in town to take care of trouble. I want to head out. Who knows how many are injured?"

Corey nodded. He gestured to his truck. "I brought some supplies from my old man's shop."

"Good," Terry replied, then walked over and took a look.

The street was dark except for several flashlights being held by those who were out. No lamppost lights were on.

A number of folks were chatting among themselves trying to figure out what was happening. It was to be expected. Corey knew the signs of an EMP. He wasn't trying to be argumentative with his father but if he'd agreed with him, he would have been heading for the cabin instead of trying to help folks. "We might want to get going before the cops confiscate this vehicle," he said.

"What do you mean?" Terry asked.

"Look around you, Terry. You see any other vehicles in operation?"

"Actually, I saw Dave Michaels out in his banged-up old truck on the way in."

Corey hopped up into the driver's seat. "New vehicles, Terry."

He frowned. "Well, no."

"And you won't. At least not for a while. Jump in, I'll explain on the way."

The group squeezed into the cab of the truck, and they rolled out heading towards Highway 2. Those on the street looked on, a couple tried to flag them down but

Corey acted as if he hadn't seen them and kept accelerating. The sooner they were out the better. He could have stayed but he knew it would only be a matter of time before the local Whitefish Police Department would be looking to detain any vehicles that were operating. He had no problem with them using his once they got back but for now, they needed it. The radio in the front of his truck crackled. "Come in, Corey."

It was his dad. He picked it up and pressed the button. "Go ahead."

"You took the utility," his father said.

"And you took mine."

"Where are you now?" he asked.

"Heading towards McDonald Lake."

"Are you kidding me?"

"I told you where I would take it."

"You're wasting gas and valuable time. Turn around and head back."

"Once we have checked on the downed plane."

"No. Now."

"I'm not fifteen anymore, Dad," he said before he turned off the radio. Terry looked at him. He was all too familiar with Andy Ford. There wasn't anyone in town who didn't know him. With a population of only 7,000, word got around. When he wasn't dishing out advice from behind the counter at his store, he was running survival workshops twice a month and his flyers advertising the events were seen flapping in the breeze on telephone poles. Beyond that he was often found arguing with residents. Corey couldn't keep track of the number of times over the past year he'd been called out to give him a ride home or break up a fight. His father was brash and unruly, and had earned a bad reputation in town. Because he had a background in the military, a number of the sixteen cops who worked for the department would call Corey instead of arresting Andy. It was easier that way. Less paperwork. The warning was always the same.

"So?" Terry asked as he lit a cigarette. "He's riled up about this, isn't he?"

"Yep," Corey replied. "He thinks it's an EMP."

There was a long pause before Terry replied. "And you?"

"Had you asked me that before I went away to the military, I would have given you the same answer but..." he trailed off.

"You don't believe him?"

"No, I'm not naive. Vehicles don't stop by themselves in a power outage but uh..."

"You don't want to be pegged as paranoid like him."

Corey glanced at him. "Crazy, huh?"

Terry laughed and blew out smoke from the corner of his mouth as Corey brought his window down. "No. I get it. You might be his son, Corey, but you're not Andy Ford, neither is your brother. Which reminds me. You heard from him?"

"Not for a long while."

Terry nodded looking out as they drove east in silence. The road was deserted and dark, nothing but ranches, forest and mountains on either side of them as they drove northeast up into the Haskill Basin and around to West

Glacier. He was interested to see how some of the other villages and towns in the area had fared. Even though he was convinced that some kind of EMP had occurred, he was hesitant to jump on his father's bandwagon. Since returning from the military he'd tried to rebuild a different kind of relationship with his father, one that didn't revolve around survival workshops and prepper talk. It was as if his dad didn't know anything else but that. Nothing else seemed to be important. It almost reminded him of some of the religious folks he'd met in town who spent all their time trying to reach people with the gospel. He wasn't against either but there was a big difference between being mindful and fanatical. Besides, his father's incessant need to pump them with information and the necessary skills for surviving had come at a great cost, but he couldn't see it. It had pushed his family away, driven Tyler to Las Vegas, and Corey off to the military. Any attempt at trying to have that conversation with him was shot down. It was never his father's fault. He couldn't see the forest for the trees. In his eyes, caring meant imparting valuable skills for life, forget spending time playing ball, teaching your kid to ride a bike or hanging out together at the local movie theater — that was wasting time in his eyes. Unless it had some correlation to survival it was considered a waste of time.

Corey gripped the wheel and curved around the roads, every bounce a reminder of the many times his father had brought them up this way as kids. Most who visited Glacier National Park, which was located to the east of Whitefish, with Kootenai National Forest off to the west, probably conjured memories of hiking, backpacking, cycling and camping. Not so for the Ford family. It was a place to push the limits, to experience isolation, hunger, thirst and pure fear. Corey knew his father was extreme. Not all preppers were like Andy, even though Corey assumed they were until he got older and met more of them.

A flashback of rowing into the middle of a logging lake under the premise they were going fishing stuck out in his mind. Somehow, he honestly believed his father wanted to spend a lazy summer day fishing with his sons. But it was all just a ruse. When they reached the middle of the lake, Andy handed over scuba BCD jackets and filled the weight-integrated pockets with enough weight to make them drop like a stone. Next, he instructed them to get out of the boat. Tyler was petrified, already nervous about water from a previous incident where he'd nearly drowned.

"Dad. Why?"

"Biological warfare. You need to be able to hold your breath longer than others."

"But we have masks for that."

"Yeah, you do. But they only benefit you if you can get to them in time, which means holding your breath." He reached around and tossed two masks overboard. *"Go get them. Don't come up until you find them."*

Corey was fourteen at the time, Tyler twelve. "Are you serious?"

"Boy, do I look like I'm joking?"

He was out of his damn mind but he didn't see it that way. No, somewhere in his brain, it all made sense. Corey had tried to convince him to just let him go and leave Tyler onboard but he wouldn't have it.

"You think you can hold your breath for the two of you? Don't be stupid. Get over there."

Corey rolled over the side. He kept a firm grip on the boat, waiting for Tyler, but he straight out refused, gripping the boat tightly and shaking his head. That's when their father took matters into his own hands and picked Tyler up and hurled him over the side. There was no questioning him. No trying to reason. Both of them sank to the bottom with little effort. How Corey managed to spot both of the masks before they ran out of air was a miracle but he made sure Tyler had his before they breached the surface, otherwise, he knew their father would have made Tyler go down again. That was just his way.

That wasn't the only time he did that. There were many days that followed and each time he made it more difficult, pushing the envelope on how long they had to stay beneath the water. Did they learn? Yes. But not what he thought they had. They learned to hate. Every day, every experience, deepened their hatred for their father. Tyler took it harder than him, bottling up his rage until he was of an age where he could leave home.

Corey had left a few years before that, seeking freedom in what others considered a rigid way of life. To him it was nothing. Mentally and physically he was already prepared for the Marines.

"Corey," Terry said snapping his fingers in front of his face. And just like that he was back in the present moment, the memory fading to the back of his mind. "Heads up," he said pointing to a police blockade near the small village of West Glacier.

Chapter 11

Las Vegas Boulevard was like a graveyard of stalled vehicles. They witnessed several fights breaking out but that was to be expected with so many people scared, frustrated and unsure of what was taking place. Erika began coughing. Gray smoke from downed planes that had taken off from McCarran Airport and veered into the city swept through the streets, a toxic blend that was making it difficult to breathe. The air was thick. Tyler reached into his bag and pulled out a gas mask and handed it to her.

"What the hell," she said taking a step back. "You brought that to our date?"

"Put it on, there's no telling what is in this smoke." He coughed, reached into his bag and pulled out a half face respirator to cover his face.

"I'm not putting that on."

"I will," Nate said holding out his hand. Tyler glanced

at him but kept offering it to her. She looked at his bag and before he could tighten his grip, she snatched it out of his hand and began rooting through it.

"What the hell have you got in here?" Erika expected to find some kind of weird rape kit, or something but the rest of it was relatively normal, if normal meant carrying a medical kit, flashlight, headlamp, two-way radio, smart charger cable, a knife, hand sanitizer, toothbrush, toothpaste, deodorant, wipes, campers toilet paper, LifeStraw Go water bottle, a 2-liter hydration bladder, four snack bars, what look liked a small portable cook set and… when she pulled that out, Nate started laughing.

"Shit, you've got Mary Poppins' bag. What else is in there?"

Tyler stood there as Erika pulled one item after another out onto the sidewalk. Socks, pants, shirt, underwear in a compression sack, sunglasses, a magnifying glass, a nylon poncho, a high visibility reflective vest, light sticks, emergency food bar, a flare, a solar charger battery, a tarp for shelter, a micro whistle, a mirror, a thermal blanket, a survival novel, playing cards, a compass, paracord, pandemic kit, LED light, an emergency Bivy for sleeping in, a map of the local area, steel fire starter flint, waterproof lighter, gloves and several other items she wasn't sure what they were. But it wasn't that which freaked her out the most, or even the knife that had given her cause for concern, it was what was at the bottom. She pulled it out slowly, holding it by the grip. As soon as Nate caught sight of it his eyes widened. "Holy shit. You're packing a piece."

"Alright, that's enough," Tyler said taking it from her and shoving everything back in. He crouched on the sidewalk as Erika looked at him. "It's legal in the state of Nevada to open carry or have a concealed weapon."

"I know it is. But do you always carry that bag with you everywhere..." she shifted her body with some attitude, "... or only on dates?"

"It's..." he trailed off pushing items into the bottom, trying to find the words to explain.

She didn't know what to make of it but in all her time

dating people, she had never seen anyone carrying what amounted to camping or survival gear. If that was what it even was? "Are you living on the streets?" she asked.

"No. I have an apartment just like you. Well not as upscale as Lyons but…"

She turned and began walking away, quickly.

He put a hand out. "Hold up, Erika. You don't understand."

"I don't want to know."

"There's a very good reason why I have this."

"I'm sure there is." She threw a hand up but didn't look back. "I'd like to say it's been a great night but I'd be lying. Take care."

"Wait up."

She turned to see both of them jogging after her. That's when she decided to slip out of her heels and break into a run. She didn't even pick them up. All she could think about was getting as far away from both of them as possible, more so Tyler. What a freaking weirdo carrying a backpack with a knife and gun. Vegas was full of freaks, and potential serial killers. Maybe he was one of them? What would have happened if the date had gone well? She could have ended up dead and buried in the desert. Amid the smoke she could see the hotel, a fifteen-story red and brown monstrosity that stood out from its competitors. Before she managed to make it to the entrance, Tyler grabbed her arm and spun her around. "Just wait a goddamn minute and give me a chance to explain."

"I don't care. I don't. Really. If you want to carry a knife and gun, and all that shit… that's your prerogative. I just want to go home," she said. Tears began to well up in her eyes. The stress of the night had taken its toll and she just wanted to get inside, and close the door on the chaos of the city. "Please. Just let me go home."

Nate placed a hand on Tyler's shoulder. Tyler nodded and released his grip.

Before he could change his mind, Erika walked away, then broke into a jog heading into the building. Inside it was a noisy circus. Lights were on in the lobby powered by a portable generator that was humming. It was strange as she knew the hotel had a permanent backup generator in the basement. All their hotels did. But for some reason it wasn't working. Guests had filled the lobby and were crowding around the front desk, voicing their complaints. Were they utterly oblivious to what was taking place outside? Luanne, the hotel concierge, spotted Erika and raised a finger. *Oh God,* Erika thought as she tried to make a beeline for the stairwell. The last thing she wanted to do was crowd control. However, two words caught the attention of the angry group. "Ms. Lyons!" Erika caught her reflection in the gold metal of the door she was about to go through. Her hair was a mess, her face blackened by smoke, and she had no shoes on. She was in no state, physically or mentally, to deal with anyone. Under any other conditions she might have turned, smiled and done what she was best at but that was then, this was now.

She darted into the stairwell and took the stairs two steps at a time. It was going to kill her legs to reach the penthouse suite but what other choice did she have? Even if by some miracle they'd managed to get the elevator to work she couldn't stand there waiting for it or risk getting trapped inside.

Several floors below she heard some of the guests enter the stairwell. "I saw her go this way. I want my money back," she heard them say. Erika ran faster, her thighs burning with each floor she ascended. When she finally reached the top, she hurried to the double doors at the end of the hallway and banged on them, looking over her shoulder. She expected to see the angry guests but the door opened and she pushed her way in past Maria, a woman she employed to watch over Bailey. Within seconds, Bailey came trotting over. She was a large German shepherd, only four years of age. Erika had grown up wanting one for as long as she could remember but her parents always said no. Too messy. Too big. Too loud. Too much work. So as soon as they put her in charge of the hotel in Vegas, she went about getting one from the local animal rescue. There wasn't much information, only that the last owner had tied her to a lamppost and walked away. It was hard to believe there were such heartless people in the world.

"Hey girl," she said crouching down and wrapping her arms around her thick dark black and brown hair. Bailey nuzzled her and smelled her feet. "Yeah, I know. I've been…" She looked around and noticed that Maria had set up candles all over the apartment, and a few crank-handle lanterns.

"Ms. Lyons. Are you okay?"

"Yeah. I guess. I just need to get out of these clothes, take a shower and…"

Before she had taken a few steps inside there were several bangs on the front door. Bailey growled and then started barking. The sound of angry guests could be heard on the other side. "Ms. Lyons. Open up. We know you're in there. We want a refund. This is unacceptable."

Maria looked at Erika and she motioned with her head to take Bailey into another room. Erika wasn't fearful of facing angry people, her parents had schooled her in the art of facing the uncomfortable. From an early age she was looked after by someone else, and when she reached the age of fourteen, she was sent off to boarding school, a decision that she wouldn't have made had she had a choice in it. After she graduated from a hotel and hospitality program, and studied advertising the following year, her mother was quick to integrate her into the family business. Unlike others who had to work their way to the top, she began there. It was all about appearances. Her mother wouldn't have her daughter handling menial duties. They pushed her to the front of her comfort level and initially had her handling the promotion of the hotels as well as management of one of the hotels in Vegas. She was told if she could prove herself with one hotel, they would give her more responsibility. Oh, responsibility? Like that was what she wanted out of life. Please. They had it ass backwards. She wanted freedom, adventure, and as strange as it sounded, uncertainty. It felt like everything had been planned out for her life and she was just along for the ride. Perhaps that's why she was drawn to Tyler's profile. It wasn't just that he was a good-looking guy but he came across as a kindred spirit. Pity, she thought.

"Ms. Lyons. Open up!"

Erika hurried over to her shoe closet and slipped into a pair of flats. She snatched up a long coat to cover the dust that had turned her black dress gray. She darted into a bathroom and turned on a tap. It spluttered a few times, and some water came out. Good. At least the water was working for now. A quick splash of water on her face, then she ran her fingers through her hair and grimaced. God, she looked awful.

Another bang, followed by another.

It would have to do. She took a deep breath and tried to channel her mother's attitude as she ambled up to the door and swung it open. Outside there were roughly ten people, men and women, mostly husbands sent by their wives to deal with the situation. It was always the same.

"We are sweltering hot in our rooms. There is no air conditioning. No lighting and…" One after another they voiced their complaints until it just became a crescendo of noise.

"Okay. Okay!" she bellowed. "Now I've been out. I am not unaware of the situation but maybe you are. Do you know that we aren't the only ones who have been affected? The entire city is darkness, planes have dropped out of the sky, and people are lying dead, and trapped beneath rubble. Have you considered that? You should consider yourself grateful you're alive."

Okay, she laid it on a little thick but after the night she had, she was in no mood for crap, and hospitality had dropped to the bottom of her priorities. Still, she expected them to take a step back, perhaps apologize, or grumble and walk away but they didn't. They stood fast. In fact, one of them jabbed his finger at her with a scowl on his face. He was a foreigner from Ireland who by the smell of his breath had been hitting the whiskey pretty hard. "Now listen here, you prissy little cow. How dare you tell us we should be grateful to be alive when you're living in the lap of luxury? Where are our candles? We haven't been offered any. Huh? Where are our flashlights? All we've been told is to go back to our rooms and be patient.

Well I can speak for all of us when I say, our patience has run out. We expect a refund immediately, not a credit, not a we'll do that once the machines are up and running. Now. Cash. Got it?"

"Sir, I don't have cash."

He scoffed and turned and looked at the others. "I'm sure you've got plenty inside there. What do you say, guys?"

"Yeah. Cough it up now!" They all began jeering and pressing forward.

"Step back or I'll be forced to call security."

"Security my ass. I saw your security leave within the first half an hour. Obviously you aren't paying them enough. Now get out of the way. I'll find my refund myself," he said pushing her back.

"This is my apartment. Now get out!"

But they weren't listening. Anger had taken root. The product of too much to drink. Several of the guys from the group followed after the Irish asshole who pushed his way inside and was now pressing into the main room to search for cash.

"Maria!" Erika yelled. She didn't want her getting caught up in it, neither did she want them encountering Bailey. A door opened and Maria came out with Bailey on a leash. The second the dog caught sight of the intruders she started barking furiously.

"That dog bites me and I sue you!" the man yelled.

What should have been a cordial exchange with her guests had turned into a breach of privacy, and threats. She went over to the phone to call down to the front desk but one of the men yanked the phone out of the wall and tossed it across the room.

Forced back to control her dog, all she could do was watch as they rooted through her belongings searching for anything of value. "Get out. I will call the cops!"

"Go ahead. I might do it myself."

"Get out of here."

They refused to listen to reason.

That was when the door eased open and Tyler emerged holding a pistol. "You heard the lady. Time to leave. Now!" His voice didn't get the attention he thought he would, so he fired a shot straight into the ceiling. "Out. Now!" he bellowed holding the gun on them.

Chapter 12

Strange. She looked pissed. Tyler thought she would have appreciated the support. After the knot of guests left her apartment, she slammed the door and got right up in his face. "Are you out of your goddamn mind?"

He grinned. "Obviously," he said before continuing. "Listen, you were a stone's throw away from things getting ugly. Had we not shown up who knows what would have happened."

"I had it under control."

Nate walked by her. "Oh yeah, you had it under control," he said sarcastically, snatching up a grape out of a fruit bowl and tossing it into his mouth.

Erika looked on. "Excuse me, do you mind?"

"Very much," he said before slumping down into the sofa. He patted either side of him. "Wow, now this is luxury. Quite a pad you got here. You want to give us the tour?"

"No. I want you both to leave. Now!" she said walking over to the door and placing a hand on it.

Right then Maria came out of the room she'd taken Bailey into. Bailey came bounding out and charged towards Tyler. He didn't flinch as the dog began sniffing him then wagging her tail. Tyler stooped and ran his hand around the back of the dog's ears and started scratching. "Hey there," he said.

Erika looked on completely stunned.

"Weird. In all the time I've had her, Bailey has always barked at males. I figured it was because of her last owner but…" she trailed off as she came over.

"Ah, dogs like me. They know when a person is a threat."

"Yeah same here," Nate said peering over the back of the sofa. As soon as Bailey spotted him, she started barking furiously. "Or not." He slipped back out of sight.

"It's okay," Tyler said calming the dog almost immediately. He looked up at Erika and she had this stunned look on her face.

"Why are you here?"

"To explain," he said rising to his feet. "Look, I know this has been one hell of an evening. I probably would have been freaked out if I'd seen someone with all this crap in their bag but there is a good explanation for it all. I wasn't going to harm you, Erika. I just wanted to get you home."

"Well I'm home and you can go now. I'll be fine. Thanks for your concern."

"You sure about that?" he asked thumbing over his shoulder.

"I'll phone down to the front desk. Security has to be around here somewhere. They wouldn't leave their post."

"Yeah, they might," he said walking over to the nearest window and looking out. All across the city, there were fires raging. Smoke billowed up spreading like a ghost.

Nate sat up and leaned over to grab the phone. "You mind?"

Erika made a face but waved for him to go ahead. He tapped in a few numbers and then reached for another grape.

"You got a dial tone?"

"Yeah," he said. "Seems Tyler here was right."

Tyler could see Erika in the window turn and look at him. "All that stuff in your bag. It's survival gear, isn't it? Did your work give you that? I mean you're a tour guide, right? It was only after, I thought that perhaps maybe they'd given you that and you'd been in a rush to get from work to the restaurant."

Tyler saw his way out. He could have lied in that moment. Being a tour guide he frequently took tourists to the Grand Canyon, the Joshua Tree National Park and even to Area 51. Long hours out in the desert meant he had to be mindful and carry some of the bare essentials for survival but that wasn't where the bag came from.

He cast a glance over his shoulder. "It's not from my work. It's a long story but I don't go anywhere without it. It's force of habit more than choice though. If I had my way, I would toss the damn thing but… now I'm beginning to see the value of it. He said it would go down like this."

"He?"

Tyler turned and walked past her. "My father."

"Is he from Vegas?"

"No, farther north. Whitefish, Montana. Look, I would love to explain in detail but we are burning time here and things aren't getting much better out there. Downed planes, a blackout, cell phones not working, stalled cars. I'm all for calling bullshit on my uncle and father but even I have to admit this has the makings of an EMP."

She frowned. "A what?"

"An electromagnetic pulse."

She shook her head. He didn't expect her or anyone to really know what it was. It wasn't like they taught you this in high school, or college. "It's a burst of electromagnetic radiation that usually follows a nuclear detonation. In simple terms it screws with electrical and electronic systems. There are a lot of factors involved that determine the effects, some of which rely on the altitude of detonation, energy yield, gamma ray output, distance, its interaction with the earth's magnetic field and the shielding used by people. It basically has the power to fry computers, phones and newer vehicles that use computer circuitry."

Erika crossed her arms and walked over to the window. "But I didn't hear an explosion."

"You might not. Again, it depends where, when and how high or low it occurred, and to be frank, there is the possibility that it's not even that. It could be something else, but without some connection to what is happening across the country, it's hard to know. But what I can tell you is the results will be the same no matter what caused it."

"Which are?"

"Panic. Chaos. Desperation. Murder."

She snorted. "I might have seen some desperation and panic out there but murder? Come on. Aren't you taking things a little too far?"

"That's what I said to my father when I was younger."

Her brow furrowed as if she was trying to understand. It was too much to unload on her, or anyone. The things he went through with his father should have put him in therapy for years but he hadn't gone that route. What was the point? He didn't want to remember it and that's exactly what a therapist would have made him do. Tyler looked over at Nate who was talking on the phone. "Look. Right now, I don't want to believe this has happened but it has and what we do in the next twenty-four hours will determine whether we live or die."

Erika scoffed. "I will admit planes dropping out of the sky is bad but what are you expecting me to do?"

Right then Nate got off the phone. "Well, I'm all set. Ready to leave whenever you are."

"Leave?" Erika asked, her eyes darting between the two of them.

Tyler was about to explain but he didn't need to, Nate did it for him. He rose from the sofa and scooped up a handful of grapes, tossing a couple in his mouth. "We're heading north."

"I didn't say I was heading north," Tyler said. "I said, I'm going to speak with my Uncle Lou, and then decide after that."

"Right, but you said if he plans on going to Montana, you'll go with him. So you're going my way. I'm going with you."

Erika cast a glance at Maria and then stepped forward. Perhaps it was her interaction with the unruly guests, the view from her window or the mention of an EMP, but her concern for the situation was evident in her voice and questions. "I thought you lived here in Vegas?" she asked Nate.

"I do. My mother is…" He glanced at Tyler. "North. Spokane, Washington. I'm going to travel with Tyler if he leaves. You should come too," Nate said. "Probably safer out there than in the big city." He paused and both of them studied her reaction. She swallowed and looked at the ground.

"No. I can't leave. I have responsibilities. Who would run this hotel?"

"I hardly think it matters now," Nate said. "You heard what he said."

"I heard what he said, but I heard a lot of things from him tonight, and not all of it was true." She glanced at Tyler and walked over to Maria and told her that she was free to go for the night. Maria gave a nod, collected her coat and told Erika if she needed anything to let her know. The door clunked shut behind her. "Anyway, this is where I live. I have no reason to go north except…"

Tyler frowned. "Except?"

"Ah, it doesn't matter," she said crossing the room and picking up the landline phone. She pressed a number and waited a second. Tyler looked at Nate who was now leaning back in a chair, tossing the remainder of grapes into his mouth. "Luanne. What's the update?"

There was a pause. He couldn't hear the reply.

"Just tell them they will be compensated but until the system is back up, they will have to wait. Nothing we can do about it." More silence then Erika nodded a few times. "Yeah, that's fine. I appreciate that." With that said she hung up.

"Things okay?" Tyler asked.

Erika didn't reply. Instead she walked over to the window and looked out into the night. The city was unlike anything they'd seen before. It was usually lit up like a Christmas tree at night but now the only illumination came from a smattering of buildings that had generators, people on the street using their phones as flashlights, and fires blazing out of control.

Tyler walked over and stood beside her. Silence stretched between them for a good minute before he said, "My father used to say that there would come a day when society would break down. Most people would be unprepared. Most would expect the lights to come on, stores to continue to sell goods, and the government would ensure everyone was safe, and that was the reason people would die. Not being prepared. Not being mindful of what could happen. Reliance on the system would be society's downfall." Tyler leaned against the window ledge. "People won't start to unravel right away and that's the problem. What you did tonight, helping I mean, it's good but it only goes so far. At some point you have to start thinking about your own safety. It's just as important, if not more important." He breathed in deeply, then exhaled. "Tomorrow could be different. Yeah, things could be better. This could all just be one big mistake and the lights could come on, and cars begin working again, and the nation might rally together but what if that isn't the case? I just want you to think about that. I'm heading over to my Uncle Lou's. He owns a surplus store about a twenty-five minute car ride from here on the north side just off Lake Mead Boulevard. It's called Lou's World of Surplus. It's sandwiched between Bighorn Casino and the Santa Fe Medical Center. If you change your mind you can find us there until morning."

She nodded but didn't look at him.

Tyler turned and made a gesture towards Nate and they headed for the door.

"Tyler."

"Yeah?"

"Close the door on the way out please," she said.

For a second he thought she was about to change her mind. She didn't. He nodded and they exited the room. Immediately outside, Nate patted him on the back. "Some you win, some you lose. Don't worry, bud, there are plenty of fish in the sea. Anyway, she probably did you a favor. It's very rare that a woman like that ends up with a guy like…" he trailed off looking Tyler up and down. Tyler noticed, so he clarified as they descended the stairwell. "No offense. I'm just pointing out the obvious. She's from another world. One in which only those with money understand. And by the looks of it, she's got a lot of it. Not that it's going to be much use if these lights don't come back on." He chuckled. "Which I might add was a nice touch."

"What was?" Tyler asked.

"You know, the whole EMP. Doom and gloom. The world is going to end speech you gave her back there. I'm not sure I would have gone that route but it was unique. I'll give you that." He tapped the railing as they went down. "Ah, the things we do for love," he muttered. "So. When do you think the lights will come back on. In a day or two?"

Tyler shook his head. "Don't hold your breath."

"What? But I thought…"

"You thought I was making this shit up?" Tyler asked.

"Well not all of it but c'mon. We always bounce back. That's what makes this nation so great. California fires, yearly hurricanes, tornadoes sweeping across the land, it's all par for the course. We lose a few lives but what country doesn't?"

"In your life, how many times have you heard it reported on the news that cars have stalled, cell phones no longer work, planes have dropped out of the sky and there is no power?"

"Um… well…" Nate stumbled over his words. Tyler didn't have to clarify, eventually the penny would drop. The truth was everything that had taken place so far was almost word for word how his father had depicted it. That's what scared him the most. It was one thing to watch, read and hear about it, another to be living it. He wasn't sure if he would head north to Whitefish. The thought of returning after so many years sickened him. He needed to speak with his uncle. Although he knew he was probably climbing the walls by now with worry, Lou was different to his father, more level-headed. But that's not to say that he didn't have his moments when he acted like his father. Lou had been the one to put together the bag for him. The original that his father had made was back in Whitefish, tucked in a closet, out of the way. When he left the town, he thought he would never pick it up again. But old habits die slowly. It had become ingrained in him, carrying the backpack wherever he went. It might seem unnatural and to some probably unbelievable that he would lug it around, but his father believed that time was a person's worst adversary in a crisis. The longer it took to get to a shelter, the longer it took to find that bugout bag, the higher the chance of dying.

It was a fear-based mentality his father had instilled in

him, no different than religious people's beliefs about hell. The fear of what might happen was a strong motivator. It would make seemingly sound of mind people do all manner of ludicrous acts, most of which they would justify later.

Tyler adjusted the backpack on his back, handed the gas mask to Nate and slipped his half face respirator on as they reached the ground floor and pushed out into the smoke-filled night.

Chapter 13

It was like walking through hell. Vegas had a sleazy feel to it at the best of times but with thick black smoke rolling through the streets, and fires raging seemingly every few blocks, Tyler expected trouble. That's why he kept his Glock at the ready. Whether the bottom feeders of society weren't along the same stretch they traveled, or fear of reprisal from police officers kept the lawless at bay, they arrived two hours later without incident.

Uncle Lou's military surplus store was a one-story light brown building that crouched at the corner of Lake Mead Boulevard and Statz Street. On the outside, large red and white signs advertising security equipment, tactical gear, work wear, surplus, MREs, knives, dog tags, bags, BDUs, webbing, tents, maps, books, mining supplies, binoculars, compasses, jackets, tarps, patches and ammo cans, stood out in almost a distracting manner. Either side of the double doorway entrance were two large, green imitation missiles that he'd had a local artist in town create. Covering the windows were graphics of military personnel in action. Unlike his father, Lou had served his country, giving eleven years of his life to the army. It was him who inspired Corey to think about a career in the military. When they were younger, they would often dine at his home in Whitefish. Their Aunt Barb would cook up a large crockpot of chili, and Lou and their father would throw back alcohol like water and he'd recount his tours and the lives he took overseas. Whether there was truth to the tales or it was the beer talking, it didn't matter. They lapped it up and hung on every word — especially Corey.

After their mother passed on, and their home went into foreclosure, Lou and Barb were like an anchor in their life. They'd extended a hand and offered to house them but their father was too proud. When he eventually accepted help, it was from a local church member, not his brother. Still, Lou invited them to their home any chance they got and tried to provide some stability at a time when their father struggled.

Tyler went around the side of the building as shutters were covering the main door and windows. Like many of the businesses in Vegas that had the good sense to act fast, Lou knew his establishment would be one of the first places people would hit after grocery stores. Even if someone could get through the shutters at the front of the store, they would have to make their way through ballistic glass. His uncle had thought of practically everything. While not as paranoid as his father, Lou was a firm believer in having a contingency plan. Down the right side of the building was an entrance where he could drive vehicles in and out. Military vehicles were hard to get and few people wanted them so the ones he had were mostly used for display or for parades in the city.

"Are you sure he's here?"

"Trust me. He'll defend this place to his last dying breath."

Tyler banged his fist against the garage door. "Uncle Lou. It's me."

He looked up at a surveillance camera that moved ever

so slightly. A generator was powering it. "Come on. Open up." Tyler looked around nervously. The motor powering the shutters kicked in, and they stepped back as the shutters were raised. It was dark inside but along the floor Lou had installed tiny strips of lights like in an airplane to help with navigating the aisles just in case they had a blackout. Even if you have power, never turn on lights in a blackout — you'll attract unwanted attention; Tyler's father would say. The familiar smell of musty old clothes and aged metal lingered. There was a buzzing noise behind them as the shutters came down and it sealed closed.

Lou emerged from a darkened aisle with an M4 in hand. The first thing he did was launch into a tirade. Tyler knew it was coming. "Tyler, how many times do I have to tell you…" Before he finished, he squinted then asked, "Who's that?"

Tyler thumbed behind him. "Oh, uh. This is Nate. He might leave with us."

"Friend of yours?"

"Not exactly, let's say we dug him out of a hole."

Lou came over and raised his gun at him. "Put your hands up."

"Uncle Lou, it's fine."

"Why, you patted him down?"

"No but…"

Lou didn't wait for an explanation, he began patting him down and going through his pockets. "Widen your legs." He pushed him up against a shelf and kicked his feet apart.

"Is this really necessary?" Nate asked.

"If you want to leave, no. If you stay, yes."

With that said Lou continued. As he came around the back of him, he tapped and lifted his jacket. "Oh, what have we here?" Before Nate could react, Lou pulled a Sig Sauer out of Nate's waistband. He'd tucked it into the small of his back.

"Do you mind? That's mine."

"Yeah, and you'll get it back when you leave, no sooner. Got it?"

"Tyler," Nate said.

Tyler piped up, "Lou. It's not like it's unheard of."

"Of course not but that doesn't make me feel any safer, now does it?"

He pulled out a pack of cigarettes, and a water bottle, and what looked like a small women's purse. "Hmm. I'm guessing this isn't yours."

Tyler squinted at the nearly empty water bottle and noticed something. He walked over and picked it up and turned it around. There was a logo on the side for Lyons Hotels.

"You grab this while you were there?"

"No."

"So where did you get it from?"

"I already had it on me."

"That doesn't answer the question."

"Look, it's just a water bottle, what's the problem?"

Tyler scooped up the small plaid purse and opened it. There was about a hundred and eighty bucks in cash, and several credit cards. After he pulled one out and read the name, he turned around. "You stole her purse?"

"I..." Nate spluttered trying to turn around but Lou had a firm hand on his back keeping him from going anywhere. Then it dawned on him. Earlier that night Erika had said her bag, and purse had been stolen. Tyler looked Nate up and down and the pieces started to fall together.

"Wearing motorcycle gear. I should have figured. You drive a green Kawasaki?"

With his head slightly turned Nate flashed a thin smile and Tyler shook his head. "Listen, I can explain."

"Where's her bag, Nate?"

"In the rubble."

"And the phone?"

"In the rubble. Well, I think it's there."

"You think?"

He hesitated for a second then bellowed, "I sold it. Okay? You happy?"

"You really are a piece of work. So, this is what you do. You're in the habit of snatching bags?"

"We all have to earn a living. Besides, it's not like she's hurting for cash, now is it?"

"Geesh. Are you serious?"

"Look, if it's any consolation, I was thinking of getting out of the game."

"Just like you're trying to talk your way out of this," Tyler said coming around to look him in the eyes, and shake the purse in his face.

"Well, c'mon then," Lou said grabbing him by the collar and pushing him towards the exit. "Time for you to go."

"At least give me my gun back." Lou turned and snagged it up and handed it to him but not before removing the magazine.

"Tyler. Please. Come on, man. I didn't know it was her. It takes us seconds to snatch bags and phones. I don't focus on faces, I look at the item I'm taking."

Tyler didn't reply as he watched Lou guide Nate over to the side shutter. Lou punched a large red button on the wall and the steel clattered as it rose. He tossed out the full magazine. "Look. I was planning on giving it back but in the heat of the moment I just forgot."

"Yeah. I bet you did," Tyler said as Lou shoved him out into the night and brought the shutter back down. They saw him snag up the magazine and slam it back into the handgun.

"Tyler. Please, man. I don't want to stay out here. I don't have a place to stay."

Lou walked towards Tyler. "Nice choice in friends. Maybe next time you'll remember to pat them down before bringing them back here. Who knows how many others he could lead here?"

"I'm sorry, Uncle Lou, I screwed up."

"Yeah, well, come on back. Barb has some soup ready. After that I need you to give me a hand loading some of these products into the bunker." Tyler could still hear Nate outside asking him to give him a chance. He banged a few times on the shutter and Lou bellowed that if he continued, he'd regret it. He wasn't a violent man but under these conditions Tyler wouldn't have put it past him. Tyler followed Lou out back trying to forget Nate. He liked the guy but if he couldn't trust him, that could make life dangerous, and it was already ramping up in the city.

* * *

Erika poured herself another full glass of red wine and knocked it back. Since they'd left, she'd planned to handle the guest issues, first by trying to get in touch with the contract security company to find out why their guy had left and second by changing out of her clothes into something more professional and speaking with them down in the lobby. Well, that was the plan. Unfortunately, no one answered the phone and after what she experienced in her room, she wasn't willing to go through that again. In the first hour with the landline still in operation she phoned her mother in Utah. According to Luanne, her mother had been trying to reach her for several hours but because she didn't have her phone on her, and only recently returned to the hotel, Erika decided to call her.

Although her parents were still involved in the decision making of running the hotel chain, they had reached an age where they preferred to be as hands-off as possible. That for them meant frequent vacations to Aspen and overseas when they weren't living out a quiet life in Midway, Utah.

"Yes, I'm okay, Mom."

"And the hotel."

"It's still standing though security appears to have vanished."

"Well what do you expect after hiring that company? I told you to hire…"

"I know what you told me. They were recommended to me by a friend and I was trying to be frugal."

"Darling. Frugal is what gives hotels bad ratings. There is a reason why we are number one in the country and it's not because we are penny pinchers. Now I want you to phone the company I recommended. Would you do that for your mother? Unless of course you want to deal with the blowback of bad reviews."

Could she be any more condescending?

"I don't think it's going to matter. People have been irate all this evening. Once the net comes back up, we are screwed."

"Don't say that. We'll handle it."

"I'm sure you will," she said. "But what am I meant to do in the interim?"

"Leave it to Luanne. She's more than capable of running that hotel. Remember, she was doing it long before you got there."

"How could I forget? You remind me every week."

"Oh don't be so dramatic. I'm just reminding you that she's a well of experience that would be better served if you gave her more leeway."

"If I gave her more leeway, I wouldn't have a job. Wasn't that the reason you put me here?"

She heard her mother snort. "Look, if you can't handle it—"

"I can handle it."

"I'm just saying. Your brother Chad would be more

than happy to take over the reins."

"Have you heard from him?"

"Not recently. I thought he was with you."

Erika frowned wondering if she even knew what was going on.

"Mother. are the lights out where you are?"

"Yes. Darn things have been off for several hours. I have candles on all over the house. Your father has been trying to get hold of the utility company but no one is answering the phone and our cells aren't working."

"What about downed planes?"

"Downed what?"

"Oh, forget it. Is the internet working?"

"No. Nothing is. It's utterly frustrating."

"Yeah, first world problems can be like that."

"Don't be facetious, Erika, I get enough of that from your father."

Erika groaned and ran a hand through Bailey's hair. "Where is he?"

"Digging through the garage for the generator. It took

him this long just to remember we had one. I don't think he even knows how to operate it. Uh, look, I'm going to…" she paused. "Henry?" More silence followed by the sound of her mother walking. "Henry? Is that you?"

"Mother. What's going on?"

"Dear God. Who are you? Get out of here."

"Mom?"

There was a loud crash and then she heard her mother scream.

"Mom. Mom!"

In the background she could hear her mother struggling and crying, and then a loud thud. A few seconds after someone picked up the phone as she heard heavy breathing and then the line went dead. "Hello? Hello, Mom?" She tried phoning back but no one answered. Erika called her three more times before she put the phone down and paced back and forth. Her fear turned to panic, and she tried to contact the local police to see if they could alert the Midway Police Department as she didn't have their number or any way of finding out what it was because the net was down. Unfortunately, she couldn't get through to emergency services. The lines were jammed. Thousands were probably overwhelming the switchboard. "Damn it!" she bellowed slamming the phone down. She tried her mother's one more time but only got the answering machine.

Gripped by the unthinkable, Erika hurried into her bedroom and rooted through her closet for her old backpack. She pulled it out and stuffed it with some underwear, a couple pairs of pants and socks, and then rushed into the bathroom. She scooped up her toothbrush while Bailey followed her, sensing something was wrong. All the while Erika kept muttering to herself. *This can't be happening. This can't be happening.* Flustered and overwhelmed she snatched her jacket off the hook, picked up Bailey's leash and crouched. "Bailey. Come on, let's go." She trotted over, wagging her tail. Erika quickly clipped the leash to her collar and headed out the door.

All she could hear in her mind was the sound of her mother's scream.

Utah was a long way away. Traveling there by car would have been stressful, but by foot and in these conditions? She had no idea how she was going to get there but she knew who might help.

Chapter 14

There were several officers from Columbia Falls and the Flathead County Sheriff Department blocking the highway. All of them were carrying Remington 870 shotguns or Colt M4 carbines — certainly heavy firepower for run-of-the-mill checkpoints. One of the officers gestured to get them to slow down as they got closer. They'd expected to see police out patrolling and making sure that looting didn't happen but there was something very different about this.

Corey brought his window down.

"Good evening, gents," the officer said shining his flashlight beam into the vehicle. Another officer did the same on the other side, while a third went around the back and investigated the contents of the truck.

"Where are you coming from and where are you heading?"

Terry piped up, "Whitefish. We're from Flathead

County Search and Rescue. We got a call that a plane went down near McDonald Lake." He handed over some identification and the cop scanned it before handing it back.

"License, registration and proof of insurance."

Corey pulled down the visor and handed him what he needed.

The officer glanced at it. "Were you given any more details than that?" he asked while keeping his eyes on them.

"No. It was very general."

The officer looked off towards his fellow officers. "Well, before the power outage we'd received a call from several residents near the lake to report a low-flying 737. Air traffic control provided information that it was carrying inmates from a different jurisdiction. Hence the reason for the blockade," he said gesturing over his shoulder. "A number of our officers were on our way up there when our vehicles stalled. Strangely you are one of only a handful of vehicles we have seen operational since the event. Because of the danger of the situation we have to commandeer any vehicle available at this time. That would include yours, I'm afraid."

"You can do that?" Terry frowned as he asked.

"Yeah, they can," Corey replied. He'd learned about police being able to commandeer a vehicle a long time ago so there was no point in arguing. "Look, I'm a former Marine. If it's okay I would like to go with you. I might be of some help, and being as this is my father's vehicle, I'm not too sure he would be too pleased if he knew I'd handed it over to the boys in blue without going along."

The officer pulled a face. Obviously they weren't in the habit of pulling regular citizens into their work, however, under the circumstances there obviously could be some benefit. Having a search and rescue crew on hand might come in handy.

"Hang tight, while I speak with my superior," the officer said before walking off.

While they waited, conversation swirled around what the officer had shared.

"Prison inmates? Holy crap," Vern said. "Can you imagine if we'd made it all the way up there and…" he trailed off thinking of the possibility of encountering them and the worst outcome. While the second officer kept an eye on them, the third one was eyeing some of the gear in the back. Corey glanced in his rearview mirror and watched him hop into the rear of the truck and fish through it.

A few minutes later the original officer returned and tapped the truck. "All right, if you want to just pull off to the side over there, we have a few things to do first. You'll be taking a few of the officers from Flathead County up there. You have any weapons in the vehicle?"

Corey nodded. "A rifle."

"You have a permit?"

He pulled out his wallet and showed him.

"All right. Just move ahead."

Moments later the truck idled at the edge of the road while the officers discussed among themselves who was staying and who was going. It couldn't have been easy.

With all the lights out in every town in the region, the need for officers patrolling the towns had increased. Many would be pulling double shifts, and feeling stretched. It was like throwing policing back to the 1800s. While waiting for them to decide who was going, Corey used his two-way radio to update his father. It was not that he had to, but in light of the fact that the cops were going to take the vehicle for a while he thought it was best.

"They are doing what?" his father bellowed.

"Nothing I can do about it."

"I told you not to go. Didn't I say this would happen? If anyone should have known better it was you. Now how are you getting back here?"

"I'll find my way."

"You'll find your way. Really? That's great. That means I'm going to have to collect you and risk losing the 4 x 4. Dear God. Didn't anything of what I taught you sink into your thick skull?"

"You're skating on thin ice, Dad."

"No, son. You are, and it's cracking beneath your feet.

For God's sake. Where are you now?"

"West Glacier and about to head up to McDonald Lake but you won't get through the roadblock here. They see that truck, they'll take it."

"Like fuck they will."

"Dad, don't do anything stupid."

His father scoffed. "What, like you just did? I should—"

"Calm down," Corey muttered. Terry looked at him and shook his head. They were all too familiar with Andy Ford's outbursts. He wasn't always that way. When their mother was alive, she kept his ego in check but after she died, that all went to shit. The drinking didn't help and his paranoia only got worse. Except now, this had all proven that he was right.

"Well, I'm on my way." He cursed one more time before the radio went silent.

Moments later, several of Flathead's finest hopped into the back of the truck and beat on the top to let him know to head out. Corey rolled out, his mind now preoccupied by the danger up ahead. It was one thing to search and rescue those in need, another to go up against people who had nothing to lose.

* * *

Although there was a good chance no one knew about their presence in the mountains and they could probably hunker down in the cabins for a few days, Gabriel was eager to move on. It was harder to catch a moving target. He'd sent a couple of the guys ahead to scout out the ranger station just in case that ranger wasn't lying and he'd managed to get word out before the power outage.

The door burst open and Bryan Hauser came in out of breath. "There are two rangers at the station. What do you want to do?"

Gabriel cast a glance at the old man and woman and told Torres to tie them up.

"You're leaving them alive?" Marcus asked with a look of confusion.

"They've been helpful. I don't expect anyone is going to make it out of here for some time, and like you said. If they could have walked out of here they would have by now." Gabriel gathered up a backpack of food and a first-aid kit, and headed out. Torres was given the additional rifle and they moved out planning to meet up with Jericho and Bill who were doing some reconnaissance on the ranger station. Several of them were still wearing prison garb. That would make blending in a problem. So the first thing on their list was to get to the nearest home and change out. Gabriel was fine, he was wearing one of the old man's leather jackets and even though the jeans were a bit tight and long, they were dry, warm and he'd rolled up the bottoms.

A short distance down the road, Hauser led them to a thick grove of trees where Jericho and Bill were waiting. He ducked down and through the tree branches observed movement inside. One ranger was in his mid-forties, the other a female, much younger, both were armed. Behind the station, at least another two hundred yards away there was another building, a home. He'd seen the properties dotted around the edge of the lake. Marcus came up behind him, hunched over and placed a hand on his shoulder. "What have we got?"

"A male and a female."

"A female. Nice."

Gabriel glanced at him. "Stay focused."

"Oh I am."

Gabriel made a gesture and they moved out into the clearing, nothing more than dark bodies running through the blackness of night. As soon as they made it to the wooden porch that wrapped around the property, Gabriel had Jericho slowly turn the knob on the door while Bill kept an eye on the rangers through the window. As soon as he had the door ajar, Gabriel was the first in. Kicking in the door might have led to one of them getting shot, instead he took the subtle approach and slipped in, moving quietly towards the main living room.

"I still think we should have gone with him," the female ranger was saying.

"No point. Rescue will be up here soon and…"

Before he could finish what he was saying, Gabriel

emerged aiming his rifle at him.

"No sudden moves and no one gets hurt."

"Who are you?"

That was soon answered when Marcus and Jericho came into view still wearing their prison garb. The ranger's hand lingered near his sidearm while the female looked terrified. "Don't do it," Gabriel said.

"Where is he?" the ranger asked.

"Your colleague? Ah, he's fine. You should worry about yourself. Now take your hand away from your firearm." He made a gesture with the barrel of his rifle. "Don't make me do it."

The ranger's hands went up and Marcus hurried in to restrain him. He threw both on the ground, they were face down while Marcus tied them up. He took extra time doing the female and seemed to be enjoying himself a little too much. Marcus bent down and whispered something in her ear while running his hand over her ass.

"Marcus," Gabriel said in a reprimanding way. His brother looked at him, gave a devilish smile and got up.

Jericho hauled them to their feet and sat them on a large sofa in the center of the log cabin. Wood crackled and spat out a few hot embers from a roaring fireplace as the rest of the inmates went through the cabin gathering together anything that could be of use. On the far side of the room were two tables with a ham radio, a TV, a computer and a half-finished jigsaw puzzle. There were a couple of beer bottles out, and a bowl of nachos. There was a reason he kept the rangers alive. He wanted to know what they knew. Instead of asking if they had called for backup, he made the assumption they already had. "So, who's coming?"

"What?"

"You called for backup. From where?"

"West Glacier. That's where the park's headquarters are. Where are you from?"

"Isn't obvious?" Gabriel replied getting tired of the same dumb question, especially since most of them were still in prison garb. He went over to the ham radio to see if it was working. It powered on without any problem.

Outside he could hear a generator running. "How many ways out of here?"

"Two. You can go north to Red Rock Point but beyond that you have to go south using the road around the lake. It will take you down to the village of Apgar. There are several trails off this road but those are the only ways in and out from here. Once you hit Apgar you can go south to West Glacier or north up Camas Road."

"When you got the call from your buddy, who did you speak to?"

"Headquarters in West Glacier. It's about twenty-five minutes by car from here. At least four hours if you hike. We handle everything related to the park."

Gabriel walked up and down and looked out the window. What smidgen of peace he'd felt before was now gone. "You have a vehicle?"

"Yeah but it's—"

"Not working," Gabriel said, finishing what he was about to say. Frustrated, he scooped up a pair of binoculars that were on the table and went outside to have a smoke. He walked down to the water's edge in the hopes of a getting a better look at the area. They were in a basin surrounded by a hilly landscape covered with thick forest. He brought up the binoculars and peered through. He could see a few homes had lights, where people had been smart enough to buy gas or solar generators. He squinted to see the area between the trees further across the lake. He was sure he could see movement, two yellow headlights gleaming through the trees heading their way.

He flicked the remainder of his cigarette into the water before heading back up to the cabin. No sooner had he got within a few feet of the cabin than he heard a woman screaming. Gabriel hurried inside to find the woman had been bent over a table and his brother was unbuckling his belt. Without a moment of hesitation, he lunged forward, grabbed him by the back of the collar and hurled him across the room straight into the ham radio. The whole thing slid off the table and crashed on the ground. He shouted at the other inmates to get out. They backed up and he slammed the door closed so he could have a moment with his brother. Turning to speak with him, he was met with a sharp jab to the face. The punch was hard enough to rattle his brain and buckle his legs. While he was on the ground trying to get his bearings, his brother came at him again. Before he could get another punch in, Gabriel kicked his legs out from underneath him and jumped on top. Straddling his chest, he held out his arms and pinned him down like he had many years ago as a kid. Back then they fought all the time. Their fights were vicious and often ended with one of them losing a tooth or being knocked out. The years hadn't changed much between them.

"Stop. Stop, Marcus!" Gabriel yelled. He glanced over at the female ranger who had already covered herself up and was cowering in the corner near the male who looked furious.

"Get off me."

"That shit might have flown before they put you inside but you are not doing it again."

"Get the fuck off me."

Gabriel slapped him on the side of the face as if trying to wake him from his madness. "You want to live that way, you do it once we are free but until then you do as I say."

"Screw you. We are free!"

Gabriel grabbed him by the throat. "What happened to you?"

"Don't give me that self-righteous attitude. You were inside before I was."

"Yeah. And you should have learned from that. But no, you had to go fuck things up and look where it got you. Had I been out I would have…"

"Would have what?" Marcus asked.

Gabriel stared at him and then rose to his feet and offered him a hand. Marcus batted it out of the way, got up and stormed out. Gabriel looked at the woman and apologized, reassuring her that it wouldn't happen again. He might have robbed banks, killed a cop and a ranger, but he was no rapist and he'd be damned if he'd let anyone do that while he was calling the shots. His mind went back to the lights between the trees. Someone was searching for them and he wouldn't be here when they arrived. He headed for the door. Torres was outside smoking a cigarette. "We leave now. Deal with them."

He didn't need to ask what he meant. Seconds later, two gunshots were heard.

Chapter 15

Crime existed in Vegas long before the blackout — robberies, murders, kidnapping, home invasions, there wasn't any reason why that would stop now. In fact, everything that had taken place so far had only stacked the odds in favor of criminals. Darkness shrouded the lawless, communication was dismal at best, roads were clogged with stalled traffic, and emergency services were overwhelmed by downed planes. It was a perfect environment for the greedy. The first sign of trouble began with someone shaking the shutters on the outside of the building. It had triggered the silent alarm system. Tyler had been scooping hot soup into his mouth and relishing every drop when a red light on the wall started pulsating. Lou turned his head and grimaced. "For God's sake. Your friend is going to end up with lead in his ass." Lou shoved his chair back causing it to screech, and grabbed up his rifle.

"Darlin', your soup will go cold," Barb said.

Tyler took off after him. "Hold up, Lou, I'll speak to him."

"No, he's had enough chances."

Since being kicked outside, Nate had been banging on the garage door for the past twenty minutes. When that didn't work, he'd gone around the front and tried there but when he got no response, it went quiet. They thought he finally had given up and left, leaving Tyler feeling somewhat guilty. He was of two minds about it all. He wasn't opposed to letting Nate back in and giving him another chance, but Lou wouldn't have it.

Tyler followed him into a small room out back that had multiple monitors displaying various views of the outside. He had cameras set up on the roof pointing down to prevent anyone from stealing or damaging them. That was when they got their first glimpse of the problem, and it wasn't Nate.

"I knew it. I told you, Tyler, he would bring people back."

Tyler leaned forward and looked at the screens. Four Asian men wearing red and black bandannas over the lower half of their faces were attempting to gain access to the front of the store. One of them was beating on the lock with an ax trying to get it to snap while another had hooked up a chain to the shutter and tossed the other end to a guy waiting by an old pickup truck. "Lou, Nate's not even out there. And he's black, not Asian."

"Black. Asian. White. They're all the same," he said brushing past him. Tyler heard the sound of a magazine being slapped into place. "These bastards are in for a big surprise if they think they are getting in here." Lou double-timed it to the front of the store, where he entered a door off to the right. It was the stairwell to the roof that was used as an additional fire escape in the event that any of the lower exits couldn't be reached. He tapped in a code to unlock a large metal flap and pushed it open. Tyler followed him just to see what he had in mind. He figured he would open fire on them but that wasn't to be. As soon as he reached the top, he swept his jacket to one side and yanked off what looked like a smoke grenade. They sold Enola Gaye products in the store. The damn things could kick out a lot of colored smoke within a matter of seconds. They were often bought for sports venues, nightclubs and festivals because of the sheer amount of smoke they produced in less than a minute. "Here, catch," Lou said tossing one to him. "You take that side, I'll take the other."

He already knew how to use it. It was as simple as pulling the ring to the side and away it went. Not making a sound they crept up to the edge of the building. They could still hear the guy hacking away at the lock. He'd be doing that for some time as Lou didn't install low-end locks, only quality. Lou gave a nod and pulled the ring, then tossed it down, while Tyler lobbed his towards the truck. Thick, blue smoke erupted, filling the air and creating confusion. A few rounds close to their feet and those assholes were scrambling to get the hell out of there.

Lou cracked up laughing as the truck tore away with one of them hanging on to the back for dear life. He unloaded a few more rounds their way for good measure before heading back for the opening. "Oh man, the look on their faces. They didn't know who the hell was shooting or from where. Amateurs," he said. Tyler took a moment to see if he could spot Nate. He went to the far side and looked down but he wasn't there. He figured he'd given up and headed home.

"Tyler. Come on, we have a lot to do before morning," Lou said crawling down into the shaft.

"Yeah, I'll be right there."

He crouched at the lip of the store and used a pair of binoculars he'd grabbed off the counter on the way up. Even though Lou was convinced they were out of hot water, Tyler wasn't. The smoke grenade he'd thrown had landed in the back of their pickup truck so even though it was dark, he could still see the smoke billowing in the distance as they swerved to the edge of the road near Bighorn Casino and one of them tossed it out. Had he got back in and driven off, Tyler might not have given it another thought, except that wasn't what he did. The guy turned and looked towards the store. Another one jumped out the passenger side and they reached into the back of the truck and pulled out what appeared to be AR-15s with bump stocks, which would allow the semi-automatic rifle to fire bullets almost as fast as a fully automatic. They left their vehicle where it was and running at a crouch all four of them crossed the road and fanned out into the adjoining lot that was used for car sales.

Tyler hurried over to the opening and yelled as he scaled down the ladder taking him back into the stairwell. "Lou. Uncle Lou! They're not gone."

He almost bumped into him as he hurried into the store. Lou was already on it, carrying another M4. He handed it to Tyler without even asking him if he knew how to use it. It was a given. Tyler had been given lessons since he was old enough to hold a gun safely. It was the only thing his father taught him that he actually enjoyed. It let him release his frustration and pent-up anger. There were often days he would go out the back of their home in Montana and line up bottles just to unleash a few rounds. He'd become very adept at firing from a kneeling or standing position as well as moving. Left handed, right handed, with or without support. His father made damn sure they knew guns like the back of their hands.

* * *

The soles of her feet ached more than her thighs. While hiking was a favorite pastime for tourists and residents of Vegas due to the immense number of trails in the area, she'd never had the time to waste. Waste. That was what her mother called it. Wasting time. What was the purpose of walking somewhere unless you have a reason? Why walk when you can drive or catch a plane, she would say. Her father wasn't much different. Raised in a wealthy family, he knew nothing more than the silver spoon.

Erika reached down and scratched the back of Bailey's ear and pulled her in close. Even though she felt moderately safe walking the streets at night with her dog, the breakdown of power made her feel uneasy. With no lights on, and only the fires burning brightly throughout the city, the sense of impending doom felt ever present.

She was halfway through the Art District when she saw a group of thugs coming out of the Gold and Silver Pawnshop dragging a man by the back of his collar. They were laughing and beating him with their fists while several others cleared out whatever they could from the store. Those not a part of it slipped by quickly, not wishing to get involved and not hanging around long enough to give the thugs a reason to turn their anger towards them. What caught her attention was that they weren't what she would have classed as gang members, they looked like ordinary bystanders, the kind of people you might see waiting at a bus stop, or staying in her hotel. Erika crossed the street to avoid walking into them and tried to turn a blind eye but when Bailey started barking, one of them looked over.

"Shh. Bailey. Quiet," she said picking up the pace.

"Hey. Hey wait up," she heard one of them say. Out the corner of her eye she caught him jogging towards her.

Before he could get close, Erika fished into her jacket and pulled out pepper spray. Trish always carried one in her purse, and she was mortified to learn that Erika didn't. She'd never needed to. In all her times of traveling she'd been driven across the city. "Well you can use it when you take Bailey for a walk. You are planning on walking her yourself, yes?" Trish had said.

"Of course," she remembered saying.

Spinning on the balls of her feet she didn't hesitate for a second to threaten him with it. "Back off. I'll spray." Trish had told her numerous times that if she was ever attacked to spray and run, never give them the option to walk away. It was her first time being approached. In theory she hadn't been attacked but there was the potential. Bailey tugged hard on the leash, baring her teeth and lunging at the guy.

"Whoa!" he said backing up with his hands raised. "I thought you were someone else. My bad." He backed up a little more but still wasn't interested in walking away.

By now his friends were looking over. Erika knew time

was of the essence.

She took a few steps back and then turned and hurried down the street. She went at least six blocks and found herself downtown before she dared looked back. They were gone. She stopped running and placed a hand up against a tattoo store to catch her breath. Bailey took a piss, and she looked around. Most if not all of the stores on the street had their shutters down. Besides the pawnshop, she hadn't seen anyone else breaking into stores though she imagined it would only be a matter of time if the lights didn't come up. Her thoughts returned to her parents as she trudged through the downtown weaving her way around stalled vehicles. On the way she passed by several people, folks who had common sense not to attack others. She felt like warning them about the group she'd passed but opted to say nothing and press on. A few tears welled in her eyes as she recalled her mother's scream. Had someone broken in? It was possible. Their home in Midway was in a well-to-do neighborhood. Had someone taken advantage of the moment?

As she came up to Stewart Avenue the Zappos building was on her left, and a huge open lot to her right. She crossed the street and turned her head at the sound of a bottle smashing, that was when she caught sight of the same group she'd seen looting the store. A shot of fear went through her as she became aware that they were following her.

Erika swallowed hard and burst into a full-out sprint.

No sooner had she started to run than she saw them take off after her.

What did they want? She didn't have anything of value on her. Across the street were a couple hurrying. She called out to them hoping they might listen but they were too gripped by fear to stop. They darted down another road and left her running towards a gas station on the corner of Las Vegas Boulevard and Mesquite Avenue. She had cut around the back hoping to find somewhere to lay low when she noticed they'd divided and two of them had circled around to cut her off.

Her eyes darted back and forth as she tried to dash

between the gas station and Money Gram. It was pointless. Bailey began tugging hard and trying to scare them off but it wasn't working. "That dog bites me I will kill the damn thing," one said.

"I don't have anything."

"Yeah you do, Lyons."

Then it dawned on her that they knew her. Her stomach sank.

"Yeah, I thought I remembered you. I saw your billboard over on Clark Avenue. I don't forget faces. Now come on, what have you got?"

"I don't have anything."

Bailey was now pulling to the point that Erika could barely hold her.

While the group didn't look like they were carrying any weapons, that didn't mean shit. She saw what they did to the pawnshop owner. One of them came at her, a large guy, greasy hair, overweight and all hands. He didn't get within spitting distance before Bailey pulled so hard that the leash slipped through her hand and she attacked the man, latching on to his wrist. He let out a wail as he stumbled back, falling over.

That was when she saw one of them produce a tire iron.

"Bailey," she yelled as one of them struck the dog. Fortunately, she moved otherwise it would have nailed her head. It was the worst thing they could have done. Instead of cowering back, Bailey pounced on the tire iron-wielding lunatic and started snapping up her shit. As Erika tried to get Bailey off, someone grabbed her from behind and dragged her to the ground. She felt a hard whack against her head and then heard her dog let out a loud yelp. Erika blacked out at that point.

How long she was out was unknown but when she came to, the people were gone and a familiar voice could be heard nearby speaking softly to Bailey. "There, there, it's okay, girl." As her eyes adjusted and the world snapped back into view, she saw Nate down on one knee, a gun in one hand and the other stroking Bailey.

Chapter 16

Rounds snapped overhead, a torrent of gunfire that would have easily forced the Las Vegas SWAT team into action, except not that evening. "Tyler, one of them is going around the front. I'll hold them off here," Lou said. Tyler nodded and took off at a crouch. He spotted the guy darting from one vehicle to the next, using them as cover to close the gap between him and the store. The other three were nothing more than a distraction. There were only two ways up onto that roof. They had used the one through the store, and the other was around the west side of the building. There was a staircase that led up to a side door. If a person balanced on the metal railing they could easily haul themselves up. Tyler figured that was what this goon had in mind.

For a brief moment, as Tyler tried to get a bead on him, he felt as if he was back in Whitefish, thirteen years of age with his father bellowing at him. He'd constructed an elaborate homemade shooting range out back of the home. It was on a level that even the FBI and CIA would have been impressed. There were buildings they had to clear, obstacles to shoot around, lateral moving targets and a few surprises that their father threw in each time to try and catch them off guard. Tyler had excelled in shooting stationary targets but it took him years before he could proficiently navigate that course without error. Throughout those early days he never heard his father once say well done, or good job, or you're getting better. It was always the same shit — you missed that target which means you're dead. How does that feel? Or what kind of shooting do you call that? Or you're lacking focus. It was rare he heard any positive words. Even when he finally completed the course, his father simply snorted, got this half smile on his face and walked away. It had been his brother who had championed him, patted him on the back, told him he was getting better. Had it not been for him, he often wondered if he would have turned the gun on his father. It was crazy to think about that now but back then there were many times he felt as if he'd reached his breaking point.

In his mind's eye he could see the targets springing up into view from behind bushes, and moving along a rail his father had made. The anxiety back then was not about being killed but about getting it wrong. Missing the target. Firing too many rounds. Showing a lack of situational awareness. Being judged by his father. His palms would sweat and his pulse pound as he darted in and out of bushes, trying to hit targets while making sure that he didn't trigger a trip wire and end up with a branch slapping his face or chest.

Tyler squeezed off a three-round rapid burst, smashing the side windows of cars before a round struck the guy in the shoulder spinning him to the ground. His instinct or the memory of his father told him to climb down and finish the job. *"You leave them alive, you die. You got it?"* he recalled him saying after Tyler hit a target only to be shot with a rubber bullet. Yeah, his father didn't do it by halves. Forget using paintballs. How could he forget the bruises all over his body? The pain of being shot with rubber bullets. That alone motivated him to get it right.

At the lip of the roof he scanned for movement. He knew the guy wasn't dead as he'd clipped his right shoulder but he also wasn't lying down as his feet had disappeared out of view. Tyler looked back towards Lou who was taking care of business. "You okay, Lou?"

He gave a thumbs-up before unleashing a burst of gunfire.

Tyler hurried over to the side of the roof, swung his rifle behind his back and climbed over. He slid down and made his way to the front of the store. He cut the corner and pulled back before pivoting around and making a mad dash for the vehicles on the other side of the road. As soon as he was over, he dropped down and checked his ammo before looking to see where he'd gone. A quick peek showed no sign of him. *Where are you?*

His mind flashed back to the past.

After Tyler successfully completed his father's shooting range multiple times over the years, Andy Ford looked more annoyed than pleased. In an attempt to ramp things up, and take difficulty to the next level, he'd invited buddies of his from a survival workshop and told Tyler he would be going up against six of them in a forested area, north of their home. It was a location he hadn't ever been to but his father was all too familiar with it. Also, what he hadn't told him was that he would be doing it at night, his attackers would be camouflaged, and he would be wearing a bright orange vest. Tyler would get five rubber bullets and he was to use nothing but the environment to evade and conquer. That was it.

"But that's unfair," Tyler had said.

"Life is unfair, kid. Get used to it. You think when this world goes to shit, people are going to ask themselves if they are giving you the advantage? No. You have to be ready any place, anytime, with whatever you have."

"But there are six of them."

"I guess you'll have to adapt."

He spoke with him as if he was just a stranger who'd walked into his store to get survival advice. Corey of course had passed with flying colors, he was a natural, someone who took to any environment he was placed in. But Tyler. It was always an uphill climb. None of it came to him naturally. He made more mistakes than his father's worst students. Dumped off in those woods later that evening, with no previous experience on what to do, he adapted by removing his orange vest, stuffing it in a bush and then climbing a tree and listening for movement. He took out three of them before they realized where he was. After that he dodged, hid in the dirt and leaves and even waded into a freezing cold river up to his neck in order to elude his pursuers. When he was out of ammo and down to the last man, he wielded his rifle like an ax and stayed low to the ground until he saw his window of opportunity. Now he would have liked to have said he passed that day but he didn't. After knocking out the guy with his rifle, he met his father in the parking lot of the forest where he chewed him out for removing his vest.

"Did I tell you to climb a tree or wade into the river?"
"You said use the environment, I did."

"Did I tell you to remove the vest?"

"You said adapt."

"Well you failed. Failure to follow the rules is failure in my book. Failure to—"

Tyler cut him off. "I did what I had to out there and I'm the one still standing."

He knew there was a good chance he would get a beating for speaking out of line but at that point he didn't care. Cold. Hungry. Tired, and miserable with spending hours and days doing everything his father said with little praise, eventually got the better of him. His father didn't wait. He lashed out and slapped him across the face, knocking him to the ground.

"Not standing now, are you?" his father said, leering over him. The smell of alcohol was thick on his breath. It wasn't him talking but the whiskey. Tyler's hands balled in the dirt, gripping wet leaves. All he wanted to do was knock his teeth out, make him understand what it felt like. His father saw his reaction and beckoned him to take a swing. "Go on. Do it. It will be the last thing you do."

He was baiting him.

Corey had been waiting in the idling truck. He'd watched it all play out but did nothing. Tyler looked his way expecting him to intervene as he usually did but he didn't that evening. He assumed his father had told Corey to stay put or his punishment would be even more severe.

Instead of taking that swing, Tyler released the leaves and rose to his feet, brushing himself off and gritting his teeth. He scowled at his father before saying, *"You know what, Dad — fuck you! And fuck your rules of survival."*

His father attempted to strike him again but he ducked his open hand and bolted into the dark forest. Back then he was certain his father would chase him down and give him an ass whopping. But he didn't. Instead he let him stay out there for close to forty-eight hours in the worst conditions of rain and cold. Miles and miles from the nearest town, in a landscape that looked the same everywhere he turned. In those two days he learned more about surviving against nature than he had from his father, all of which led him to believe that his father had purposely set him up, knowing he would bolt. He'd played so many head games with him he didn't know whether he was coming or going.

When Tyler finally emerged from the forest and arrived home, his father didn't lay into him, neither did he greet him with open arms. He just acted as if nothing had happened. It was business as usual. But it had happened, and those events and many more had stuck with Tyler, eaten away at who he was, and for better or worse shaped him into the man he was today.

Movement off to his right snapped him back into the present.

"Arggh," he heard as the Asian guy catapulted himself off the top of a truck landing on top of him. Tyler's rifle was knocked from his hands as they rolled across the sidewalk into the road. Bleeding badly from his wound, the guy had his hands wrapped around Tyler's throat and was trying to choke him out. Tyler reached up and jammed his thumb into the man's bullet wound, causing him to cry out in agony. He followed through by striking him in the eyes and digging in his finger so deep that he could feel the bone. They rolled again, and now Tyler was on top. Without hesitation he reached around, pulled his pistol and fired three into the guy's stomach. His body went limp beneath him and Tyler stared down at the first person he'd killed. Shock quickly set in as he crawled off, rose to his feet and stared blankly. He staggered back trying to come to terms with what he'd done. It didn't matter how many times his father had told him he'd have to kill someone one day to survive, it didn't register in that moment.

Fear gripped him. He was thinking the cops would show up any moment and toss him in the back of a cruiser. He looked down at his bloodied hand and felt his stomach lurch. With one hand on a car trunk he retched before wiping his lips with the back of his hand. Tyler hurried over and retrieved his rifle, then he ran to the far end of the store and took up a position to help Lou. Fortunately, two of them had already been taken out.

"Where's the third?" Tyler yelled scanning his field of

vision.

Lou replied. "He bolted. Your guy?"

Tyler cast a glance back at the body. He hesitated before saying, "Dead."

Over the course of the next ten minutes they hurled bodies into the back of Lou's old military Jeep, then unloaded the corpses in a dumpster at the back of a Chinese restaurant. Even though Lou believed that the lights weren't coming back on again, he didn't want to have dead bodies outside his business. Tyler didn't get into it with him. He was just glad to no longer see the guy he'd killed. As Lou closed the steel lid on the dumpster, he glanced at Tyler who was staring at his hands.

"You know, the first time I killed someone overseas I puked my guts up. It's perfectly normal, Tyler." He walked over and took a seat beside him on an overturned milk crate.

"Does it get any better?"

Lou snorted as he pulled out a cigarette and lit it. "If you're the one still breathing. Yeah." He then chuckled to himself. "No, look, in all seriousness. It was either him or you and that's the way you have to look at it. But a word of advice. Don't spend a long time mulling it over. It will only eat away at your soul. Those men had a choice to walk away. That's why I didn't kill them when I could have. You see, any fool can kill, Tyler. You just point the gun, and squeeze the trigger. But to stay alive you've got to know how to use this," he said tapping his finger against Tyler's head. Tyler nodded. "I know your father was hard on both of you and I know you might not see it but he loves you boys. What he taught you when you were young was to prepare you for this. You see, there is a lot of people out in the city that aren't ready for this. Oh, their parents made sure to pay their way through college, buy them their first car, and maybe even pay off some of their debts, but what use is any of that if you can't stay alive long enough to enjoy life? Your father taught you the most valuable lesson. How to survive." Lou blew out some smoke. "You can't put a value on that."

After they made it back to the store, Barb warmed up

what remained of their soup and they began to finish it off. Once they'd eaten, he returned to his room at the back of the store and settled in for the night. He sat there thinking about all that had played out over the course of the night and the man whose life he'd taken. The look in his eyes as he breathed his last.

Tyler had begun to nod off and drift into a state of sleep when Lou knocked on the frame of his door. "Tyler."

He raised his head. "Yeah?"

"Come with me."

He glanced at his watch. It was close to midnight. "What? Where are we going?"

Lou led him to the front of the store. As he came around a corner that led into the heart of where all the merchandise was stored, his eyes fell upon Erika and Bailey.

"Erika?"

She gave a warm smile and he was about to approach when Nate emerged from a bathroom off to the right. He was doing up his pants when Tyler saw him.

"What are you doing here?" Tyler asked.

"If it wasn't for him, I probably wouldn't have made it," Erika said. "That goes for Bailey too."

"Ah, I don't know," Nate said. "I think she would have something to say about that, wouldn't you, girl?" he said crouching down and running his hands through her hair. That was a big change from the reaction he'd got out of the dog the first time they'd met.

Tyler frowned. "Does she know?" That was the first thing that came out of his mouth. He expected Erika to frown and looked at Nate perplexed but she didn't.

"He's already told me."

Nate looked down at the ground.

"And you trust him?"

She took a second before she replied. "I owe him," Erika said.

Tyler huffed. "Well I don't. You can stay but he can't."

"Okay," she said nodding and then turned to leave.

"Let's go, Nate."

Tyler's brow furrowed. "Erika! C'mon. I…"

She whipped around. "If I stay, so does he. That's the deal."

"Just like that?" She nodded. "You forgive him that easily but you couldn't forgive me for a bad date?"

She offered back a deadpan expression then threw a hand up. "Look, forget it. I thought you could help but maybe I was wrong."

"With what?"

Erika brought him up to speed on the phone call to her parents and what she had in mind. "I figured if you're traveling that way it would be easier to go together."

Lou was perched on some boxes with his arms crossed. He didn't say anything but his eyes kept darting between them. "Yeah. Fine. If that's okay with you," he said making a gesture to Lou.

He shrugged. "We'll put her in the spare room. Dickhead here can bed down with you. Grab yourself a sleeping bag," Lou muttered motioning to a stack on a shelf. Nate grabbed one up and they followed him out back. Tyler glanced at Erika as Barb guided her to a separate room next door to his. He bid her goodnight before entering his room and watching Nate roll out a fresh sleeping bag on the floor beside his bed.

"Well isn't this a turn of events," Nate said with a grin on his face. Tyler cut him a glance before lying down for the night. He locked his fingers behind his head and stared up at the ceiling wondering what the next day would bring. As glad as he was to see Erika, his fears over what trouble the road ahead would present kept him awake long into the night.

Chapter 17

Flames licked up into the night sky. Wood popped, and crackled. Charred pieces glowed in the darkness. The ranger cabin had been turned into an inferno. They had spotted it in the distance long before they arrived on site. Along the way, one of the officers had attempted to get the rangers on the radio but failure led them to think the worst. As soon as they arrived, the three officers from Flathead County Sheriff Department fanned out. Unfortunately, the heat was so intense they couldn't get close enough to see if anyone was inside. Corey jogged down to the shoreline and looked out across the glistening lake. A full moon reflected on the calm surface. If a plane had gone down, it was now resting at the bottom. They had in the past been called out to situations that required donning scuba gear and searching, but that was only done in the day. Had any of the inmates survived? One glance at the burning log cabin answered that. The question was, where were they now?

"Anything?" he asked Officer Ferris, who had gone to a few of the log cabins down the road to check if anyone was there.

"Nothing. We'll sweep the perimeter, go door to door and check that residents are okay but that's all we can do. Three blockades have been set up, one in Glacier, the others were north of Apgar but there is a good chance if anyone has survived, they have pushed east towards St. Mary. Hopefully officers will stop them there but my guess is with all these cabins around, they've probably changed out of their prison garb. Finding them is going to be hard. If they're on foot they'll get around the blockades and blend in with the town folk," Ferris said.

"You think that's wise?" Corey asked.

"What?"

"Going door to door at this hour. These guys don't have anything to lose and we don't know how many were on that flight. No doubt by now they're armed."

"Not much choice. It's our job."

"Why not wait until morning? For backup."

"We are backup," Ferris said walking over to him and looking out across the lake. "Since the power has gone out, our landline has been off the hook with requests for assistance. Officers in every town are pulling double shifts and that's just to provide protection to locals. Why do you think they agreed to let you come with us?" he asked, turning and walking back up the steep incline. Corey surveyed his surroundings. The thick woodland of Glacier National Park swallowed them and the surrounding cabins. The inmates could be anywhere. It would be like searching for a needle in a haystack.

"Hey, I've got something over here," Noah hollered.

The group hurried back up to the main road and found him holding inmate clothing.

"I just found it out in the open, right over there."

"Well I guess that answers if anyone made it," Terry said, turning and eyeing the perimeter. The ever-present sense that they were being watched had all of their nerves on edge. With the fire burning brightly and illuminating the clearing, Corey's mind went on high alert remembering his time in Fallujah, Iraq. *He and his platoon had been sent in to clear the city of ISIS militants. He'd seen it all; car bomb attacks, women and kids with bombs under their clothing, and large caches of weapons stored in homes beneath flooring. He remembered them getting a lead on a cache and group that was supposed to be in a home on the west side. A Blackhawk had dropped them off in the dead of night inside the courtyard of walls. Dust whipped up in their faces as they entered the unknown, feeling exposed and vulnerable. Their team had navigated their way down squalid alleyways, past wrecks of old cars, slipping through half-completed houses and wading through garbage heaps to find the secret location because they couldn't use a vehicle without being fired upon. They had been preparing their plan of attack for months, using another team who would perform a preliminary feint from the east to draw away a large number of jihadists while an armored brigade had formed a tight cordon around the city to prevent them getting reinforcements or additional supplies.*

The thunderous and sustained bombardment of artillery from warplanes shook the eastern side, obliterating everything in its path while they made their way to the location.

They found the two-story concrete home and a cache of weapons, but what they weren't aware of was it was a trap. Nothing more than a means to lure in a large group of Marines, get them out in the open and then surround them on all sides. Within seconds of emerging from the home carrying out weapons, the earsplitting din of simultaneous fire from weapons rained down on them. Corey had dropped a rifle and was picking it up when his buddy in front of him was killed. Had he not lost his grip on one of the weapons he was carrying out, he would have joined eight of the men who fell that night.

Instantly the rest of them were embroiled in brutal, close-in fighting through the labyrinth of a city as they tried to push back and escape the insurgents' grasp. Another four died as they walked into ambush sites, some of which were booby trapped houses. He could still remember the smell of blood on his face as an IED planted in an alley blew apart his friend.

He learned a lot that night. The junk cars that littered the streets weren't there by chance but had been created to block roads and funnel Marines down into kill zones.

"Move," Corey said, beckoning the others away from the clearing.

"What?" Terry asked.

"Move, now." He waved them towards the darkest areas of the forest, where none of the light from the cabin would reach them.

Swallowed by the darkness, Ferris frowned and squinted at him. "What the hell is the matter?"

Corey didn't respond but was focused on the road, and kept scanning the tree line. "Where are you?" he said under his breath. Ferris overheard him and grabbed him by the arm. Their truck was still out there.

"You want to tell me what is going on?"

"It's a trap. I think."

"You think?"

"No one just leaves their clothes out in the open. They could have tossed them in the fire, thrown them in the bush."

"Maybe they didn't have time," he said, not seeing the obvious. How could he, none of them had served in the military or done any time overseas. The training they got in the academy, though good, didn't account for underhanded tactics used by insurgents. It had cost many a Marine's life to learn what not to do. And in his mind, this was no different. The odds were stacked against them and until he knew how many they were up against they had to be overly careful.

They remained there for several minutes until Corey collected the vehicle and brought it over. They hopped in and drove off further down the road. Even as they drove away, he had a sense they were still under a watchful eye.

* * *

"I don't get it. We had them right there. We should have killed them."

Under the cover of darkness, Gabriel was swift to act. He shoved Torres back against a tree with a hand gripped around his throat, and pressed the barrel of his pistol against his temple. "You want to bring down the full arm of the law on us?"

"But why would you let them go?"

"Did you see what kind of weaponry they had? Have you seen what we've got? There might be more of us but believe me, you don't go into a firefight with nothing more than a rifle, a handgun and a shotgun. Besides, now we know what we're dealing with. Six people. We take them out on our terms."

"So, you drew them out just to see how many there were?"

"No. Not just to see that."

He cast a glance over his shoulder before releasing him. He didn't bother to explain. A man like Torres wouldn't understand or appreciate it. He was a gangbanger. An opportunist who was used to doing drive-bys and making bad choices. He didn't see that this was a game, a chess match and whoever was in the position of power would win. A sudden or wrong move wouldn't mean going back to the pen but it could end their lives. He wasn't ready to kiss his freedom goodbye and he damn well wasn't going to die out here. Gabriel just needed more time. Time to think and that meant keeping them all alive. They were no good to him dead. Besides, now he knew which way they were going, he could go in the opposite. It would buy them some time. He was exhausted and badly in need of sleep.

"Let's go," he said leading the way. If the others doubted him, none of them said anything. They trudged into the woodland, searching for the next cabin and the next unsuspecting homeowner.

* * *

Farther down the road they came across three more cabins. Ferris, determined to do his duty, wanted to stop and check in with the homeowners. That was when they found a cabin door ajar. At first, they didn't enter but surrounded the cabin and observed it from a distance. Satisfied, Corey and Ferris moved in to try and see if they could hear anything. It was only when they got close did they hear a muffled cry. Having experience in clearing homes in Iraq, Corey was the first in the door. He moved with purpose, keeping his rifle out front of him as Ferris followed. In the living room they found an elderly couple. Corey squeezed the bridge of his nose as Ferris untied them.

Ferris crouched in front of the couple. "It's okay. What's your name?"

"Mitch Sampson," the old-timer said.

"Who did this?"

"Inmates," he replied, reaching over and consoling his wife who was now in tears.

"How many were there?" Corey asked.

"Um six, no, maybe ten?" the old man responded. "Not all of them came inside. So there could be more. I don't know. They kept us here."

"How long ago?"

He shook his head, a look of uncertainty spreading. That was when his wife spoke up. "Roughly thirty minutes ago." She wiped blood from her lip and Corey went into the kitchen to find a cloth. Ferris continued to talk to him as he tried to wet the towel. The faucet spat. The pressure wasn't very good but there was still some water coming through. That wouldn't last. Eventually the backup systems would stop at the water plant and they would have to resort to getting water from streams, rivers and lakes, or collecting rainwater the way his father did in large barrels.

When Corey returned, he handed the lady the cloth and she used it on her husband's head before tending to her lip. He had a nasty gash. It had swollen, and looked badly bruised under the light of their flashlights.

"Did they take anything?"

"Some clothes, food. They wanted the truck but it's not working. Do you know what's going on?" the man asked the officer.

"The power is out across the county, or at least in our neck of the woods. We'll know more soon. You both live here permanently or are you from one of the towns?"

"Whitefish."

"Same," Corey said.

"Yeah, I thought I recognized you. Your pap is Andy Ford, right?"

He nodded, waiting for a derogative term to follow. Not many people had good things to say about him. It wasn't that he went out of his way to be nasty to anyone but his reputation of being outspoken had landed him in hot water within the community.

"He's a good man," Mitch said taking the cloth and wiping dried blood off the side of his face. The response caught Corey off guard. He was so used to seeing eye rolls, and people shaking their head when he told them where he worked, that hearing anything good was rare. "Yeah, many years ago he lent us his generator when ours broke down. We were waiting for a delivery on a new one but it was back when we had that cold weather."

Corey nodded. "That's right. I remember that. That was you?"

He smiled. "You were young back then."

Corey was in his teens when Mitch had shown up at the door to speak with their father. He recalled his father telling them that they would be without heat for a while but that it was fine, a few extra layers on the bed, and an extra top would do the trick. He never explained why he'd given it, or how he knew Mitch but that time had stuck out in his mind, as it was freezing cold. He thought his father was being an ass, or that Mitch held lent him their generator and was wanting it back, but that wasn't the case. How many other times had he helped others in the community?

Ferris tried to get Mitch back on track.

"Were they armed?"

"Two of them were. They also took my shotgun."

"Did you see what direction they went?"

"I heard one of them talk about the ranger station." Ferris glanced at Corey, a look of confirmation as to who was behind it. "But I don't think that's where they're planning on staying. They took the keys to our house in Whitefish. My guess is they are heading that way."

As Ferris continued to pepper him with questions, Terry came in the door, a look of concern on his face.

"Uh, Ferris, you might want to see this."

"What is it?"

Terry looked at the old couple and motioned for him to step outside. One of the other officers watched over Mitch and his wife while he and Corey ducked outside. Vern and Noah were chatting and having a cigarette. Terry pointed southwest. "Found two bodies down by the water a few hundred yards from here. One is a ranger, the other an inmate. Both were shot."

Ferris made a gesture for him to lead the way. They hurried through the forest, a sense of dread washing over them. The thought of them making it to Whitefish rocked him to the core. The department only had sixteen officers to police the ski resort town. It was challenging at the best of times but now? The thought of Ella and his unborn child came to his mind.

"If they weren't armed before they are now," Terry said as they trudged through the darkness. Terry wasn't aware of what Mitch had told them, or the danger they posed if they managed to make it to Whitefish.

Chapter 18

Vegas was gone in a cloud of dark smoke. The glitz and glamour had been reduced to rubble, and a smoldering mess. Unable to sleep, Tyler had been up early that morning to witness the first rays of light as it gave way to the horror of a world without power. He pawed at his eyes, wiping away sleepy dust and hoping to forget the faces of the Asian men. Most of the night he'd expected the fourth guy to come back with even more gang members. He didn't. Some learned their lessons fast while others preferred to fall rather than admit defeat. Tyler sat alone on the roof watching the sun come up over a smoke-filled city looking for a glimmer of hope, a sign that this had all just been a bad dream. But there was nothing. There were no sirens. No cavalry to save the day. No FEMA. Just a deafening silence. He was used to the hum of the city, the clatter of workers and seeing the sidewalks filled with tired folk nursing coffee on their way to work. But the streets were barren. Although the military weren't roaming the streets, he knew it wouldn't be long before they would.

It was still hard to believe it had happened at all. Fires burned out of control, smoke drifted and then the echo of a gun firing alerted him to the harsh reality of a nation in distress. This was just the beginning, the tip of the iceberg, his father would say. It wouldn't take long for a city to unravel. A few fires, a lack of police, plenty of people injured, and desperation would soon kick in. No surveillance cameras in operation presented new opportunities for criminals. Looting of businesses and home invasions would come first, followed by rape, murder and gangs seeking control of neighborhoods. An initial show of force by the government would be next but by then chaos would have spread across the nation, and America would become a war zone as people fought for control.

When his uncle appeared beside him holding a cup of steaming hot coffee, Tyler thanked him. They sat on the lip of the roof drinking and talking about the future or lack thereof. Although Lou was a diehard prepper, his military background meant he believed the nation would bounce back from it. He had hope. Tyler's father? For him, it couldn't be further from the truth. He was anti-government. He didn't believe for one minute they would help, and if they did, it was only as a means to continue to control the masses. That's where he and Lou didn't see eye to eye but they never let it come between them.

Blood was thicker than water.

"Oh, here," his uncle handed him a set of keys to the 1979 CJ5 4 x 4 Jeep and informed him that he wouldn't be going with him.

"You want me to take it? Ah man, I can't take it, Lou. It's all you've got," Tyler said giving the keys back to him. Lou placed them back in his hand and wrapped his fingers around them tightly.

"I can't go with you, kid, but I can prepare you for the road."

"Why? Come with us," Tyler said gripping the keys.

"Corey and my father would want you there."

"She won't make the journey, Tyler. And everything we need is here anyway."

"Then I'll stay."

"No. You need to go. For your brother's and father's sake."

Tyler snorted. "He'll be fine."

"He will. You won't," Lou said taking a sip of his coffee and looking out across the city. "We aren't getting any younger, and I know your father has regrets over the way he treated you."

"Regrets? Please."

"He told me."

"Yeah, in between bellyaching about my choice to leave?"

"Every time he phones."

"Which is basically never."

Lou chuckled. "Your father calls every couple of weeks to touch base and see how you're doing."

"And yet he never asks to speak to me."

"He won't. He's a stubborn man, Tyler. I've told him he was wrong to force his ways onto you boys but you've got to understand. In his mind he was doing what was best — what was right by you."

"Right for him, you mean?"

"For all of you."

Silence stretched between them.

"It's over a thousand miles. If you rotate driving, and you don't stop except to gas up, and you avoid the main cities, you should get to Whitefish in about sixteen to twenty hours from now, give or take. Worst-case scenario it takes you a couple of days. But don't give anyone a ride or help. No matter what situation they're in. Don't trust anyone." He looked out again. "It's going to get a lot worse before it gets better. I've already put together some food for you to take, a few bags of gear with several rifles and handguns, and plenty of ammo. I want you to head north on 318 then switch over to I-15 once you hit Pocatello. That route will keep you away from Salt Lake. It's a straight shot, mostly small towns but don't underestimate them. I mean that."

"I won't."

After finishing his coffee and tossing the dregs over the edge, he pulled out a pack of smokes and lit one. Lou looked at his watch. "The others are still sleeping. You should head out soon. Get a head start before the rest of the city stirs."

"I doubt they've rested," Tyler said. "Lou. Are you sure you won't come with us? What happens if that guy comes back?"

"He'll regret it."

"I won't be here to help."

"Kid, I did five tours in the forces. I think I can handle myself."

Tyler smiled as Lou got up and patted him on the back. "Don't sit out here long. I want to show you the route on the map." Just as he walked away, he stopped and turned around. "She's a good-looking woman, Tyler. Give her time. Sometimes that's all they need." Tyler's lip curled as Lou disappeared down into the store. He downed the rest of his coffee and headed down.

When he came back into his room, Nate was crawling out of his sleeping bag. "For such a hard floor I slept considerably well."

"That's good to know," Tyler said. "Roll it up. You'll need it."

"We having breakfast?"

"If you're lucky," he replied. He snatched up his bag from the end of his bed. Taking that damn thing with him everywhere he went had become ingrained in him like a habit he couldn't get rid of. Now he was grateful.

"What's your problem?" Nate asked as Tyler went to head out. "I apologized to her. Anyone would think I stole from you."

Tyler turned, walked back over to him and squinted at him. "Trust is earned, and you might have won her over but it's going to take more than swooping in to save the day to earn mine."

"And I thought she was the one with high standards," he said with a smirk.

Tyler narrowed his gaze then exited. As he came out into the corridor he nearly walked straight into Erika as she came out of the bathroom. "Whoa, sorry," he said.

"Morning," she said in a low voice, diverting her eyes and raking a hand through her damp hair. She was fully dressed in casual clothes and he hardly recognized her. She was wearing tight jeans, a thin long-sleeved green top and flats. Erika flung a white towel over her shoulder as she walked on. There was a sweet scent to her like apples. He breathed it in and smiled as he stepped to one side. He took a moment to glance at her ass before heading up for breakfast. That morning Barb had put on a big spread — bacon, eggs, toast, beans and fried tomatoes. The sweet smell of coffee permeated the air.

"Ah you shouldn't have."

"You got to have something in your stomach before you leave."

Barb was a few years younger than Lou, a white-haired beauty that often reminded him of Paula Deen, with her big personality and infectious smile. Barb suffered with

MS and had for years been fighting the crippling disease. Her ability to taste anything had gone, she'd lost a considerable amount of weight and she wasn't very steady on her feet anymore. He understood Lou's reasons for staying. A sense of the familiar was often enough to keep a person content even in the worst circumstances but he wished Lou was coming. Having him riding shotgun would have certainly put his mind at ease, especially when he didn't know where he stood with the other two.

After he took a seat at the table, Nate and Erika joined them a few minutes later. Erika had a smile on her face and was laughing at some joke Nate had told her on the way in. He eyed Tyler with a smug look that made him second-guess his decision to let him stay.

"Now you take as much as you want," Barb said. Lou had everyone link hands and he prayed, thanking God for what they had, and asking for his help for the journey ahead. Unlike his father, Lou was a firm believer in God.

"Dear, before you go, let me take a look at that arm of yours. We'll clean it up and I'll wrap it in a new bandage," Barb said to Erika. She nodded and cut Tyler a glance.

Over breakfast, Lou showed him the route on the map and pointed out a town that a fellow Army buddy lived in. "His name is Ralph Brunson. I've tried reaching him by ham radio but I'm getting no answer. He could be dead for all I know. I'll keep trying while you're on the road but if I don't get through and you make it there, you just tell him that I sent you, and you'll be good. No doubt he would replenish your supplies and hopefully give you some gas. We go way back. But just a word of warning. He's not all there. He suffered a fair amount of head trauma from tours overseas. I mean, the times I have chatted with him it's not been too bad but the years haven't been good. Oh, and don't stare too long at his scar."

"His scar?" Tyler asked.

Lou made a gesture to his forehead. "He's a little self-conscious and… well, just don't."

"Roger that."

Tyler glanced at the other two. Nate was stuffing his face with food and paying no attention. Erika was listening intently, nodding her head. Right then, Lou turned to Erika. "You know how to fire a weapon?"

She shook her head. "No."

"Okay. Before you head out, Tyler here will show you."

"I can do that," Nate said with a mouthful of food.

"No. I need you to give me a hand loading up the Jeep."

"Look, is that necessary?" Erika asked.

"Loading up the Jeep or knowing how to fire a gun?"

"No, I meant, don't you think we might be taking things a little extreme?"

Barb placed a hand on her shoulder. "Darlin', had your friend not been there brandishing a gun last night, things would have got real extreme. It's important to learn. I wasn't one for guns but once you learn how to properly use one, you'll feel safer. Trust me. You understand?"

Hearing it come from another woman must have helped as she nodded. Once breakfast was finished, Tyler took her up onto the roof and lined up some bottles on one of the steel air vents. "Okay, it's pretty simple." He took her through the basics. He wasn't expecting miracles from her but as long as she knew how to hold a gun, load, unload, clear a jam, and fire, she would be good to go. The chances of her having to use it were now high and the more people who knew how to shoot, the better chance of their survival. "So remember, focus on the front sight and maintain equal height and light between the front and rear sights. That's it. And then slowly breathe out as you squeeze the trigger."

Crack.

The bottle smashed into pieces. Tyler squinted. "Not bad. Okay."

Another shot and she missed, the next one she got it. "That's good."

He stood behind her and provided guidance. She leaned into him and he caught the aroma of her perfume.

He felt his pulse speed up as she fired a few more rounds until she had taken out each of the bottles. "Well damn, girl, you are a natural."

Her cheeks flushed. "Yeah, right."

"No, I'm serious. You should have seen my first shots. I think I took out a bird, a bicyclist and a stray cat before I hit the target."

She started laughing as he continued to take her through some safety steps to ensure that she didn't shoot herself or anyone else nearby. Once finished, she thanked him and headed down to prepare to leave.

Tyler thanked Lou, and gave him and Barb a big hug before slipping behind the wheel. Lou leaned against the Jeep and gave them a reminder.

"Remember. You stick together out there. Don't leave anyone behind. Watch their back, and they'll watch yours. And if you find yourself in trouble, and you have no other choice but to kill, do it without hesitation. I don't want to find out you never made it. You hear me?"

They all nodded, and he patted the top of the Jeep and

then went over and hit the red button on the wall. The garage door went up and Barb walked over to Lou and wrapped her arm around his waist. The Jeep rolled out and Tyler gave one final glance in his rearview mirror. Would it be the last time he saw Lou alive? That uncertainty bothered him. He'd become like a father to him. As Lou and Barb bid them farewell, and Tyler gave the engine gas, he felt his stomach churn.

What if they didn't make it?

Chapter 19

"We can't go that way," Erika said, motioning for Tyler to take a different route. They'd only been on the road a couple of minutes, and made it a few miles from the surplus store, when she was barking orders. She had the map spread out on her lap and even though Lou had marked out which roads to take in red, and had made it clear not to take I-15, she wanted to go against that.

"But..." Tyler began to say.

"Midway, Utah, is a straight shot up I-15 then onto 189. If we take this route, we will be way off the beaten path."

"Why didn't you say something back at the house? At least then we could have got Lou's input," he said gripping the wheel tightly as he swerved around stalled vehicles. He glanced at Nate in the rear with Bailey. He had this permanent grin on his face as if he found it all amusing.

"He seemed pretty adamant. I didn't want to interject."

"But you have no problem doing it now."

She folded up the map and tucked it between the seats. "You said you wanted to give me a ride. This is the direction we need to go." The next ten minutes was spent in silence as they navigated the barren streets of North Vegas and looked on in shock at what had occurred within the first twenty-four hours. People weren't rioting but looters had taken to the streets and busted into different stores, dragging out appliances, boxes of sneakers and electronics, but that wasn't the worst of it. It looked as if someone had purposely pushed vehicles across the road to block off the ramp to I-15. Why? He wasn't going to keep going to find out. Tyler yanked the wheel hard to the right and headed up Gilder Street, into a typical residential area.

"Where are you going?" she asked looking back over her shoulder.

"Seriously, we have a lot of ground to cover. Are you

planning on being like this all the time?" he asked, focusing on the road ahead. "I'm the driver. I make the decisions. The road was blocked. I picked a different route."

She unfolded the map again and he could see the wheels in her brain turning over.

"But we could have gone south, then hung a right and tried the other exit."

"You know what, how about you leave the driving to me, and you just keep your eyes out for trouble."

Bailey barked once and Tyler smirked. "See, even your dog agrees with me."

Her eyes narrowed and she put her feet up on the dashboard.

Tyler had to take the Jeep up onto the sidewalk to get around several of the vehicles. The Jeep handled it with ease, bumping back down on the road. They'd only seen three other older vehicles working that morning which meant they would be a target. If not now, soon. As they drove past some of the residential homes, things looked moderately calm. Vehicles were in driveways, curtains pulled back and some of the homeowners were outside talking among themselves. He figured by now someone would have attempted to stop them and ask for a ride, or at least try to take the vehicle, but that hadn't happened. For a brief moment he couldn't help but feel his thoughts as a kid had been validated. His father was wrong. Sure, he was right about a disaster happening but he was wrong about people. Inherently, humanity came to each other's aid. Of course those Asian men at Lou's had a different take on it and that was to be expected, but overall, the general population gave a shit about each other, at least that's how it had appeared the night planes crashed into buildings and tore through the city like a hot knife sliding through butter. The truth was, in a city of 641,000, people would be more focused on getting what they needed to survive the first couple of days than on escaping or attacking others. They would be locked into a short-term plan — find food, medication, hygiene products, water, and make sure they could last until the lights came back on — but that was faulty thinking. Survivalists thought long term, and in doing so their short term would be fine. People like his uncle and father were already ahead of the curve.

It was also the reason why they hadn't seen people breaking into homes yet. Yes, a few windows of businesses were shattered, and yes, they had seen groups of teens running out of a computer store with armloads of notebooks and tablets, but that was because they believed the nation would spring back. They were taking advantage of a volatile situation. They were of the mindset that this was temporary, nothing more than a glitch in the system. The fact was new behaviors were hard to learn, people always fell back on the system that was comfortable. Society didn't teach people how to embrace the uncomfortable but his father had. Tyler gripped the wheel tighter as memories flooded his mind. He hated the thought that everything he'd taught them growing up was about to pay off, as that meant acknowledging his father was right and for so long, he'd told himself a different story.

As Tyler veered onto Judson Avenue and then took a left on White Street he slammed on the brakes. The Jeep shuddered as the brakes squealed. Up ahead a large group had gathered in the middle of the road. These weren't gang members. Just ordinary working class folk gathered together like a neighborhood block party. Two of them were standing on the top of a vehicle speaking to the group when they caught sight of the Jeep.

Although they were a fair distance from them, he knew what they had in mind as soon as the speaker pointed at them. The crowd turned, and a few that were armed broke away and began running towards them.

"Back up!" Nate yelled.

He didn't need to tell him, Tyler was already jamming the gearstick into reverse. He crushed the accelerator to the metal and told them to hold on. The Jeep let out a loud squeal as it shot backwards. He looked over his shoulder and tore out of the mouth of the road onto Judson Avenue. Nate held on to Bailey as they spun out and powered forward. Tyler looked in his rearview mirror and saw the small group appear at the end of the road.

"Why didn't they shoot?" Nate asked.

"Would you want to risk putting a bullet in the vehicle you were after?" Tyler replied.

"You think that's what they wanted?" Erika asked.

"Well I don't think they were looking to have us join their neighborhood block party," Tyler said. His lip curled up. "Besides, not everyone is at the point of attacking. The Asian gang that hit the surplus store were highly motivated. They were probably robbing stores long before the power outage."

"Wait. You came under attack?" Nate asked.

It then dawned on him that he hadn't told them about the incident, or the man he'd killed. He looked at Erika out the corner of his eye and nodded. "It was brief."

"You managed to scare them away then?"

The memory of dumping their bodies in the trash came to his mind.

"Something like that."

He didn't want to taint Erika's view of him, at least not while it was still early days. If the lights stayed off, the time would come when they would be faced with a similar situation. Hell, it could happen today. No, it was better to remain tight-lipped. He hung a left onto Donna Street and accelerated fast knowing they were only a few blocks from the street where the group were gathered. How many others would they encounter like that? Traveling on foot seemed safer but with so much distance to cover it was out of the question. Besides, if he was going to lose the vehicle it would have to be for a damn good reason.

They drove past several schools that would have usually been busy with parents dropping off their kids but now the parking lots out front were empty.

"I don't get it. Shouldn't the National Guard be out by now?" Erika said.

"They probably are but the need is too great. Do you remember Katrina?"

"No."

"Please tell me you watch the news?" Tyler asked.

"I don't have time for it. Too busy dealing with guests."

Tyler glanced at Nate in the back. "No, I'm too busy stealing."

"I didn't say that."

"But you would have. I saw the look on your face."

Tyler shook his head. He thought back to how the government dealt with Katrina. The outcry was heavy. The country condemned mismanagement and a lack of preparation to provide relief. There had been a delayed response to the flooding in New Orleans, a communication breakdown and a lack of National Guard. When they finally got to the heart of the issue, it was quite clear what the problem was. The government had no evacuation plan even though they had ample warning what might hit the Gulf Coast. The fact was a shift in attention towards terrorist attacks had distracted them from being prepared. That was why when supplies were sent in, the first batches contained items that might have helped in a chemical attack. They had got it wrong. Then of course there was the problem with residents not taking warnings seriously. Over the years there had been warning after warning in hurricane season and many of the residents had simply shrugged it off, thinking nothing would happen. Then there was the lack of people who owned cars causing the governor to use school buses to evacuate. It also didn't take into account that many of the locals lived paycheck to paycheck and couldn't afford to move away from home. That's why people were still in Vegas. Many had no choice but to pray and hope that the circumstances would change.

Erika piped up. "You think we could stop and try a landline phone?"

"Are you kidding?" Tyler asked.

"I want to try my parents one more time. It might have been a misunderstanding. I might have…"

"Imagined it?" Tyler said, casting her a glance. "Look, Erika, I know you don't want to accept this is happening. Trust me, I don't. But it is. People might not be out of control on every street, in every city, in every town but they will get that way. And those who are smart, which includes criminals, won't wait twenty-four hours or a week. They will strike while the iron is hot." They zipped past a family that tried to thumb a ride. Tyler felt bad leaving them there but there was no room, and he couldn't trust anyone else — hell, he could barely trust those who were with him right now. "Now throw a rich family into the mix and who do you think they are going to target first?"

"They're…"

"Not rich?" Tyler asked shooting her a sideways glance.

"I was going to say that they have security."

"Doesn't matter. Hiring some rent-a-cop to man the gates isn't going to stop determined people."

"Okay, but maybe she screamed because she saw something else."

"What, and then hung up and didn't answer your calls after that? C'mon, you look a lot brighter than that to me."

Her eyes widened and he knew he had put his foot in his mouth.

"Look, just pull over, I want to at least try."

"First off, where will you find a landline? And second, the landlines might not be working now."

"They were yesterday. I thought you said they have backup systems in place to last a week?"

"They do. But that was yesterday. A lot can happen in twenty-four hours. Besides. I'm not stopping. It's too dangerous. No, we press on."

"Pull over."

"Not doing it."

"Tyler, if you don't pull over right now—"

"Princess, you can throw a tantrum all you want but it won't get you anywhere. I'm not your maid and I damn well am not going to—"

"PULL OVER!" she bellowed.

Tyler slammed the brakes on. All of them jerked forward in their seats. He turned. "Why didn't you bring this up at Lou's? You could have tried the landline there. You always have to be so damn difficult."

"Difficult. Really?"

Without saying another word, she got out and strolled off down the main street towards a convenience store that looked as if it had already been looted. Bailey jumped out to follow her but she told her to get back in the Jeep. Bailey looked at her walking away for a second and then hopped up into the passenger seat beside Tyler. Nate leaned forward and patted him on the shoulder. "I'll keep an eye on her, bro."

"If trouble shows up, I'm out of here, understand?"

"You'll be fine. Stop worrying."

Tyler pulled a face and sat there watching over the vehicle. There was no way he was leaving it alone, or the supplies. He slammed a fist against the steering wheel, regretting inviting them. He scanned the homes either side of the road, fully expecting trouble.

* * *

Roughly a hundred yards down the road, Erika

approached the store. The glass in the door was gone, shattered into thousands of pieces, scattered on the ground. The chain the looters had used to rip the shutters off was a few feet away still hooked up to crumpled shutters covered in graffiti.

Erika peered inside before entering just to be sure the owner wasn't there. Nate came up behind her and startled her. "For God's sake, Nate. Did he tell you to follow?"

"No. He wants to leave."

"Let him."

"You can't fault him, Erika. He's just trying to play it safe."

Glass crunched beneath her feet as they stepped inside and took in the sight of empty shelves. A few items were on the ground but nothing of significance. All the food and coolers had been raided. A huge bag of Doritos had been torn apart and were scattered. "What a waste," Nate said. "Listen, make this quick. I'll keep an eye out front."

She nodded and disappeared into the back where it was dark. Although she was determined to make sure her parents were okay, the thought of traveling for the next seven hours in a country now torn apart made her skin crawl. She wanted to believe that it had all been a mistake. That she'd phone this morning and her mother would pick up and tell her not to worry. At least then she could go back to the hotel and wait this out.

In the darkness of the store she spotted a landline on the wall. She came around the counter and was just about to reach for it when she noticed someone laid out on the floor. There was a large pool of blood around the middle-aged man's head. She grimaced and stepped over him. It felt wrong to be there but what other choice was there? She picked up the phone and got a dial tone. Good. That was positive. Erika punched in the number and waited. It rang, and rang and then went to her mother's voicemail. Erika hung up feeling deflated.

Nate was busy looking outside so she tried again and got the same result. "Damn it." Erika hung up and was about to head out when she heard something in the rear, like a girl sobbing. A shot of fear went through her.

"Hello?" she said in a low voice. There was no reply. She cast another glance at Nate. He had a cigarette in hand and was in the process of lighting it. Erika took a few steps down the narrow corridor that divided the front of the store from the rear. There was a door partially open at the end of the hall revealing a cramped lunch room, and off to her right was a dirty toilet. She looked in and grimaced at the smell. Again, she heard whimpering. "Hello?" As she continued down the hall, she came to a set of stairs that went up to the second floor. She contemplated going back but after hearing crying for a third time she had to know. Erika climbed the steps, they creaked beneath her feet. When she made it to the top, the door to the apartment was open. She pushed in and the whimpering stopped.

"Hello?" she asked again. No reply.

Moving in, she pulled the Glock from her side holster, and thought about what Tyler had told her. How to hold, squeeze, get rid of a jam. When she turned the next corner, she found herself looking into a kitchen that was in a state. The table and chairs were overturned, the cupboards were pulled off the hinges, and plates were smashed on the ground. It looked as if someone had taken a sledgehammer and pounded holes in the walls. She continued into the living room but no one was there. Then she headed for the two bedrooms at the far end of the hall. One of the doors was open. She peered inside. It looked as if it belonged to a teen girl. Posters of pop artists had been torn off the walls, the bed ripped apart, and there was a bag of weed on the countertop, next to a cracked notebook.

Erika was about to leave when she heard a shuffle behind her. She turned and focused on the closet. It was white, made of wood and slatted. She brought the Glock up and approached it slowly. Then, using the tip of her boot, she was just about to kick it open when a hand wrapped over her mouth and pulled her out of the room.

"Shh!"

She struggled within the stranger's grasp and was dragged out towards the main bedroom. The moment she was inside the room she managed to pry loose the hand. It was Nate. "Quiet. They're downstairs."

"Who?"

He put a finger up to his lips and told her to find somewhere to hide.

They could hear glass breaking, and loud voices hooting and hollering. Then it sounded like someone was rattling a marble in a tin can, before they heard spraying.

"Samantha. Where are you?"

Nate headed over to the window that was already open. The drapes were blowing in front of it. He gestured with a jerk of his head for Erika to head out.

"I'm not leaving. There is someone else here."

"Yeah, and they are about to come upstairs. Now…"

"No. A young girl. I heard her crying."

"That's not our problem. You heard what Lou said."

"I don't give a shit what Lou said."

Nate walked over to her. "Do you want to get shot?"

"I need to check."

"No, you don't."

He grabbed her by the arm but she pulled it away.

"Tyler was right. You're out of your goddamn mind. Now get out that window before I shoot you myself."

She threw him the bird and pulled back the door and went out to the corridor. The sound of someone coming up the stairs made Nate react fast. He grabbed Erika and pulled her back in.

"Samantha. I know you're in here. We saw you come in earlier. Come on out."

Two guys chuckled and one of them must have had a club in his hand as they heard a pounding on the wall as if he was hitting it every few seconds. Nate hurried over to the window and slipped out. There was a slanted roof that went over the front half of the store. Slide down, make the ten-foot jump to the ground and they could be back in the truck. He turned to beckon Erika and this time she listened and crossed the room and slipped out. Nate slid down the roof expecting Erika to follow but when he reached the bottom and jumped off, he looked up just in time to see her re-entering the window.

Chapter 20

It wasn't the scream of a girl she heard but of a man. Erika rushed towards the door and swung it open just in time to see a guy stumble out of the teenager's room with a butcher's knife embedded in his chest. He was in his mid-twenties, dressed in a checkered shirt and jean jacket. He was clutching the handle of the blade and staggering back. His head turned and he spotted Erika but only a gasp escaped his lips. Inside the teenager's room it sounded like a war was taking place. She heard glass breaking, then a loud thud as if someone had been thrown into a wall. Erika brought up the Glock, slipped down the hallway and sidestepped past him as he slumped to the floor, his eyes glazing over. Turning into the girl's room, she arrived just in time to see a bearded guy wearing a beanie and slamming a girl's face against the wall. "You messed up now!" he said holding a gun up to her head.

"Hey!" Erika shouted. The guy turned, shoved the girl away and without hesitation swung his handgun around at her. In that moment time seemed to slow. She felt the metal of the trigger against her finger, and then an eruption as she squeezed it. The guy dropped and she squeezed again, then again, then one more time. When his head slumped forward her hand was shaking. Her eyes darted to the girl who looked to be around fifteen years of age. She was dressed in blue jeans and a pink T-shirt with some slogan on the front.

"Erika. Erika!"

Nate came rushing up the stairs only to stop and gaze at the deceased. A second later he looked into the room and placed a hand on her outstretched arm to get her to lower it. "That's it. Relax."

Erika backed out and Nate looked at the young girl.

No words were exchanged as they turned to leave. Erika was shaking badly as they exited the store and made their way back to the waiting Jeep. Tyler had sunk down in his seat and turned off the engine to make it look like any other vehicle on the street. As soon as he caught sight of them approaching, he started the vehicle.

"What happened?" Tyler asked.

* * *

Nate shook his head and gave him an expression that made it clear that it was best to drop it but he wouldn't. He'd heard the gunshots but just assumed they were coming from farther down. Bailey hopped into the back with Erika while Nate rode shotgun. Tyler glanced in his rearview mirror at her and could see she was in a state of shock. Bailey was licking her hand but she wasn't responding.

Tyler veered out and continued on past the store, glancing in in for a second but seeing nothing unusual.

They drove on navigating through the streets of Vegas trying to get to I-15, which would take them northeast out of the city. As they went north on Civic Center Drive, Tyler had begun to notice that another vehicle was tailing them. He'd seen this old blue Toyota Hilux a few times along the streets that led to Civic Center Drive but it was only when he took a turn down a road and saw it again did he start to believe they were being followed. Whoever it was, they were keeping their distance. He could just make out two occupants but there could have been more.

"Don't look back but I think we're being tailed."

"What?" Nate said whipping his head around. Tyler shook his head.

"The blue truck?"

There had been a few others that passed them, and a couple pulling out of driveways. Anyone who didn't know would have thought that society was beginning to come to life again but that wasn't the truth. These were all old vehicles.

"Maybe they're in the same boat as us. You know. Trying to get on I-15 and get out of the city."

"Yeah. Maybe," Tyler said keeping a close eye on them as they veered left onto Cheyenne Avenue and then curved around onto I-15. That was when the real problem began. It was clogged with stalled vehicles for miles. All four lanes were filled with traffic that had simply come to a standstill. Tyler slipped onto the hard shoulder that was used for emergency services, thinking that would be open. It wasn't. Further down, vehicles that had stalled had drifted to a standstill and the drivers must have veered off to the edge. "Oh crap. So much for heading that way."

Nate said. "We'll find another. The whole damn interstate can't be like this."

"You wanna bet?" Tyler said. Erika didn't say a word. All the color in her face seemed gone, as if she'd seen a ghost.

Tyler put the vehicle in reverse and backed up. "You okay back there?" he asked her. Her eyes lifted but she said nothing. In his rearview mirror he saw the blue Toyota slam its brakes on, do a U-turn before it got on I-15 and shot off at a high rate of speed down the road before hanging a right.

He might have considered it strange had they driven up close and acted intimidating but he never got that impression. It was possible they too were searching for a way out of the city and hoping someone like themselves would find it — no different than if someone was lost and they learned that another driver was going their way.

Nate pulled out the map again and ran his finger along I-15. "If you go east on Cheyenne Avenue and come off at Las Vegas Boulevard, it turns into the 604 and runs almost parallel to I-15."

Tyler spun the Jeep around, and Erika reached out for Bailey as she nearly toppled out. "Tyler!" she bellowed. The Jeep screeched to a halt and he looked at her in the rearview mirror. Tears welled up in her eyes and he knew something bad had happened but neither she nor Nate was talking.

"Sorry," he said. He pulled away slowly.

As they drove in silence, Tyler turned his questions on Nate, curious to learn more about him. He had a sense he still wasn't telling the entire truth.

"So, when did you move to Vegas?"

Nate looked at him and then began drumming with

his fingers on his leg. Nerves perhaps? "About eight years ago."

"So before that you were living with your mother?"

He nodded.

"What did she think about that?"

"She didn't care. Anyway, I was tired of Colorado. I needed a new scene."

"Colorado? But I thought you said she lived in Spokane, Washington?"

He opened his mouth then closed it. "Um. No, she does. When I moved out here, she decided to go and stay with her sister in Spokane."

"And your father?"

"Haven't seen him since I was knee high. And from what my mother told me about him, I'm kind of glad." Nate looked away.

Tyler snorted. At least they had one thing in common, fathers they didn't care too much for. "A bit of a douche?"

"A bit? He used to use my mother as a punching bag.

Yeah, you could say he was a bit of a douche."

That put an end to the conversation immediately.

It was getting harder to make progress. With so many stalled trucks, SUVs, sedans and motorbikes clogging up the road they had to keep getting out and trying to roll them out of the way. But doing so left the Jeep exposed. One of them had to keep an eye on it, and Erika still being in a state of shock wasn't making it any easier.

Tyler put his shoulder into it while Nate guided the wheel, and the stalled vehicle veered over to the sidewalk.

"Nate. What happened back there?"

"She should probably tell you."

"I'm asking you. What happened?"

Nate jumped in and hit the brake on the Ford Edge and got out. He looked off towards the Jeep and sighed. "She killed someone."

"What? Why didn't you tell me?"

"Because it wasn't my place to."

He walked to the rear of the SUV and they crossed the road to shift a small Nissan out of the way. "There was a young girl in the store. The owner was dead. Two guys entered and were searching for the girl. I tried to get her out. Erika, I mean, but she went back inside. By the time I made it back inside, they were dead." Tyler jumped into the vehicle this time while Nate pushed. He glanced back at Erika, understanding what she felt. Killing someone even if necessary didn't make it easy. No matter how bad they were or what they had in mind, they were still a human being after all, and the weight of guilt was heavy.

"You ever killed anyone?" Tyler asked.

"Oh, so you assume because I earned my living robbing people I must have?"

"It was just a question."

Silence formed between them.

"No. No I haven't," Nate replied. "You?"

"Yeah."

He stopped pushing and came around. "You serious? Who? When?"

Tyler jammed the gearstick into park and got out. "Yesterday. When the store came under attack."

"Under attack?"

Ashamed to admit what he had done, he unloaded his burden. Once done, he kind of felt relieved. While the act of telling someone didn't change the situation one iota, it did feel good not to carry it alone.

"You did what any of us would have done."

"You think?" Tyler asked as they moved one more vehicle. It wasn't that he needed affirmation but he was curious to see what Nate might have done.

"Damn right. I'm not dying. I will do whatever it takes to survive. If that means choosing between me and some random asshole who decides they want what I have, it will be me standing at the end."

They were about a hundred yards away when Erika screamed. Tyler whirled around in time to see Bailey latch on to someone's arm. There were three individuals surrounding the Jeep, and one of them had managed to grab Erika from behind and was attempting to pull her out of the Jeep. Nate and Tyler brought up their rifles and fired off several rounds causing the men to duck and scramble. Bailey took after one of them while the other two split. The one wearing a dark green hoodie dragged Erika over to an alleyway.

"Stay with the vehicle," Tyler said, pointing to the Jeep while he sprinted for the alleyway. By the time he made it there, he saw a side doorway close. He could still hear her muffled cries as he tried to get in. "Shit!" It was an emergency exit with no handle on the outside. *How the heck did you get in?* It must have been open. Not wasting any time, he hurried up to the mouth of the alley and came around to the front of the building to see where she'd been taken. It was a block of apartments. He yanked on the front door but it was locked. Taking a few steps back he unloaded several rounds at the glass until it was completely shattered. Then he climbed in, cutting his hand in the process. "Damn it." He hurried through the darkened corridor calling out her name but getting no response. She could have been anywhere inside there. There were apartments on either side. Doors were closed and if anyone was inside, they weren't responding to the shots fired or him yelling out her name. When he made it to the far end of the corridor, he pulled open a door and entered a second hallway that had an emergency exit door at the end. Within seconds he pushed through it and found himself in the alleyway.

Just as he was turning to head back in, a guy stepped out from a doorway off to his left and slammed into him, holding a knife and trying to jam it into his heart. Tyler had released his grip on his rifle, and it was dangling around his arm as he used both hands to hold his attacker at bay. He thrust him backwards, and kneed him in the nuts before following through with an uppercut.

Without even thinking he swung his rifle around as the man tried to get up and fired a round into his skull. A quick glance to his left and right and he entered the doorway the man had emerged from. It was a laundry room with multiple washers and dryers. The smell of dryer sheets lingered. "Erika. Erika!" he yelled as he hurried through only to find her lying on her side in an adjoining room. Dropping a knee, he placed his ear near her mouth and found she was still breathing, just unconscious. Her lip was split and bleeding badly. Slipping her arm over his shoulder, he wrapped his other arm around her waist and hauled her up. As he started to drag her out of there, she began to come to. She let out a scream and tried attacking him. "It's me. It's me," Tyler said. Her eyes widened and she began to cry. "It's okay. You're safe. Come on. Let's get you out of here."

As they passed the dead man on the way out, Erika glanced down at him and then back at Tyler. "You did that?"

"Yeah. And he's not the first."

She squinted at him but he didn't explain further. It was self-explanatory, though he was sure questions would come later. They trudged out the side exit door and along the narrow alleyway that was littered with garbage and overturned trash cans. The smell of rotten meat carried on the air, a sign of the times. Garbage collectors wouldn't be coming and in a city of this size, it wouldn't take long before the streets would be overflowing with trash.

When they made it back to the Jeep, Nate was down on one knee, comforting the dog. As soon as Bailey saw Erika, she ran over and rubbed her head against her knees.

"I'm okay, girl. Thanks to you." She then looked at Tyler. "And you. Thank you."

As they climbed into the Jeep, Nate said, "You remember that blue Toyota? That was them." He pointed off towards a road just a few blocks down. "I saw the other two peel away in it."

"At least they didn't get the Jeep."

"But they took two of the backpacks."

"What?" Tyler scanned the back of the Jeep. Sure enough they were gone. Only one was left, and that was his own. "Damn it. Damn it!" he said kicking the side of the Jeep. They didn't linger but one thing they were beginning to realize was that having a working vehicle was like placing a bull's-eye on their back. Even for those that already had a vehicle. In a world without power, transportation was as valuable as food, clean water, medication, shelter and weapons. Then again it might not have been the vehicle they were after but their supplies. It wouldn't get better, and Tyler wasn't sure if the pros of having the vehicle outweighed the risk. So far they'd been fortunate but how long would that last?

Chapter 21

On the lam. Who would have thought it possible? Gabriel had spent years thinking about what freedom would feel like. This wasn't it. Oh no, this was so much sweeter. He couldn't have asked for more. With the power down and telecommunication no longer working, it only stacked the odds in his favor. Sure, cops were out looking for them but for how long? A town, a county, a state, even the nation only had so many resources to use when a prisoner escaped, and in all cases, they relied heavily on communication, volunteers, witness tips, transportation, clear roads, and most of all — order.

Where was that now?

He smiled as he lay on the bed staring up at the log cabin ceiling.

After three failed attempts to escape, he thought he'd never see the outside again. The system had taken additional measures to ensure he wouldn't get another chance and he was sure that was why his name was on the list of transfers. Oh, if they could have known. What a screw-up. A beautiful screw-up.

Minutes earlier he'd awoke to the sound of birds chirping, the scent of pine, and a faint band of sunshine filtering through the blinds. It had been the best night of sleep he'd had in over six years. He rolled off the king-size bed and walked over to the window to take in the sight of the new day. He picked up the handgun on the side table and stuffed it in the front of his waistband, covering it with his shirt. Day two of freedom was already shaping up to be good. Good weather, a great climate, beautiful views, and… He reached across and flicked the light switch up and down to see if anything had changed.

Nothing. No power. Perfect.

Gabriel leaned his neck from side to side causing it to let out a cracking sound as he worked out the tension from the crash. They'd been extraordinarily lucky. It was as if fate was giving him another chance and he planned on taking it.

After setting fire to the ranger station and witnessing the crew they were up against, they'd taken shelter inside the home of a family a few miles south, just on the edge of the lake. The large log cabin was nestled in the trees, a good distance from neighbors. Out of sight, out of sound, no one heard the family of four scream the night before as he and the rest of the vicious inmates burst in and took over.

He'd stayed awake for the first few hours, and then they'd rotated shifts to keep an eye out for cops. Gabriel made his way down the thick wooden ladder from the loft. Marcus and Hauser were awake while the others slept. "How are they?" Gabriel asked.

"Still in there." The father, mother and two boys were tied up and locked inside a large walk-in pantry closet. He nodded to the kitchen area. "Coffee is on the counter. Had to use a Coleman stove but it did the trick."

"You checked the landline this morning?"

"I pulled the cord out last night. It's of no use. Why? Who were you going to call?"

"An old friend in Utah."

"What do you think?" Hauser said opening his arms wide to show him his new threads taken from the father's closet. Gabriel smiled. "There was enough for a few more but Barret and Jones will need something larger."

They were over two hundred pounds and the father of the home was closer to one eighty. Gabriel poured himself a hot cup of coffee and took a sip. Hauser walked over. "Not bad, huh?"

"It's a mean cup of joe." He glanced at his brother just beyond the window. He was sitting in the porch rocker keeping an eye on the driveway. "How's he today?"

"Quiet. Look, Gabriel. Do you think it's wise we stick together?"

Gabriel screwed up his eyes and Hauser raised a hand. "I'm just saying. They're probably looking for all of us and traveling together as a group isn't exactly smart."

"Don't you think I know that?"

"Then why bother insisting that we do it?"

He didn't answer him, instead he brushed past and

wandered out. A warm breeze blew against his face, the sun already beginning to heat up the landscape. Gabriel took a seat beside Marcus without saying anything. He looked up the driveway and then out across the lake. A few minutes passed and then he said, "What I said yesterday. I…"

"Don't bother. I know what you meant."

Gabriel looked at him before taking another sip from his cup. "What you did before, was your past. I'm not asking for a reason why you did it, only that you leave it there, in the past. We have an opportunity, Marcus. Never before has this been presented to us, and probably never again. This is it. We need to make it count. That means sticking together, watching out for each other, and playing our cards right."

"You mean not having any fun."

"I didn't say that."

"I've been stuck in that prison for five years."

"As have I, and even longer, but now we get a chance to turn things around."

"Oh please. They are going to have us back in the slammer within seventy-two hours."

"Maybe. Maybe not."

"I need a woman," he said.

"And you will have one but not that way. We are not that way."

"You might not be but I am."

"Bullshit. I don't believe that. I don't know who skewed your mind but my kid brother is not a rapist."

Marcus snorted. "You keep on believing that."

"Then choose differently."

Marcus turned in his seat with a scowl on his face. "Why does it matter to you? It's not like we're planning on living out the rest of our lives as ordinary people. We are on the run, Gabriel. We are wanted felons. Bad shit got us where we are, and it's what we do."

"We define who we are."

"That's right. I know who I am. Maybe it's time you accept who you are."

With that said Marcus got up and walked back inside,

leaving Gabriel pondering.

Over the next twenty minutes he sat there thinking about the road ahead. There were many directions they could head. All were dangerous and had the possibility of ending in disaster. As he weighed the pros and cons of heading for Whitefish, he heard the sound of gravel crunching beneath tires. Instantly he rose to his feet and scanned the tree line. There, between the pines, a green military truck was approaching.

Gabriel dashed inside. "Wake up. Everyone. Get up."

The inmates were sprawled out on the couches, and in chairs, and on the floor. He went around and gave a kick to those who were less than responsive. "Get up now! Marcus, Hauser, get the family, take them to the back room of the house. Keep them quiet."

"What are you going to do?"

"Just do it."

He hurried over to the window and pulled back the drape ever so slightly. The same vehicle from the previous night rumbled down to a stop. He could see it between the trunks of the trees. It was parked on the main road. Several cops jumped out the back and they fanned out, heading for the neighbor's home across the way, while two armed guys walked down towards their cabin.

Gabriel heard the door shut in the rear of the home. He turned and scooped up a few of the pillows on the floor, along with blankets, and tossed them onto the sofas. He collected some of the used cups and took them out to the kitchen and hid them inside the dishwasher. Quickly, he poured himself another cup of coffee, and looked in a mirror on the wall. He ruffled his hair a little more, and grabbed up one of the throw blankets and wrapped it around him. He adjusted the Glock in the front of his jeans and made sure it wasn't visible. Just as he was doing that, he heard footsteps approach the door and then two knocks.

He scanned the room for anything that looked out of place, and then spotted a photo of the family. He grabbed it and slid it behind a pillow.

Another knock, then he saw a face at the window

trying to peer in

"Yeah, just coming."

He shuffled over and cracked the door open, taking a quick sip of his drink to appear normal. "Damn, it's bright out," he said as he squinted and gave his best performance. Outside there was a guy in his early thirties, dark eyes, a thick beard, swept-back hair, athletic in appearance and rugged-looking in jeans and a thick sweater. He noticed tattoos on his forearm, and the carbine rifle he was carrying. The other guy looked weedy, spectacles, salt-and-pepper hair and wearing clothes that looked like they'd been bought by an overly protective mother.

"Morning. Sorry to bother you. The name's Corey. I'm working with the local police to check on the well-being of those with homes in the area. Wanted to know if you have seen or heard anything unusual in the last twenty-four hours?"

"Unusual. Like a power outage?" Gabriel chuckled.

Corey smiled. "Well that of course but I'm referring to

a group of individuals."

Gabriel frowned. "Who are you?"

"Sorry. We're volunteers with search and rescue. We had a plane go down in the lake last night. We were wondering if you might have seen anything, or anyone."

"Oh that, did anyone survive?" Gabriel asked.

"Well that's what we're trying to establish." Corey looked past him. "You home alone?"

"Yeah. Just me. The wife is at her mother's. I've been trying to get hold of them but haven't had much luck. You know when the power is coming up?"

"Have you tried the landline?"

"Yeah. It wasn't working."

"Strange. As it usually works for at least a few days after a power outage unless there has been a flood. The power is supplied by backup generators. It's actually the one thing that tends to work for a while. You mind if I check?"

"Um. Sure. Come on in." He opened the door and was about to head in when someone called out to him.

"Hey Corey. You want to come and check this out?"

The guy had one foot in the door when he looked over his shoulder.

"I can check," the other guy said. "You go."

"You sure, Noah?"

"Yeah, seems fine."

Corey looked at Gabriel again, made a face and nodded.

"All right."

He jogged up the driveway while Gabriel welcomed Noah in. "Sorry, I didn't get your name?"

"Noah Peterson."

Gabriel shook his hand before closing the door behind him.

"Nice place you got here."

"Yeah. Was gifted to us by a close family member," he said, watching as Noah walked around and observed.

"So, where's the phone?"

"Oh, it's over here."

As he led him across the room, he suddenly

remembered what Hauser had said about yanking out the cord from the wall. Thinking fast, he slapped a hand against his head. "Damn. I forgot. We're in the middle of upgrading. Yeah, getting a whole new system. Satellite phones because reception is crap out here."

"But it's a landline."

"Yeah but we get our landline through the internet. So, when the internet goes down so does the phone." He groaned. "Sorry. Completely slipped my mind."

Noah looked at him skeptically, his eyes darting to the phone. He saw the exposed wires. "You do that?"

"Oh that. No. We had the guy in a couple of days ago but he got called away at the last minute." Noah pursed his lips, narrowed his eyes and nodded. Gabriel leaned against the counter, and his eyes fell upon a magnetic wall bar that was used to hold large kitchen knives.

"Well, I guess I will let you get on with it," Noah said turning his back and heading towards the door. Gabriel grabbed one of the knives off the bar and put it behind his back so it was out of sight. He followed Noah to the door as he opened it.

"I hope you find them."

"Yeah," Noah said looking one final time around.

Right then, just as he was about to go out the door, a noise came from the back of the house. It sounded like something had dropped on the ground. Noah let go of the handle and frowned.

"I thought you said you were alone?"

"I am. It's probably boxes I stacked up. Too many."

"Right. And, uh, what was your name again?"

"Gabriel."

"Gabriel…" he fished for more.

Instead of saying Johnson, he glanced at a stack of mail on the counter and used the last name of the family who lived there. "Rickman. Gabriel Rickman."

Noah extended a hand. "Well, Gabriel. Have a good one."

Again the noise came, this time it was louder followed by a muffled cry.

Gabriel acted fast before Noah could say a word. His

hand came around with the blade in one smooth motion and jammed it into his gut. He used his other hand which was shaking Noah's hand to pull him in close. Noah let out a gasp, and Gabriel twisted the knife and pushed it in even deeper. "That's it. Just relax," he said guiding him down to the floor. Then he called out to Marcus. "Marcus. Get out here now."

The door across from them opened and he emerged.

"We need to leave immediately."

Chapter 22

The journey out of the city to Midway, Utah, wasn't easy. They stayed on Highway 91 traveling northeast, parallel to I-15. For many hours all that separated them from the clogged interstate was a wide, flat dirt median covered with green desert shrubs. Though contrary to Nate's advice, others had the same idea and so they spent a great deal of time swerving around vehicles. Tyler kept a close eye on the gas gauge. They had a five-gallon drum of gas in the back, enough to keep them going for a while. The only upside to being out of the city was there was less chance of someone hijacking the Jeep.

"This road just seems to go on forever," Erika said. An hour ago, she and Nate had swapped seats as Nate wanted to get some shut-eye. He curled up in the back under a blanket.

"Why didn't you tell me about killing that guy?"

She glanced at Tyler. "For probably the same reason

you didn't tell us. It's not exactly our finest moment, is it?" She breathed in deeply. "Can we just avoid the subject?"

He shrugged. "Sure." They drove for another ten minutes in silence, the wind whipping around them. Tyler had given a lot of thought to what Erika might do if she found her parents dead. There was a strong possibility that a home invasion had happened.

"About your parents. If..." he trailed off rethinking talking about it.

"If they're dead?" she asked. Her response caught him off guard. "I've thought about it. I don't know what I'll do."

"Look, if they are, you know you are more than welcome to return to Whitefish with me."

Her eyebrow went up. "You'd like that, wouldn't you?"

He caught an edge to her tone. Tyler considered calling her out on it but understood that she wasn't in a good place mentally. How could you be after hearing your mother scream on a phone, getting no response from repeated calls and by day two of the blackout killing someone? Strangely he didn't need to say anything as she must have picked up on her own attitude. "I mean. I appreciate that offer. Maybe I'll take you up on it. So, what brought you to Vegas?" she asked.

"Wow. If I wasn't mistaken, Erika Lyons, you almost sounded interested in me."

She gave him a nudge and smiled. "No seriously. Montana is beautiful."

"You been there?"

"Twice." She ran a hand through her hair. "We have several hotels in the state."

He nodded. "Of course you do." He bit down on the corner of his lip and thought back to the last day he left Whitefish. "I…"

"You had problems with your father?"

He turned his head and frowned. "How did you…?"

"I overheard you talking with your uncle. I didn't want to intrude."

He nodded and gripped the wheel a little tighter giving it a bit more gas. "Yeah, we had a bit of a falling out. It was a long time ago. I left when I was eighteen. I headed to Vegas to go to college."

"Why Vegas?"

"My uncle was already there and I think that kind of helped convince my father."

"But you were old enough to make your own decisions."

"As were you," he said. "And look where you ended up."

She nodded, and a faint smile appeared. "Point taken."

"Unless of course you had an interest in hotel hospitality?"

She stuck her tongue out and pushed a finger into her mouth and made a gagging noise. "I did what made them happy. I figured if I took on some responsibility and they saw how bad I was at it, that they would be more than happy to pay for what I really wanted to do."

"Which was?"

"You're gonna laugh."

He smiled. "No. Go ahead. Can't be much worse than being a tour guide."

"Hey, don't knock it, it piqued my interest."

"Ah, so it wasn't all bad," he said.

"The date yeah, your profile no."

He laughed.

Their smiles soon faded as they took in the sight of more stalled vehicles — cars, trucks, 18-wheelers and delivery vans dotted the highway. There were many families trying to hitchhike on the side of the road, carrying luggage in the hopes of reaching the city. Some of the RV owners were still there. Someone had used clothing spread out on the ground to form the word HELP just in case the government sent in rescue helicopters. Others stuck a thumb out expecting Tyler to stop but he zipped past them without even slowing. Erika looked in her side mirror. "That's gotta suck."

"Yeah, being stranded in the middle of nowhere. I don't envy them but that might be us by the time the day's out."

They passed a few older vehicles still in operation — Tyler figured they were heading back to the city — probably expecting it to be better, not worse. His thoughts switched to his father. He hadn't thought about what he would say to him when he returned. For the longest of time he'd kept his distance, and the few times he'd seen his brother Corey, he'd steered the conversation away from their old man.

After being on the road for several hours they agreed they would stop, so they all could all take a piss and stretch their legs. There was only three hours left to go before they hit Midway so when they saw the rest stop near Quail Creek State Park and saw how few vehicles were in the vicinity, Tyler pulled off the main stretch of road that cut through the red rock mountains. He weaved the Jeep down to what appeared to be a quiet lake and parked just a stone's throw away from public toilets. According to a sign nearby it wasn't a lake but a manmade reservoir that diverted water from the Virgin

River and transported it using buried pipeline. Tyler got out and stretched, looking around for any sign of trouble. On any other given day it might have been busy with campers, boats and anglers but it was absent of all three. There were only a few buildings nearby; one was for a service that rented canoes and kayaks, the other one was a restroom. Close to that was a large pavilion with BBQ amenities, coin-operated showers and a concessionary shop. Much further down near a steep grassy hill was a campsite, where there were six RVs. Smoke was coming from one of the BBQ areas.

"Okay, don't take long," Tyler said, holding his rifle nearby and keeping a close eye on the campsite. He sat on the front of the Jeep and brought a pair of binoculars up to see if anyone was near the concession area. On the outside it didn't look as if anyone had broken in but the doors were locked. Was it possible that those who were camping had opted to take time out from civilization and unplug completely? If so, would they have even been aware of the situation? No, the main road was just up from them. He figured they would have seen vehicles stall or a lack of vehicles on the road.

Nate came out doing his zipper up. "Ah man, it's surprisingly clean in there." Tyler directed his vision towards the campsite. "Any trouble?"

"Doesn't look like it."

Tyler headed into the bathroom. He entered one of the stalls and tried flushing the toilet. It was no longer working. Some would see that as a problem but a simple bucket of water flushed down it would do the trick. He closed the door and set his rifle down beside him. After sliding down his jeans he squatted and checked to make sure there was paper. When he was in there, he heard someone come in and go in the stall beside him. "Nate?"

There was no reply. He tilted ever so slightly and looked at the boots of the person that were partially visible beneath the raised panel. He heard him grunt and went back to focusing on finishing his own business. Every few seconds he would glance down to check if the man was still there. The boots weren't moving but he could hear movement.

Just as he reached for a handful of paper, a thin wire appeared in front of him. It happened so fast, before he knew it the noose went over his head and he found himself pulled upwards. Tyler flailed around, his pants around his ankles as one hand held on to the wire trying to pull it away from his neck and the other stretched for the rifle. He supported himself on the toilet seat for a second, but another hard yank and his feet slipped away and he slammed into the main door. He turned his head upwards to see who his attacker was. Gritting his teeth together, a long-haired, greasy-looking fucker with wild eyes was pulling tight. He could feel the wire tearing into his skin as he struggled to pull it loose. As darkness crept in at the sides of his eyes, he knew he was going to pass out if he didn't get free. His fingers touched the tip of the rifle leaning up against the wall but as he was moving around so violently, his leg ended up kicking it and it landed flat on the ground. As desperation kicked in, he pushed his feet against the panel across from him and instead of fighting the man pulling him up, he used his feet to springboard himself back towards him, essentially over the top.

"Arrgh," he cried out as he thrust his legs like a piston and went over the top, landing on top of his attacker. They both crumpled to the floor in the cramped space, Tyler with his underpants down and the man out of his boots. The bastard had slipped out of his boots and pretended as if he was sitting on the toilet when he was preparing his wired noose. Not even thinking to call out for help — something that was foreign to him after what his father had taught him — Tyler yanked the wire free from his neck just as the man was trying to go for his rifle under the raised panel. Tyler crawled on top of him and slung the noose over his head as the man's finger reached the trigger. He managed to fire off a few rounds but because he couldn't get his arm out from underneath, it did him little good. In fact, he was in a worse position because now he had Tyler's full body weight on top of him and the same weapon of death wrapped around his neck.

Tyler began yanking hard even as he heard Nate's voice.

"Tyler. Tyler!"

All Nate would have been able to see was legs flailing around and them banging against the door as he tried to kill the man. He was gripping so hard on the wire, it began to cut into his hands as he fought for control. The man reached up and scratched his face, trying desperately to stick a finger in his eye. Then he felt the man grab his balls. With his underpants down, he was fully exposed and the guy was using it to his full advantage. Tyler screamed in pain and released his grip on the wire in an attempt to pry loose his grubby hands around his junk.

A second later, Nate appeared above, leaning over the stall from the adjoining one. He aimed a gun and before Tyler could say no, he fired twice killing the man instantly. A mist of red hit Tylers face. It wasn't that he didn't want Nate to kill the asshole but it was the fear he would miss and shoot him. Fortunately, that hadn't happened.

His attacker slumped down beside him and Tyler felt the pressure between his legs vanish. However, the pain was still there. It felt like he'd been kicked in the nuts.

"So, this is what you get up to in your spare time," Nate said, smiling before disappearing out of view. When Tyler was able to stand, he opened the door and Nate pulled the guy out.

A few minutes later, once he'd cleaned himself up and gathered what was left of his dignity, Tyler came out gripping his crotch and moaning. "Don't you say anything," Tyler said.

He thumbed off to his right. "A little late."

Tyler turned his head to see Erika standing in the doorway of the men's restroom.

He groaned and shook his head as he went over to the sink and tried to get some water. It coughed out some dirty pipe water and he splashed it over his face. Tyler gripped the sides of the wash basin and looked at himself in the mirror.

Tyler glanced at Nate. "Who the hell was he?"

"No idea," Nate said.

"How the hell did he get past you then?"

Nate shrugged. "I don't know."

"I do," Erika said shooting Nate a stern look. Nate looked as if he was trying to signal to her to not say anything but she did. "He went to see if any of the campers had a cigarette. The Jeep was out of view of the entrance. I couldn't keep an eye on both the Jeep and the entrance to the restroom. I looked that way but he must have slipped past me when dumbass here left to get his cigarette."

Tyler gave Nate a dirty look and he threw his hands up. "What? I needed a cigarette. I was out. I figured…" Tyler wanted to grab him and smack him around but it wouldn't have helped and besides he was in too much pain. He winced and screwed his eyes up as he exited the bathroom that was now covered in blood and smears of shit.

"I think we should lay down some ground rules,"

Tyler said.

Nate frowned. "Rules?"

"For survival."

Nate shook his head and brushed past him. "I should drive," he said, offering to get in the driver's side.

Tyler tossed the keys to Erika. "Like hell you will." Tyler slipped into the passenger side and laid back his head trying to forget the pain.

"Just wanted to help," Nate said in a half-ass manner before hopping in the back.

"Yeah? You can help by digging into my backpack and finding some Advil. And Nate. Next time you decide to walk off to bum a cigarette, you won't need to wait for cancer to kill you, I will do it myself."

Chapter 23

The utility truck idled on the main road as they waited for Noah to return. Terry had been chatting to Officer Ferris about diving into the lake to check on the plane and see how many had died. Ferris was against the idea until the power came back on. "No point lugging the dead back to the surface at this point. Let's hold off until the power comes up and we can determine how many were on that flight."

"You knew inmates were on it but didn't know how many?" Corey asked.

"I didn't speak to them directly. We just get our marching orders." He nudged him. "Look, just go and get Noah. We still have a lot of ground to cover. These assholes could be anywhere by now."

Corey nodded, and hopped out. His mind was distracted with thoughts of how the town of Whitefish would cope when they realized the power wasn't coming back on. He and Ella would be fine as would his father as their entire lives had been building up to this point. Although his father had invested a great deal of time in building a home with every amenity to help them ride out a disaster, and even though he'd lost it in the foreclosure, business had been exceptional and as soon as he was able, he'd funneled profits from the store into turning a cabin located north of Whitefish Lake into a fully functional shelter with all the bells and whistles. Others would have seen it as a waste of money, in fact there were many in town that mocked him for his choices, but were they laughing now?

As Corey approached the door, he noticed it was partly open.

"Noah."

He gave a short knock on the door before stepping inside. "Hello?"

The moment the door opened wide his eyes fell upon him. His initial reaction was to raise his rifle and call out for additional backup, while taking a few steps back for his own safety. "Ferris!"

Back outside he scanned the windows, then went around the side before heading in once the three officers came down. Vern and Terry stayed with the vehicle. Corey motioned with his head and Ferris entered followed by Corey.

"Shit."

He dropped to a knee and checked his pulse.

"He's gone."

Quickly they moved through the cabin clearing each of the rooms. When Corey made it to the rear, he walked in on the family who were lying on their sides, gagged, with their hands and ankles hogtied. They let out muffled cries. Corey reassured them they were safe. At first they didn't look convinced until Ferris walked in. Just seeing a uniformed officer set them at ease. They untied them and began peppering them with questions.

"Where did they go?"

"No idea," the father said.

"How many?"

"We didn't see all of them. I don't know. Maybe six or eight?"

Ferris hurried out, barking out orders to the other officers.

"Look, down the road is an elderly couple. The Sampsons. You know them?"

He shook his head. "No."

"I'm sure they would appreciate the company, and you'd feel better being with more people. You have a firearms license?"

His eyes screwed up, his cheeks became flushed. A look of embarrassment formed. "Yeah. I never got to my Glock in time. It's up in my closet, in a lockbox."

"Take it. Head to house number 112. Let Mitch know I sent you. Barricade yourselves in. Don't let anyone inside except for police."

Corey gave his shoulder a reassuring squeeze. He could see by the cut on his lip, and his red knuckles that he'd put up one hell of a fight. Corey couldn't fault the man, being caught off guard was common. His wife was in tears. She immediately wrapped her arms around her two boys and thanked them. Corey didn't wait around. After exiting, he could see the officers had pressed into the forest making their way over to the next cabin. Corey ran up to the utility truck where Vern and Terry were waiting, oblivious to what had occurred. He didn't mince words. "He's gone."

"What?" Terry asked.

"Noah is dead."

The color went out of both of their faces as he told them to jump in. They couldn't have had more than a five-minute head start on them. Rage began to form in the pit of Corey's stomach. He'd known Noah since he was a young kid. All of them had grown up in the town. Noah was married, and had three kids. He didn't want to even think about dropping that bombshell on them.

He slammed his foot against the accelerator and tore away.

A mile or two down the road, he swerved to the side of the road to touch base with the officers. "Anything?" he yelled from the truck. They shook their heads and banged on the door of another home.

"They could be anywhere."

"Corey, no offense, but I'm not trained for this. I have a family at home. I thought I was coming out to do a search and rescue, not join a hunt for armed criminals," Vern said, adjusting his faded red ballcap. When Vern wasn't volunteering, he worked as a barista at one of the local coffee stores. The youngest of the group, he too was married with a young kid.

"I understand," Corey said.

"Maybe you can drop me back in Whitefish."

Corey cast him a glance. "I'm afraid until we know where they are, we aren't heading back."

"But—"

"Vern. There is no time. They've already killed rangers, and Noah. They won't hesitate to kill again. We need to find them before they do."

"And how do you expect to do that? There are too many homes, too many trees. It's like trying to find a needle in a haystack. Even if you know what one of them looks like, it won't matter. We would be better heading back to Whitefish and preparing the town for their arrival. You heard what Sampson said. That's where they're heading."

"Maybe not," Terry said. "They might hunker down in West Glacier, St. Mary or Columbia Falls. And that's if they go to a town at all. They could quite easily vanish in this national park. "

"Exactly," Corey said.

"However Vern is right about one thing, Corey. We need more people. Six of us aren't going to find them and even if we do. What then? A firefight? I can shoot but this is not what I signed up for."

"Do you think any of us signed up for this?" He glanced at them as they drove down the winding road and he scanned the tree line. There was a strong possibility the inmates had made their way down to the water's edge and were using the steep incline as cover. There was no way to see the shore unless they got out and made their way down through the thick pines. "The fact is in the coming days you might have to take on jobs you never thought you would do just to survive. This is just the beginning."

"No, they'll get the power on."

"Terry. Pull your head out of your ass. You took my father's course. At least you should know better. This has all the signs of an EMP. Whether it was caused by a nuke detonated high in the atmosphere, or by a coronal mass ejection, the outcome is still the same. The country won't be able to bounce back from this. We may only be two days into this but you know what to expect."

Terry shook his head, running his hand over his wedding band.

Corey could see his emotions getting the better of him. Like many others he would experience going through the stages of grief over the demise of society, from denial, to anger, then bargaining to depression and then if he made it through that, acceptance. Corey swerved to the edge of the road. "If you want to get out, no one would hold it against you. But right now, the sooner we find them the safer everyone is going to be."

"Safe?" Terry said. "If this is an EMP, none of us are safe."

He stared at them both but neither one got out.

Corey nodded. "Okay. Let's find these bastards. For Noah. For our families. For Whitefish."

Chapter 24

Erika's parents' home stood head and shoulders above their neighbors. A beautiful mountain home valued at over four million dollars, it was perched in a coveted position overlooking the Heber Valley. Interestingly, the entire log home had been cut and assembled in Montana. The irony was not wasted. Like a home in the Hollywood Hills, it was just off a narrow road called Big Matterhorn Way. After several hours of avoiding trouble they turned onto the dirt road that led up to the entrance of the house. "Big place for two people," Tyler said.

She didn't reply, as worry took precedence.

As soon as they stopped, she hopped out with Bailey and hurried up to the front door. Tyler wanted to hold her back, fully expecting what came next — a scream.

Nate was in the house before Tyler. Still achy, and still in pain, he hurried to find Erika sprawled over a female body in the hallway. The dead woman wore a white blouse that was caked with dry blood, and tight blue jeans with white flats covered in droplets of blood. It looked as if someone had beaten her to death. Nate looked back at Tyler and they exchanged an awkward moment. There was nothing that could be said to ease the loss. She would be unpacking her grief for months, if they lived that long. Nate headed up a large wooden staircase that went up another two levels. While he did that, Tyler headed to the back of the home where a door was wide open providing an astonishing view of the valley. However his eyes didn't linger on the beauty but on the second body lying in the yard, not far from a gorgeous log shed. Tyler looked back to say something to Erika but she was still sobbing her heart out. Instead, he stepped outside and made his way over to check on the man he believed was her father. A full head of silver hair, a well-dressed man, wearing a shirt and well-pressed pants, his back had two bullet wounds, and there was a third behind his ear. He stood there staring at him and then looked towards the garage which was open. There were at least three sports cars inside that hadn't been touched. Had the attack occurred before the power went out, they would be gone but now they were nothing more than junk. Generators were the new asset, and he could only imagine what kind of top-of-the-line generator her father owned.

He lifted his head and breathed in the mountain air. A warm sunshine shone brightly in the summer sky. Trees rustled and a flock of birds wheeled overhead.

Tyler turned to see Nate on the balcony that wrapped the second level of the home. None of the house appeared to have been vandalized, indicating these were just kids looking to blow off some steam. Tyler sighed, dipped his chin and pressed on into the house in preparation to give her more bad news.

Her parents' home was nestled in the side of the mountain, and because it was shrouded by trees it would have made it a prime target for anyone wanting to get in and out without being caught. And, with the power out, the security lights and cameras would have been useless. That's when it dawned on him, how had they got in? The home was perched high enough that the intruders would have had to climb over tall stone walls, or work their way down through the thick brush that surrounded the west side. Unless of course the security guard had let them in?

Tyler strolled around the home to see the front again. That was when he saw it. The small booth was shrouded by a canopy of trees, just off to the right of the driveway, in front of the now open black iron gates.

One glance made it clear security didn't escape unscathed. An arm of a security guard was the first thing Tyler saw. As he came around, he grimaced at the sight. He'd been shot in the face. A single round drilled into his forehead before he'd been able to draw on the intruders.

It was a sign of the times, the beginning of the downfall.

Attacks would occur all around the country, first by opportunists and criminals, taking advantage of what others believed was temporary, and then by everyday people, desperate to survive.

When he returned to the house, Nate was trying to

keep Bailey back from licking up the blood. Erika hadn't moved.

"Erika," Tyler said in a low voice. She didn't respond.

He crouched and placed a hand on her shoulder.

She shrugged it off. "Go away."

"They're gone, Erika. There's nothing you can do."

"Just leave."

"Not without you."

"I'm not going with you."

He hesitated before rising and wandering around the room. Nate leaned against the staircase banister, glancing towards the door. There was a large stone fireplace at the center of the room, multiple sofas around a slate coffee table and an expensive-looking tapestry rug beneath that. Hardwood floors, granite counters in the kitchen and state-of-the-art appliances conveyed their wealth. Large windows went up to a cathedral ceiling allowing in the natural flow of light. On either side of the walls were stuffed animals — a fox, a goose, and two deer heads. Had her father or mother hunted, or were they just people who appreciated those who did? Had they taken the time to furnish the place or paid someone to do it for them? A number of questions went through his mind, the typical ones that one might ask when invited to someone's home, except now they would go unanswered.

"Okay. We'll stay then," Tyler said, removing his jacket and throwing it onto the couch. "I'll go get what supplies we have from the Jeep and bring the vehicle into one of the garages."

"What?" Nate asked.

That caught the attention of Erika. She looked up, her clothes stained with remnants of her mother's blood. "I meant to say I'm not going to Whitefish."

"I know," Tyler said walking backwards towards the main door. She studied him as he exited. No sooner had he stepped outside than she followed him out.

"What are you doing?"

"Getting my bags, storing the Jeep. Like I said."

"No, I know that. I meant. What are you doing? You said you were heading for Whitefish," Erika said.

"Change of plans."

"You can't stay here."

He was still walking backwards towards the Jeep when he replied, "Neither can you."

"It's my home."

He turned, reached into the Jeep and pulled out his bag. "No, it's your parents'."

As he returned, she blocked his path, putting out a hand against his chest and scowling. "I know what you're trying to do and it won't work."

His lip curled as he walked around her. "And what would that be?"

"You think I'm going to change my mind."

Tyler walked back into the house not replying to her and dumped his bag on a chair. She hurried over and grabbed it up and tossed it at him. "You're not staying."

He dropped the bag on the ground and looked her sternly in the eyes. "How do you expect to survive? Money has no value now. So you can forget that."

"I'll trade."

"That might work but how will you protect yourself?"

She crossed her arms and her lips pursed. "I can take care of myself."

"Yeah, like you did back in Vegas? Cause I'm pretty sure the only reason you're alive is because of me."

Erika narrowed her eyes. "You self-righteous prick!"

"Well. Am I right?"

Without warning she swung at him and he stepped back. Her fist missed his chin by a few inches. "Not bad. Now try without making it obvious you're about to throw a—" Before he finished what he was saying, she fired an uppercut, then followed with two jabs and a hook. Each time he shifted to avoid the blows. Two more attempts and he slipped around her, and held her arms tight to her body. "Now what do you do?"

She wriggled within his grasp and then told him to let go.

As soon as he did, she stormed off towards the kitchen.

"And that's if they're not armed. By the looks of what happened here, you aren't dealing with people who mess around. This isn't a game, Erika."

She didn't reply.

"We're staying," Tyler said.

"Whatever," she replied.

Nate shrugged and Tyler shook his head as he turned to head out and park the Jeep in the garage. Erika muttered something. Tyler didn't catch it. "What did you say?"

"This pot of coffee is still warm. If they died over twenty-four hours ago, how can that be?" She glanced at Tyler, and his mind began to turn over. What if those who were responsible for her parents' death hadn't left? What if they planned on returning?

"Bailey, come here, girl," Nate said, noticing she was standing by the doorway growling. "What is it, Bailey?" The hair on the back of the dog went up. Tyler glanced over, his pulse began to beat faster. He started crossing the room towards the door when Bailey began barking furiously, and hurried out.

"Bailey. Come back here," Tyler yelled.

Erika turned to see what all the commotion was about.

Tyler ran out after the dog and found her a few yards outside barking at the entranceway. There was no one there. He caught up with her and grabbed her collar and was trying to tug her back to the house when a bullet snapped overhead. It hit the wall just beyond and took out a large chunk of concrete. That was when he pulled his weapon and fired in several directions as he pulled Bailey back into the house.

He didn't see the assailants but they were under attack, and he figured it was the same people, returned to take back the property.

Chapter 25

A deafening cacophony split the silence. Windows on every level shattered under the relentless spray of rounds. Tyler hit the ground sliding across the tiled walkway, his shoulder slamming into a wall. Above, Nate jammed his rifle out a window and returned fire then pulled back behind a stone wall. "Get this dog out of here," Tyler yelled. Erika beckoned Bailey her way. The dog knew better than to ignore her.

He had to get the front door closed, and get to his rifle which was with his backpack nearby. Tyler fired a few shots towards the opening and dashed across, diving over a sofa and colliding with a glass table. It buckled beneath him, smashing into hundreds of tiny shards. Not checking to see if he was cut, he scrambled over to his rifle and made sure the magazine was full before making his way to the wall that divided the living room from the entranceway.

More gunfire made it clear that attempting to shut the door was a useless and deadly endeavor. Instead, he slid his back to the wall and made his way over to the window.

"You see anything, Nate?"

A few seconds of silence.

"I got two, one at your eleven o'clock, the other is at three. Could be more out there."

Another sudden flurry of rounds, this time from the rear, answered that.

More glass shattered. Erika had taken Bailey and placed her in a room at the rear of the house before re-emerging. She pulled the Glock from her holster and dropped down trying to watch the rear entrance.

For close to ten minutes they exchanged gunfire until it went quiet. Erika gave Tyler a terrified glance. He wished he could put her mind at ease but maybe this was for the best. He could tell her all day of the dangers of staying on her own but sometimes people only learned when their lives hung in the balance. Their best chance of survival was to stick together, watch each other's backs and hope to God they made it to the next day. Another assault of rapid fire. His heart sped up as drywall dust scattered, filling the air like emptying a bag of flour. Suddenly, Erika unleashed one round after the other, five, maybe six shots. Tyler wiggled across the floor trying to make his way over as he could see her hands were shaking. She was doing the best she could and it wasn't her inability to fire that worried him as much as it was having her go into shock. It had happened to him a long time ago, he knew the signs. All the color draining out of the skin, sweating, nausea, and darkness creeping in at the side of the eyes.

"I'm coming to you."

She nodded but said nothing.

Nate fired a few more rounds.

"They're trying to gain ground," he yelled. "Pushing forward towards the Jeep. Please tell me you have the keys."

"Of course," he said. They could try hotwiring it but

that took time and exposing themselves to Nate's line of fire, and no one in their right mind would attempt that. Erika popped her head around the corner and fired again, two more rounds. When Tyler got close enough that he could see the rear door, he spotted a dead guy laying in the doorway. She'd taken one of them down. No wonder she was shaking.

"Remember to reload," he said pressing his back against a wall across from her. "Okay?" he asked, trying to reassure her and get her to focus on him instead of the ever-present danger.

More bullets tore at the wall near them.

Tyler fired back and saw a large guy run for cover.

"Speak to me, Nate."

"I'm still here."

"Good." Tyler nodded. "Conserve your ammo. Only fire if you have a clear shot." Since losing the other two supply bags, they now had a minimal supply of everything — bullets included. Although if they made it out of this unscathed, they could take their attackers' weapons, and whatever else they had on them.

There was a long period of silence. Every few minutes, Tyler would peer around to see if anyone was trying to get by undetected. He looked over at Erika who was staring at her dead mother.

"Tell me something," he said trying to distract her. "You never told me why a woman like you is single." Tyler took another peek around the corner. It was still clear. "It wasn't on your profile or in any of your texts. A lot of the other women gave some blurb about how long they'd been out of their previous relationship, and you never said anything. I figured you'd have a ring on that finger of yours by now," he added. She gave him a confused look as if she was juggling thoughts of her mother and what he was saying.

"I did have a ring," she said looking down at her hand. "I gave it back after I found out the asshole cheated on me."

"Your fiancé cheated on you?"

"Yeah. Clichéd, right?"

"Common, you mean," he replied. "Well his loss, right?"

She got this smile on her face. It was brief but enough that he caught it before she nodded and looked back at her mother. Again, he tried to shift her focus. "At least you made it to that stage. I know you think our date went bad but to be honest, it went pretty well compared to my past ones or lack thereof."

Erika snorted. "Are you joking?"

"I wish," he said taking another look. He wanted to get closer to the rear entrance. Drag the dead guy in, collect his weapon and close the door but he couldn't see the other guy. "Let's just say I've not had much luck with women."

"I would have thought someone like yourself would have had women fighting for your number."

He laughed. "You're a good shot but a terrible liar."

She chuckled then it faded. It wouldn't be easy to recover from losing her parents but it was possible. "I lost my mother a long while ago," he said thinking back. "She suffered a stroke, and never really recovered. The doctors gave her a year. She lived more than that and then succumbed."

"Were you young when you lost her?"

"Too young," he said. "My father worshiped the ground that woman walked on. After she died, he went to pieces. Kind of unraveled like society is now. Anyway, he was a survivalist, a prepper you might say, though to most of the townsfolk he was a headcase." Tyler shuffled into another position to get a better look at the rear yard. He continued talking as he moved. "From an early age he would take me and my brother out and run us through these insane survival-based scenarios. You name it, he took us through it."

"That's good, right?"

"Now, yeah, I see the value in it. Back then I didn't. I just wanted a normal life, a father I could throw a ball with and someone who would show up at my school and be proud."

"He wasn't? Proud I mean?" Erika asked.

"If he was, he had a weird way of showing it."

His mind flashed back to multiple instances of getting homeschool exam results, or achieving any of the goals he'd set for them like memorizing the sixty-eight medicinal plants that could be substituted for drugs, and which state they could be found in. That was just one of the hundreds of things he'd drilled into them like a boot camp instructor. Even after years of living away from home they were still there at the forefront of his mind, as fresh as the day he learned them.

"Is that why you carried that bag around?"

Tyler chuckled as he returned to the wall and slumped down across from her. "It became a habit, almost like a security blanket, or a crutch, you could say. Better to walk with the devil you know than the one you don't."

He often felt like an outcast. Even on the few occasions he managed to lie to his father and spend time with some of his old pals from school, he quickly learned that he didn't have anything in common with them. They would talk about music, movies, TV shows and the latest sports but he'd fallen out of touch with that. Those were a distraction. Nothing good came from them, his father would say. It dumbed them down and took away from time that could be spent memorizing radio frequencies, what to do before, during and after every natural disaster, hand signals, trail signs, Morse code, first aid, gun and fight training, and survival skills.

"Sounds like he had a lot of rules."

"He did."

His mind began going through them like a Rolodex — having the right mindset, practicing awareness, sharpening senses, avoiding automatic behavior, avoiding knife fights, throwing a power punch, adapting and overcoming, masking up, not being a hero, using paracord, tying knots, defending yourself, using first aid, using plants as meds, collecting and purifying water, staying dry, lighting a fire without matches, handling guns, target practice, signaling and navigation, setting up a campsite, food prep, fishing, firearm maintenance, reinforcing a home, stocking the right supplies, wound control, setting broken bones, treating for shock, using solar power, staying clean, and the list just went on and on… There wasn't a day he wasn't learning something new or having to prove to his father that he could remember what had been taught to him. Even when they knew the basics, his father could find ways to take it to the next level. He was a wealth of information, and when it came to survival there wasn't anyone he knew who was more prepared.

Another eruption of gunfire, then Nate shouted out, "They've backed out."

Tyler peered around and made a dash for the door. He dropped down, and waited before cutting the corner to make sure the coast was clear. The guy Erika had killed was a run-of-the-mill Caucasian guy, no different than someone he might see walking down the street in Vegas. He retrieved an AK47 from him, then shoved his body outside before locking the door behind him. Nate dealt with the front door. It wouldn't stop them from getting in, as the home was spacious and most if not all of the windows had been shot out. But he certainly wasn't going to make it easy.

"We should leave," Nate said. "Before they come back."

Tyler looked at Erika who was fixated on her mother. "In the morning." He glanced at Nate and he acknowledged the request with a nod. That evening they buried Erika's father and mother out back. As the sun set and another day gave way to darkness, they listened to her say a prayer before sobbing over their shallow graves. It didn't matter what her background was, or how wealthy, arrogant or self-entitled they had been in life, no one should have to lose parents that way.

Erika placed a few wildflowers on their graves and then they went back in and settled for the evening, hoping their attackers didn't return.

Chapter 26

Without a vehicle, covering the forested landscape was slow and cumbersome. It would only be a matter of time before they were spotted. A large group drew attention. And now they knew what Gabriel looked like, he would have to reconsider his original plan. It was then he began to entertain the initial idea of splitting up.

Many hours after leaving the last family they had holed up inside a cabin several miles away so he could think. Inside, he found a map of the area. Gabriel swiped off cutlery and plates from the kitchen table and laid it out. "Okay, listen up," he said looking at Marcus. "I want you to take Hauser, Perry, Manning, Rutwig and Davis. Use the boat down at the dock and head across to the other side then, go south towards Apgar, north on Camas Road. That will take you around onto 486, then you'll get on to Cedar Lake Road and that will lead you into Whitefish."

"And what about you?" Marcus asked leaning back in

his chair.

"Torres, Bill, Jericho, Owens, Reid, and Lee will come with me."

"Oh c'mon, let me take Torres and Jericho with me."

"I need them."

"But I don't trust these other guys. If we get pinned down, we don't stand a chance."

"You won't. Hauser has spotted the group just north of here. They are still going house to house. You will cross the lake and come out on the northwest side."

"And you?" Marcus asked.

"We're heading into Glacier."

"But you heard what that old man said. That's where the ranger headquarters are. That town will probably be crawling with cops."

"You have too much faith in the system."

"The system is what caught us in the first place."

"Marcus."

He shook his head. "I don't like it. It doesn't feel right. Why do you want us to divide now? You were adamant that we were stronger together."

"We are. But there are too many of us to avoid detection. If there are blockades set up along these stretches of roads, we need to stay low key, blend in, not stand out."

"And you think dividing will do that?"

"Divide and conquer, brother," Gabriel said taking a hit on a cigarette.

Marcus frowned. "Why do I get a sense this has more to do with the fact that they know what you look like and they were last seen on the north side?" He raised an eyebrow at Gabriel and waited for an answer.

"You want us to go across the lake and you head into Glacier, fine."

"No. We'll go that way." He jabbed an accusing finger at him. "But I don't like this one bit. I think it should be down to the group to decide."

"Too many views. It will only complicate things. We need to be decisive. They are looking to us to lead them."

"No they're not. Hauser would have gone with Jesse,

and I'm sure some of the others would. You have been playing them since we waded out of the lake."

Gabriel looked off to his right and left. The rest of the men were outside keeping an eye out for the cops. He was concerned about what they heard. If they even sniffed weakness or sensed that he and his brother weren't on the same page it could get ugly. It was the same in the can. Leaders rose not because they were put there by others but because they chose to not follow. It was a power move. Marcus was right. He had been playing them since the crash but if it wasn't him, one of the others would have taken the mantle.

"Decide what you want, Marcus, and go with it, but don't sit there griping."

With that said, Gabriel got up and walked over to the window and looked out. The cabin they'd raided was empty and nestled into such a thick area of the forest, they had almost walked by it without noticing. It was perfect but it wouldn't last. Eventually the cops would come across them. The only way forward was to keep moving.

He heard his brother come up behind him.

"Why Whitefish? Why not another town? Columbia Falls or West Glacier seem as good as any other."

"I talked to the old man before we left and had him fill me in on the details. Its size, its location near fresh water are something we need to bear in mind when trying to establish ourselves and take control."

"Take control?"

He glanced at Marcus. "Never before has an opportunity presented itself like this. There are sixteen police officers in Whitefish, and no means of communication to surrounding towns. If the lights come on tomorrow, do you want to be caught hidden away in some dusty old cabin, cowering? Or do you want to go out in a blaze of glory and be remembered for all time?"

Marcus chuckled. "I want to live."

"For how long? Running from town to town? State to state? What life is that? But think about this brother — if the power grid doesn't work again, do you want to run a town? Hell, run a county?"

Marcus scoffed. "You know, brother, I can appreciate your fortitude and vision but don't you think you are asking for trouble?"

"Have you forgotten your own advice?" Gabriel asked, turning and facing him. Marcus gave him a look of confusion. "You said, *'I know who I am. Maybe it's time you accept who you are.'* I know who I am, Marcus. Who we are. But I'm not willing to accept that as my lot in life. Now I don't know what act of God, nature or man that caused the blackout, or how many hours, days, weeks, even months we have before society returns to normal but until that time, I'm going to make the most of it and establish new ground rules. Rules that others must live by if they are to survive in my world."

Marcus shook his head, with a look of disbelief or even amusement. "Your world? Your rules?"

Gabriel gave a nod. "You got it."

Marcus laughed and placed a hand against the wall. "And what of your world? What does that look like, huh?

Because right now I don't see anything better. In fact, I wonder if we aren't worse off for being free."

Gabriel got close to him and wrapped his hand around his brother's neck. "That's because you've become accustomed to viewing life with blinders on. You have been institutionalized. Our family, society, prison, all of them have put blinders on us. They want us to see this world through a narrow lens of haves and have-nots, do's and don'ts, and maybe they could enforce that when the power was up but not now. No." He cupped his hands either side of his eyes in a narrow manner and then removed them. "There are no more blinders, brother. Call it fate. Call it a second chance. We decide how we live, who lives among us, where we go, and who lives and dies." He wrapped his arm around his shoulder and squeezed tight. "Look at them out there," he said turning his face towards the men dotted around the cabin and porch. "They are hanging on every word we say. And that's just a few. There will be others. Our group will grow strong."

"Yeah, and how do you propose to convince people?"

"If the power stays down, people will get desperate and when they do, the one holding the spoon will be looked up to like God himself."

"You're not God, Gabriel," Marcus said shrugging his arm off his shoulder. "You can't control the outcome of this. What you speak of is nothing more than the product of an over imaginative mind. It's ridiculous. And it's liable to get us all captured or killed. So I will meet you in Whitefish but don't count on me to stay. As much as you are evaluating your future, so am I."

Marcus glared at him, then reached for the handle on the door and went outside. He was still pissed but that would change in time. Gabriel would prove him wrong and then he'd come around. They all would. Marcus called together his group and they were brought up to speed. A few grumbled at the decision but no one could deny that splitting into two small groups would be beneficial. They made their way down to the dock, and as evening fell upon them, Gabriel bid them a safe journey.

He crouched on the rickety wooden dock and gripped his brother's hand. "I'll see you in Whitefish."

A look of disbelief or concern flickered across his face before Marcus nodded, and Gabriel and his group watched as they rowed out across the silky still waters.

* * *

Corey was getting exceedingly irritated by Ferris' incessant need to be in control. They weren't getting anywhere using the same method of driving house to house and knocking. With only a few vehicles on the road, and the sun nearly gone on the horizon, the inmates must have spotted the truck's headlights from miles away. Was it any wonder why they hadn't come across them? All they'd found was a path of devastation left in their wake; a cabin on fire, residents beaten and tied, and now Noah wrapped up in a tarp in the back of the truck. Instead of traveling together down the same road, Corey had suggested using two-way radios and splitting up. Ferris wanted more specifics on what that involved but he couldn't give it to him as his own idea simply went against what Ferris wanted, and anything that went against that was shot down. In his mind, the truck was the property of the county police and he would do whatever the hell he liked with it.

Instead of fighting him on it, Corey agreed and while Ferris was checking on another cabin, Corey wandered down to the water's edge with a pair of night vision binoculars. He figured in a lake this size, the plane and its debris couldn't have been entirely submerged so he began scanning the surface, looking for the tip of a wing, luggage or flotation devices, anything to give him an indication of where they would have to dive once they'd arrested or killed those they were following.

A green hue engulfed his field of vision as he gazed out.

He adjusted the diopter and then the focusing ring as his eyes caught sight of an object in the distance. He rotated the ring until the object became clearer.

It was a boat manned by one person, and carrying five others. Was it them? Again, he made an adjustment but it was hard to tell in the low light. Then again, who would be crossing the lake at this hour? They weren't heading for Apgar but the other side of the lake. Was it possible? No. He shook his head and lowered the binoculars. Corey glanced at Ferris as he came out of a cabin, barking his orders for them to move on to the next property. Then he looked again through the binoculars. If he used the truck he could probably make it around to the other side by the time they reached the shore. If it was them, they would have no other choice than to surrender. Stuck in a boat, exposed in the open, it would be madness to fight back. Corey gritted his teeth knowing what he had in mind would land him in hot water but the alternative could be worse. He had to find out. Vern and Terry had just come out of a cabin adjacent to him when he hurried over and told them to head up to the truck.

"But Ferris wants us to check in on the homes across the way."

Corey walked past them motioning towards the truck with a finger. "Change of plan, guys."

"What?" Terry asked.

He didn't tell them any more than that. As soon as they were out of Ferris' view, they hopped into the truck and he fired it up and did a U-turn in the road, heading back up around the northeast side of the lake. As the truck picked up speed, Vern and Terry gave him a concerned expression. "You want to fill us in on what is going on?"

"I think I've spotted them."

"Okay good, then let's tell Ferris and let them handle it."

"I'm afraid it's down to us, guys."

"Hang on a second, Corey. You expect us to go up against eight or more armed inmates without backup?"

"Six."

"Six what?"

"Inmates. At least if that's them."

Terry frowned. "You don't even know?" He waited for a response but Corey didn't give one. Terry let out an exasperated sigh. "Ferris will blow his top. Turn the vehicle around. Take us back."

"No time," Corey said turning off his headlights. If it wasn't for the shine of the moon, he would have had a hard time seeing the edge of the road. Vern started to get nervous.

"Corey, he's right. We need to go back."

He was no longer listening to them. His eyes were scanning the forest as the truck roared down the road. He knew he would have to ditch it a fair distance from where they might come ashore, otherwise they would hear them coming and right now the only thing they had going for them was the element of surprise.

Terry slammed his hand on the dashboard. "Have you heard a word we have said?"

Corey nodded but kept scanning.

"Pull over."

"In a minute."

"Now!"

"Terry. I like you. I really do. But if you two don't man up and grow a pair, it won't be just six inmates you will have to worry about, it will be an entire town. What is coming down the pipeline is far worse than what is rowing across this lake. Stop thinking of yourself for once, and think about Noah. Think about his family. Think about all the other families that might die if we don't stop these assholes." He paused. "Can you do that?"

There was silence. He knew they were pondering it.

Suddenly his father came over the radio.

"Come in, Corey."

He scooped it up and pressed the button. "Yeah, go ahead."

"It's too hot. Too many cops out."

"Where are you?"

"I made it to West Glacier but had to pull to the side of the road. I'm heading for the cabin instead. I'll meet you there."

"I told you you'd be wasting your time."

"They still got my truck?"

"You still got mine?" he tossed back.

He waited for a response but his father didn't answer

so Corey finished with, "Don't wait up. I still have to collect Ella and…" he trailed off looking at Terry. "I have one last thing left to do." With that he signed off.

Corey accelerated and the trees whipped by his peripheral vision. Judging by the lay of the land and glancing at the water between the trees, he could just make out where he was. Yanking the wheel to the left, he veered to a standstill, killed the engine and jumped out. Reaching into the back of the truck bed, he glanced at Noah before scooping up an AR-15 rifle. He made sure he had enough ammo before walking back to the driver's side and looking at them inside the warmth of the truck. "It's decision time, boys. Pick a side."

With that said he didn't stick around for an answer. Corey turned and sprinted towards the dense tree line in preparation for war.

Chapter 27

It had only been a few days since the EMP and already people were killing one another. Maybe not on the scale his father predicted, but it had begun. Tyler had climbed up to the slanted roof of the home and was using night vision binoculars to get a better lay of the land. His thoughts went to Erika. There was such a stark difference between her parents and his and yet in some ways they had both taught them how to survive but for Erika it was all about keeping her head above the water in the corporate world. She said her father didn't know how to use a gun, his weapons of choice were money, a pen and high-paid lawyers. He didn't have much need beyond that.

Tyler heard a shuffle behind him and turned thinking it was Erika, but it was Nate.

"How's the view up here?"

"A few fires burning in town but it's nothing

compared to Vegas."

Nate blew out his cheeks and wiped off his hands as he pitched sideways and made his way over. "Shit this is high." He took a seat beside Tyler.

Tyler nodded and looked again through his binoculars. "I thought you were trying to sleep."

"Trying would be the appropriate word," he said. "I can't. Figured I would come up here and have a smoke." He pulled out a pack.

"Those her old man's?"

"Yep."

"How is she?"

"Bailey is watching over her." Nate cupped a hand around the end of the cigarette and lit it. Gray smoke drifted into the air, along with the fresh aroma of tobacco. "She's stopped crying. So that's good, right?"

"Maybe."

Grief came in waves. There were only so many tears a person could release before their body became exhausted and they fell asleep. After burying her parents, they spent the next hour fortifying the house as best they could. Not exactly easy since the panes of glass in the window frames were gone. Tyler wanted to set up a few deterrents, create an alert system and block the main entrances before they retreated to the third floor so Erika could get some shut-eye. They'd put nails into a section of drywall taken from the garage and placed it below open windows, then covered them with dark sheets. There was no point trying to block the windows because unless someone had a good eye and was expecting such a trap, Tyler figured the nail board would do the trick.

Next he set up an eyehook perimeter tripwire system on the outside of the house and ran it between the trees. There wasn't much to it, just some wire, a clothespin, a simple flashlight bulb, a small piece of paper, a 9 volt battery, a battery holder, a plastic container, some electrical tape and eyehook screws. Some of the items he already had on him, the rest they found in her father's garage. Tyler didn't want anything that used sound, though that was common and useful when camping in the woods. As Tyler and Nate were going to rotate throughout the night, one of them would see the light and that would buy them enough time to wake the other two.

"Listen, I've been thinking about tomorrow. I want to come with you to Whitefish, if that's okay."

"What about Spokane? What about your mother?"

Nate nodded and screwed up his face. Tyler shook his head. "She's not there, is she?"

"No, she's dead," he said before taking another hard drag on his cigarette.

"Why didn't you just say that back in Vegas?"

"Would you have let me tag along if I had?" He tapped some ash off onto the roof and a mild wind blew it away. Tyler turned his attention to the horizon. Low clouds drifted across the sky, and a few dark birds circled nearby.

"So, what's your deal? You have any brothers or sisters?"

"Nope."

"Did you really live in Colorado?"

"Yeah, that part was true."

Tyler sighed. "Whitefish doesn't offer much. Not like the city."

"It's fine. I just need a place to lay my head, and a bite to eat."

Tyler flashed him a glance. "When we found you in the rubble. That wasn't your apartment, was it?"

He shook his head. "The guy who bought phones off me used to meet me and a friend of mine in different places. It was one of his." Nate took another drag on his cigarette and then flicked the rest out into the night. A few hot embers broke away and bounced. "I know I let you down back at the reservoir. It won't happen again."

"That's good to hear. It will be even better when I see it."

"I know, my words don't mean much. But that will change."

"Why do you want to go to Whitefish with us?"

Nate shrugged. "You know, I've spent twenty-nine

years of my life trying to fit in. Very few people have watched my back. When Erika spoke up for me, and was willing to walk away if you didn't let me tag along. That meant a lot. No one has ever done that. They've always looked out for themselves. Even my pal Zach didn't do that and believe me he had many chances."

"Don't bullshit me, Nate. That might pass with her but not me."

Nate laughed. "All right. Look, you seem to know what's going on. By the sounds of what your old man has in place, and its location in the country, well, it just makes sense."

"Right. Finally. An honest word. In the future do me the favor of saving what you think I want to hear, and only telling me what is true. It saves so much time."

Nate nodded. "Point taken."

Tyler was about to tell him that he wasn't sure his father would be very open to either of them, including himself, when there was rustling in the bushes below, a few feet from the house. "Get down," Tyler said, lying flat. Slowly, Tyler gripped his AR-15 and brought it up, aiming it in the direction of the sound. His pulse sped up as he waited for someone to emerge. He looked at the small bulb that was positioned just down from him. It was still off. Suddenly, the rustling stopped as a small dark mass came out. Squinting, he smiled once he saw it was a rabbit.

Nate chuckled and patted him on the back as he went to get up. "For a second there I thought—" Tyler laid an arm on him, preventing him from getting up. Off to the right, the tiny white light was lit up. Far below three dark forms burst out of the bushes heading for the house. All three were armed.

"Go. Wake up Erika," Tyler said. "Watch over her."

"What are you gonna do?"

"Take care of business."

Nate moved stealthily along the top of the roof and climbed over the edge, dropping into the balcony. Tyler shifted position, brought up his rifle and took aim at one of them but then decided not to take the shot. He was heading straight for the large open window. The other two were circling around. He didn't want to open fire from the roof as it would give away his position and right now he had the element of surprise working for him. Instead he made his way to the east side of the home to cut one of them off. He slung his rifle behind his back and used a thick drainpipe to make his way down.

When his boots hit the grass, old muscle memory took over, lessons he'd learned from his father came back to him. He brought the rifle around and dropped to a knee hiding in the shadows. He could hear whispering but couldn't make out what they were saying. Tyler darted over to a corner of the house expecting one of them to come his way.

Before seeing them, on the other side of the house he heard a loud cry. The nails in the board had worked. That momentary distraction was all he needed. He burst out ready to dispatch the other guy as he turned away. Finger on the trigger, Tyler squeezed off two rounds into his back, then darted back into the shadows. While he had seen three emerge on the west side, he wasn't taking any chances. He anticipated more.

Loud wailing cut into the night as one of the men obviously tried to free himself from the nails.

A quick glance either way and he slipped around the house expecting to find the second guy coming to his pal's aid. He hadn't. Under the glow of the moon he could see the man just inside the house, both feet were planted. He did the humane thing and put him out of his misery. A single bullet to the back of the head did the trick.

Above, he heard the sound of Bailey barking.

Where was the third?

Sweat formed on his brow and adrenaline rushed through his body as he hurried around the house staying close to the wall. That was when he spotted two more. "Shit!"

* * *

Inside, Erika awoke to the sound of a loud cry before Nate sidled up to her telling her to grab her weapon.

"Bailey, quiet," she said as Nate pried open the door and slipped out onto the landing. Gripping a Glock tight, her hand shook ever so slightly. She swallowed hard. "Stay here," she said to Bailey as she followed Nate out. He put up a hand to caution her to stay back but Erika paid no attention. If these were the same group that had killed her parents, she wanted revenge. Rage formed in the pit of her stomach as she navigated her way along the landing towards the stairs. She could hear movement down below and she wanted to peer over but it was too risky.

Before she took a few steps down the staircase, Nate pulled her back by the arm. She tried to shake his grip but it was firm and he was persistent. "You want to go, I'm not stopping you but you get shot, that's on you."

"Let go of my arm."

He released it and she continued on. All her life she'd been told what to do and prevented from heading in different directions because of the unknown. For the first time in her life she wanted to face her fears. Erika kept her back to the wall and came down the staircase, one step at a time. She'd taken four when one of them let out a creak.

A crack of a gun, a bullet zipped past her embedding in the wall.

Panic clawed at her throat and muscles, freezing her to the spot. Had it not been for the quick actions of Nate pulling her down, she would have been dead. Four more rounds peppered the wall where she'd been. They scrambled back up to the landing.

Gunfire erupted outside, a steady stream that abruptly stopped.

Just as she was rushing towards the room to take cover, she caught sight of the intruder. Light from candles in the lower room, and a band of moonlight illuminated his face. She couldn't believe it. It was impossible.

Suddenly she heard Tyler's voice. "Put it down!"

Stopping short of the door she walked back towards the landing banister and watched as Tyler came in at a crouch with his rifle aimed at their attacker. The sound of a rifle clattering on the floor and Tyler's reassuring words was enough for her to make her way down, even though Nate was still cautioning her to be careful.

When she made it to the bottom of the staircase, she turned to face him.

"Spencer?"

"Erika," he replied.

"You know this guy?" Tyler asked.

She nodded. "Please tell me you didn't do it."

"It wasn't me. It wasn't meant to happen. I came up to speak to your father but he wouldn't listen."

"So you shot the security guy on the way out? Bullshit," Tyler said.

Erika considered what Tyler said and said, "How did you get past Trevor?"

Spencer shrugged. "Again, it wasn't me."

"Stop lying," Erika said.

"I'm not."

"You had the same look on your face when you lied to me about that bitch." She didn't take her eyes off her ex for even a second.

"Look, I tried to reason with your father but he wanted me off his property. Erika, they had so much and all I wanted was a generator. He had two. I just wanted to borrow it. He wouldn't do it."

Erika moved around the room and walked over to the man who had come in through the window but was now lying dead. She took a candle off a side table and bent down to see who it was. Before she even had the chance, Spencer said, "It's Grant."

Grant was his cousin. "And the others?" she asked turning her head towards him.

Spencer gritted his teeth and shot Tyler a sneer. "Friends of mine."

"Which one did it?" She asked.

"What?"

Erika rose and calmly walked over.

"Which one killed my parents."

"I don't know."

She snorted, a faint smile appeared as she cast a glance down at the ground. Then in one smooth motion before anyone could stop her, she brought up the Glock and fired two rounds at him. One struck him in the chest, the other in the shoulder. She continued squeezing the trigger even as he collapsed to the floor until she had unloaded every round in the magazine.

Chapter 28

Flashbacks of Fallujah, Iraq, bombarded his mind as Corey ran at a crouch through the dark forest. Pinned down and surrounded in those dust-covered streets, visibility was often so poor he had to be careful he didn't shoot one of his own. The battle in that war zone was intense, close and without a doubt personal. Hours of fighting often led to pinning down insurgents in crumbling homes only to have them pull a cord on their suicide vest, in an attempt to take out as many Marines as possible and end their pitiful existence as a martyr. Corey could still hear the sound of air strikes, tank fire, and armored bulldozers taking out enemy strongholds. If it wasn't for having gone through such an experience, he wouldn't have had the courage to face off against those coming ashore.

Corey darted between trees, hopped over mounds of earth and pitched sideways down a steep muddy incline, before they came into view. His hope of taking them out while they were still in the boat was dashed as he watched two of them dragging the boat out of the calm water. Corey dropped to a knee near a large tree. He cast a glance over his shoulder to see if Terry and Vern were coming but all he saw was the blackness of night. He was on his own. It was a lot to expect them to put their lives on the line when they had families to think about getting home to, but that was why he was doing this. Any one of those rangers they'd killed probably had a family that would never see them again, a child who would have to grow up without a parent — all for what — freedom?

In the distance the rumbling of thunder made him look up at the angry sky.

It was as if nature itself was responding, closing in on society, ready to swallow it whole. A light rain began to fall, dampening his skin and increasing the scent of pine and fir trees around him. Corey shifted into a better position. He knew his only chance was to take out as many as he could, then move before they became aware that they were only up against one person. He brought up the rifle, and placed the fleshy part of his finger against the trigger ready to take his first shot.

A shuffle behind him made him turn.

Jogging towards him as quietly as they could were Vern and Terry, rifles at the ready, with a look of exaggerated determination to offset their fear. They crouched beside him and looked at the inmates on the shore. Corey smiled. He would have gone up against them alone but with support it just made his life easier, and the inmates' lives worse.

"Where do you want us?" Vern asked.

"If they make it into the tree line, our job gets a hell of a lot harder. Vern, you head over to my right, and Terry to the left. Don't get ahead of yourselves. The last thing you want is friendly fire. Hold your position, until I tell you to move forward."

They nodded and shifted into their assigned spots.

Corey watched as the inmates talked among themselves. They looked divided on which way to go, and at odds with each other. One of them shoved another and rifles were lifted. *Go on, shoot each other,* he thought. That would be a satisfying end to meaningless lives. But the inmates never turned and slipped forward... remaining unaware of their presence until Corey gave the word to open fire. Three of the six were hit before the others ducked into the tree line. The inmates scattered for cover, then converged slowly towards them using the trees and bushes as cover. There were no buildings for them to hide in, no vehicles to engage behind as Rocky Point Trail was strangely absent of traffic and at least two hundred yards inland.

A deluge of rain soon soaked the sand beneath their boots, giving the ground almost a mushy feel as Corey told them to move forward. It was a battle of inches. He could hear the inmates calling out to one another. He peered through his night vision scope on top of his rifle and raked the barrel over the trees. Nothing moved across his field of vision. Where were they? He shifted position again, running to the next nearest tree only to have the ground torn up by rounds near him. He dived and rolled before pressing his back against a large boulder. The shooter raked his gun back and forth spraying rounds. Bullets ate up dirt and tree bark, and chipped stone. Vern and Terry were on their faces, staying as low to the forest ground as possible.

Corey rolled out using another tree as cover, then he noticed one of them running between the trees. He squeezed off a shot and the round hit the guy in the temple sending his bald-headed skull jolting sideways before he collapsed.

Only two remained.

"Hey Hauser get back here," a voice bellowed from afar.

Corey scanned his field of vision and saw one heading back to the shore in fear. He was about to take aim when Vern bellowed that he would take care of him. He splintered off while Terry and Corey moved in on the final guy.

Confident, he used hand signals to indicate to Terry

when and where to press forward. More bullets peppered the trees nearby showering them in bark. The last guy was hard to spot. He kept moving but unlike the others who darted between the trees, this one must have been crawling back, rolling and sidling up to trees as it was hard to get a bead on him.

A single round echoed down by the shore. Shortly after it was followed by another.

Corey stayed focused, roving the muzzle over the terrain.

A sudden flurry of rounds and Terry shouted, "I'm hit."

Damn it. Zigzagging his way across to him, Corey hurried over to find him gripping his shoulder. He glanced up to check his position was covered before tearing open his jacket and getting a better look.

"Am I going to die?"

Corey squinted before patting him. "It's gone straight through. You'll live."

Suddenly he saw movement off to his left. The last guy

was up and running. He needed to tend to the wound but he was damned if he would let one of them get away.

"Take off your jacket, tie something off on that and apply pressure and keep your body upright. I'll be right back." He broke away and took off. The sound of his boots hitting the dirt alerted the inmate, and he turned and fired off another flurry of rounds, several kicking up dirt and pinging off boulders all around him. Corey jumped for cover and had to stay low as another cluster of bullets slammed into the trees around him.

He had made it to a clearing, where the trees were spread further apart, all of which meant he was in deep shit if he had to move again. He cursed under his breath and wiggled across the forest floor trying to close the gap. More rounds whizzed overhead, bark and leaves rained down. He rolled behind a tree and spotted the guy dart out, again trying to make it to the trail. He must have thought there were homes nearby but there weren't. One side of the lake was nothing but forest and trails.

He raised his rifle to take a shot but had to hit the

ground again as more rounds cut into mounds of earth only a stone's throw away. He took a deep breath and when the shooting stopped, he rose and burst forward quickly shifting away from his last position and hoping to cut him off near the trail.

Dark forms hurried through the forest. The inmate looked back and then tried to shoot but this time Corey was the one to get off a three-burst round, and this time one struck him. Where? He had no idea. All he saw was the guy hit the ground.

Corey scrambled up another dirt slope and then launched himself off a rocky edge and came down only a few feet from the man who had his back against a tree. His rifle was beside him. He went for it but Corey shook his head, keeping his finger on the trigger. In the dim light of the moon, he could see who it was. It was the same guy from the cabin, although his clothes were different. He'd changed out of the ones he'd seen.

"I would ask you why you killed him but it would be pointless," Corey said referring to Noah. He approached him, keeping his rifle muzzle trained on him. "Was it worth it? Huh?"

"You don't know what it's like to be pushed into a corner, to have the walls close in on you and know you will never get out. But you will."

Corey shook his head. "Yeah? You're all the same. You break the law and then plead for mercy. But did you show any mercy when you killed those rangers, or a friend of ours?"

"You think you're better than us, don't you?" He coughed and then grimaced as he squeezed his injured leg. The upper pant leg was soaked with blood. "Given enough time, under the right circumstances you will return to your basic instincts of killing to survive."

They locked eyes for a second or two before he dropped his chin. "Do it. Get it over with. You'll be doing me a favor."

"No," Coreys said, shaking his head. "I'll take you in."

"I'm not going in. None of us are." He reached for his rifle, and Corey had no other choice. He squeezed off two rounds, both burrowing deep into the man's chest. His body slumped to one side and Corey walked over and rooted through his pockets. They were empty except for a pack of cigarettes. He pulled one out and lit it, blowing smoke into the air as he thought about the man's final dying words. Who was he? What he had done to land himself inside?

"Corey. Corey!" Terry yelled.

He scooped up the man's gun and jogged back to where he'd left Terry but he wasn't there. He scanned the trees and spotted him standing close to the shore. He rushed over to find Vern lying dead on the ground, one round straight through the back of his head. A wave of guilt came over him. "One of them got away," Terry said pointing to the boat which was now a fair distance from shore. Corey brought up his rifle and looked through the scope at the man rowing. He was too far to take a shot.

Corey crouched beside Vern and placed a hand on his back and offered up a silent prayer, and a request for forgiveness. "He knew what he was going into, Corey,"

Terry said. "It was Vern who convinced me to come and help you."

He nodded but it didn't make it any better.

His thoughts went to all his buddies he lost in Iraq.

It was one thing to lose someone in the heat of war on foreign soil, but here in America? It should have never happened. But it was happening and that was what worried him. How many more would die before society rallied together and power was restored? How many would escape justice? One thing was sure, the future would test their mettle, pose life-altering decisions and change them. For better or worse, that was to be seen.

Chapter 29

The line had been crossed. There was no going back to who they were before this. At daybreak, as a light breeze blew across the town of Midway, Tyler and Nate loaded the bodies of their attackers into the back of the Jeep and dumped them in a river on the outskirts of town. They could have left them to rot, or buried them, because the chances of them being caught were slim to none but Erika didn't want them anywhere near her parents' home.

As they stood by the banks of the river watching the last of the men sink into a watery grave, Nate said, "You have to admit what she did was some pretty cold shit. I mean I've been pissed at exes before but that was on a whole other level. Aren't you pleased that first date of yours didn't go well?" He snorted. Without looking at Tyler he continued, "Makes you wonder what went wrong in their relationship." Tyler rolled his eyes. "Still, perhaps it's best we keep that gun far from her." Nate patted Tyler on the back and chuckled to himself as he ambled back up the steep slope to the road.

Because Erika had chosen to stay behind at the house while they disposed of the bodies, Tyler was certain she hadn't changed her mind about leaving, but not everything was as it seemed. Upon returning, she strolled out and tossed a new bag of gear into the back of the Jeep and told them she was going with them. It was a surprise, for sure. As pleased as he was to hear that, he didn't want her regretting her decision, so he gave her a way out.

"Are you sure?" Tyler asked. "It won't be easy."

Erika looked back at her childhood home with a heavy heart, nodding slowly as she brought a hand up to her head. "There's nothing left for me here. I can't stay. Not after what happened."

Tyler wasn't sure what caused the sudden change of heart as upon their arrival yesterday she had given him the impression that she wanted to remain, but that was before killing her ex in such brutal fashion. It was clear something had clicked on inside her, or switched off maybe. Was it her need to be with others? Was it her humanity? Time would tell. Killing, whether it be for survival or not, changed a person. How? That depended on the individual, who they had killed and the reason behind it. Before leaving, Tyler siphoned what gas he could from her father's vehicles and managed to fill up two five-gallon steel containers. He loaded them in the back and then fished around for some other useful items in his garage to take as he didn't want to have to stop unless it was to piss or fill up with more gas. He figured if they kept driving, they would reach Whitefish by nightfall.

Bailey hopped up into the back of the Jeep beside Nate and curled up next to him waiting to go while Erika went and paid her last respects at her parents' graves. Before the sun had fully risen, they got back on the road heading north. As they had taken a different route to the one Lou had marked out, it meant they wouldn't be able to drop in on his old pal Ralph Brunson, but based on Lou's description of his mental health, they all agreed that was probably a good thing. The fact was, the new world they had entered presented many challenges — lovers could become enemies, family could die, and loyalties would be tested.

* * *

Later that evening, the tragic news that two of Whitefish's residents had died spread like wildfire. Although Corey could have had an officer deliver the death notifications, he felt it was only right to tell them himself. They weren't just the mothers and kids of his friends and co-workers, they were family, a part of his close-knit community that he had come to call home. Over the years they'd swapped stories at BBQ's, given each other a hand when moving to a new home, looked after their kids when they wanted a date night, and attended the same church. That's what made it so hard to tell them. Many tears fell that night, and in all his years in the military nothing came close to the emotional anguish he felt when he saw their pain.

From there, friends of the family told others, and even

though Noah's and Vern's families were too grief-stricken to attend, a large number from the community gathered together on Whitefish Beach for a vigil to show its support for the fallen. With all the trouble the town was facing, and questions unanswered, Corey imagined only a few friends would attend but over two hundred showed up at the lake to pay their respects.

A roaring fire was lit, and floating candles donated by a local store owner were released on the lake. The flickering of fire mesmerized him and the crowd as he stood beside Ella, his arm wrapped around her tightly. A strong wind whipped at the crowd's jackets as prayers were offered up, and a few close friends led a church group in the song "Amazing Grace." Corey glanced at two police officers patrolling the perimeter on bicycles. Earlier that night after dropping Terry off at the hospital, he'd given his father's utility truck to the city. A decision his father would no doubt argue about. But it didn't matter. If it meant making their job easier, he would do whatever was necessary, and that included volunteering. Jim Bruce, the current police chief of Whitefish, was grateful and had said he would have a schedule drawn up within the next forty-eight hours. In all truth, the chief was of the belief that the lights would come back on. Corey knew otherwise.

"When will Terry get out?" Ella asked.

"Soon. Though he still thinks he's at death's door but he'll live. He's in good hands. The hospital is running on backup generators for the time being."

"How long do you think they can keep that up?"

"It's not the machines I'm worried about but the gas. With the power out, and little to no transportation, no trucks will be delivering fuel any time soon."

She nodded and sighed. "What about your father?"

"I'll ask him to donate what is left in the store to the city."

"He won't do that. You know him. He'll be back at that store tomorrow, loading up and carrying it away to hide in the mountains."

"Not if I can help it," he said.

"I'm just glad you're safe." He leaned down and gave her a kiss.

As they turned to leave and head back home, Corey squinted at two people and a dog standing near a Jeep parked on the road. It caught his attention as the engine was ticking over and the headlights were cutting into the night. There were few vehicles in operation and those that were working were either being used by the cops or the owners were keeping them out of sight. Someone killed the engine, the lights went out, and a third person stepped out of the driver's side. As soon as his eyes adjusted, a smile broadened on his face.

"Hello brother," Tyler said.

Corey bit down on his lower lip holding in a well of emotion before smiling. He and Ella met them a few feet away from the Jeep. He broke away and gave him a hug, holding him tight. "Steady."

"It's just good to see you."

"Good to see you too," Tyler replied.

Corey gripped his shoulder. "When did you arrive?"

"Half an hour ago. I went over to the store but it was locked up, and then went past dad's place, then yours. We got stopped by a cop heading through town and he said you were down here." He chuckled. "Said you donated a truck to the town. That right?"

"It's dad's. It's on loan."

Tyler smirked. "He'll love that. Is he up at the cabin?"

"Yeah. Still waiting for me. You… coming up?"

Tyler ran a hand over his face and looked past him towards the crowd.

"He talks about you, Tyler."

"Yeah? Let me guess, when he's giving workshops and showing them the videos of what not to do."

His father had recorded them while they performed all manner of survival lessons, like target practice, making a fire without matches, first aid, pitching different outdoor shelters, sparring etc. Tyler had thought he did it to have a memory of them. Nope. He used them in his workshops to show people what not to do. Of course, that meant Tyler was often used an example. It was humiliating and another reason why his relationship with his father had broken down. Corey pulled a face and glanced around. "He's changed, Tyler. Not entirely but… well you should see for yourself."

"Not sure I want to. I was hoping I could stay with you at least until we find out what's really happening."

Corey gave a confused look. "You know what's happening."

"You know what I mean," Tyler said. Corey nodded and looked at the others.

"Who are they?"

Tyler stepped back and pointed. "This is Erika, and Nate."

They both stepped forward and extended a hand. After a few awkward seconds of greeting, Corey turned back to Tyler. "You know you can't avoid him forever."

"I didn't say I would. But maybe just for tonight."

Corey smiled and wrapped an arm around his neck. "It's good to have you home, brother."

Behind them tongues of fire flickered up into the night

sky as smoke drifted inland. As they walked back to the Jeep, Tyler began to share what was happening in the cities and towns further afield. He spoke of his harrowing moments, and the dangers that lurked in the darkness. All of it confirmed that the nation wasn't coming back from this anytime soon. But it wasn't what was occurring around the country that overshadowed Corey's mind that night, or the words of the last man he killed, or even the knowledge that one of the inmates had escaped. Instead, it was the fear of reprisal — not only from inmates that had escaped but from all men like that — those who had nothing to lose, and everything to gain.

Corey cast a glance over his shoulder at the men and women gathered. He'd felt the sense of unity and strength. He saw how the community could rally together. His father was wrong. If he'd learned anything in battle, it was this — staying alive wasn't just about looking out for number one, it was in joining with others, standing shoulder to shoulder and if need be, fighting. And fight they would need to, in order to survive.

For until the lights came back on, Whitefish was now at risk.

* * *

THANK YOU FOR READING

Rules of Survival: A Post-Apocalyptic EMP Survival Thriller (Survival Rules Series book 1). Search for Rules of Conflict #2 now. Please take a second to leave a review, it's really appreciated.

Thanks kindly, Jack.

A Plea

Thank you for reading Rules of Survival: A Post-Apocalyptic EMP Survival Thriller (Survival Rules Series Book 1). If you enjoyed the book, I would really appreciate it if you would consider leaving a review. Without reviews, an author's books are virtually invisible on the retail sites. It also lets me know what you liked. You can leave a review by visiting the book's page. I would greatly appreciate it. It only takes a couple of seconds.

Thank you — **Jack Hunt**

Newsletter

Thank you for buying Rules of Survival: A Post-Apocalyptic EMP Survival Thriller (Survival Rules Series book 1), published by Direct Response Publishing.

Click here to receive special offers, bonus content, and news about new Jack Hunt's books. Sign up for the newsletter. http://www.jackhuntbooks.com/signup/

About the Author

Jack Hunt is the author of horror, sci-fi and post-apocalyptic novels. He currently has over thirty books published. Jack lives on the East coast of North America. If you haven't joined Jack Hunt's Private Facebook Group you can request to join by going here. https://www.facebook.com/groups/1620726054688731/ This gives readers a way to chat with Jack, see cover reveals, and stay updated on upcoming releases. There is also his main Facebook page if you want to browse that.

www.jackhuntbooks.com

jhuntauthor@gmail.com

Made in the
USA
Middletown, DE